SWEET NIGHTMARES

HAZEL ST. LEWIS

SWEET NIGHTMARES

HAZEL ST. LEWIS

Copyright

Editing:

- Developmental Edit: Charlie Knight
- Line editing & Proofreading: Noah Sky
- Proofreading: <u>Lindsey Middlemiss</u>

Design :

- Cover Design: © 2025 by Giulia F. Wille Art

For those who just want to call the villain daddy.

Nature District
University Square
Castle Hill
The Grand Library
Art Sector

New Swansea City
Marina District
THE VIRIDIAN
Pleasure District
THE STARLING
THE ROYAL BALLET
Gold Quarter
THE RUSSET
The Ruins
Estate District
Spirit Sector

Author's Note

Content Warnings:

Sexual explicit content, alcohol and drug consumption (limited), mention of off the page SA/R, mention of off the page DV, on the page DV (limited & not by MMC), abuse, fat/weight talk/shaming (by abusive husband), medical content (autopsy on the page), blood and gore, on the page violent death, vampire fangs (because daddy), suicidal ideation (limited), torture, kidnapping, discussion of past trauma, did I mention death?

This book ends where GILDED WICKED MIRRORS begins. It can be read first, but for those of you who have read GWMs, you know, Jane's story ends in tragedy—at least for now. Sweet Nightmares does not have a happy ending because it is not the ending of Jane's or Nightmare's stories.

Author's Note:

This is a much darker book than Gilded Wicked Mirrors. It was initially intended to be a novella, but I realized there was just too much story for a novella. However, the structure of this book is more episodic than other books in the Wicked Mirrors series and spans an eight-year period.

Please keep in mind, I do not name a single one of Jane's abusers in this book because I do not believe they deserve names. This was an active choice. Jane's husband does not deserve a name, so he does not get one.

PROLOGUE

Age 29.

Jane was born to die horrifically—just like her parents. So, she wasn't surprised to be looking death in the face. What *did* surprise her was whose face it was—and how much it destroyed her, knowing she had been so cruelly betrayed.

PART ONE
IF BROKENNESS
HAD A NAME

Chapter One

Age 21.

Jane Whitfield-Klein powdered her face, frantically trying to fix the smears in her makeup that her *husband* had placed there just moments before.

Only five minutes remained until Jane would debut as the prima ballerina of the Queen's Royalle Ballet. The show was *Lover's Lost*, in which she played the maiden, Isadora, who would eventually fall in love with Death.

Death...

Jane often wished she had married Death. Sure, he was a villain, but he'd do anything for the Maiden: protect her, kill for her, and most importantly, truly love her.

All things Jane's husband would never do. No, he'd rather slap her across the face, ruining her makeup just moments before the biggest performance of her life. Leaving her to fix his mess.

And that was Jane's current task: making beauty from brokenness.

It felt impossible. Her eyes were sunken and purpled from extreme exhaustion and stress, her arms were littered with scratches and discoloration, and her face was hollow. But at the very least—this time—she didn't have black eyes. She hated it when she had to cover black eyes. Because the only thing that could do it successfully was Mirror Cosmetics—cursed makeup that could erase any blemish, at a cost. The wretched stuff came from mirror deals, and everyone knew even the smallest bargain with a Mirror God—also known as Bargainers—was dangerous.

But if cursed makeup would get her on the stage, then so be it.

Jane would accept the consequences, because her dreams were more important than her rotten husband, cursed objects, or gilded, wicked mirrors.

The dressing room door creaked open, and the stage manager peeked his head in. "Five minutes."

"Five minutes," Jane said, trying to keep her voice steady. The hardest part of having an abusive husband, besides the physical and emotional toll, was hiding it from everyone. It was one thing to be a victim. It was another thing entirely for the world to know about it, and Jane would never let the world know. No, she was the perfect, beautiful ballerina, for the world to place on a pedestal and admire.

A puppet on a string for the rich and powerful to prop up and maneuver the way they wanted.

Jane rubbed her face, her elbows on the vanity. Gulping in a large breath of air, she tried to calm herself and salvage the night, which in a matter of moments had gone from a beautiful dream to a decaying nightmare, worse than any Looking Glass nightmare from the most powerful and dangerous Mirror God in the city. This performance was supposed to be the greatest moment of her career, but it was completely soured by her circumstances. Honestly, Jane shouldn't have been surprised. Her life was one tragedy after another and yet, foolishly, she'd believed this night would be different.

It was the night of her dreams. Finally, her life would get better. She'd have the career she'd always wanted, the respect she deserved, the prestige and money that she'd use to file for divorce.

But Jane was a fool.

Her life never went to plan—not a single moment of it. When her parents died, she was forced to move into an orphanage. Then, at sixteen, said orphanage married her off to a *"wealthy"* merchant thirty years her senior.

It was supposed to make her life better.

But *shoulds* and *supposed-tos* were dangerous, and they never quite panned out.

Jane sighed, pushing her middle fingers against the pressure points where her nose met her eyes, then rubbing underneath them and finishing her path by circling her temples. She found this helped calm her anxiety, especially before a show.

With another deep breath, Jane stood up, placed a resolved smile on her face, and cracked her neck before leaving her dressing room and walking to the stage.

The lights dimmed, and a chorus of strings poured out from the orchestra pit, painting the room with sweet enchantment. Jane let the music wash over her as she waited for her cue. The Maiden didn't start off the ballet, so she had some time to acclimate, stretching her feet and getting ready to do her job. But more importantly, she had time to restore her love of dance.

Jane closed her eyes. The music swelled, lighting her core with excitement. Her circumstances didn't matter when the music hit. Nothing mattered. Only dance. Only peace. Only joy. Only the magic of storytelling through movement.

The music reached its crescendo and, like lightning, Jane opened her eyes and hit the stage with a volley of fast bourrée steps to the center. The stage was hers to fill with grace, elegance, and charm. As a ballerina, she was known for her soft, captivating lines and intense artistry. No other dancer in the company could match her acting skills—none could compare to the truth she brought in every movement. When people watched her dance, they lived a little, experiencing every emotion as the character did. They escaped into the story world and lived lives they could only imagine.

Jane breathed life into the story on the stage. She made the audience's soul sing, unlike any other dancer in the company—in the country, possibly even the world. That's just how good she was.

A young prodigy.

No mirror enchantment, no spell, and no false facade could compare.

People traveled from all over the world to watch her perform, and little girls dreamed of one day becoming famous like her.

If only they knew what her life was truly like, they'd never trade places. Because, like mirror deals, her talent and fame came with a hefty price.

Not all that glitters is gold... often, it is rancid at its core.

This ballet began with a difficult variation, followed by an even more challenging pas de deux, and concluded with a quick costume change. Jane had seven costume changes throughout the show, with four people assisting her in changing her headpieces, bodice, and tutu. Often, one of the four had to cut her out of a costume and then sew her into another because the fit had to be that precise.

But Jane loved her first variation because she danced alone in front of the invisible magic mirror at the Queen's Royalle Ballet. There was something so peaceful and calming about it, and every time she danced in front of it, she felt like she was finally home. It rested at the back of the stage, and—to her knowledge—only she could see it. Jane would have thought she was going crazy if she hadn't lived in New Swansea, the country of magic mirrors.

In New Swansea, hundreds of magic mirrors held trapped gods inside, and those gods used their magic through deals, trading information, wealth, prestige, and magic at terrible costs. People negotiated to improve their lives, but the bigger the ask, the bigger the cost and unintended, unknown consequences.

Jane wasn't old enough to have made a bargain yet. Citizens weren't allowed to trade until the age of twenty-three, and then they were required to make at least one deal, called their Mirror

Rite. But people could take advantage of others' deals, and there was an entire economy built around them, like Jane's Mirror Cosmetics.

But even though she had never made a deal, the mirrors sang to her soul. They called to her, and sometimes they screamed at her to free them—like she would even know how. The Queen's Royalle Ballet's mirror was no different.

It sang soft melodies of joy and appeared to her when it wouldn't for anyone else, and it was for this precise reason she liked dancing alone to it on the stage. They shared a beautiful synergy.

The show always ended too soon. If she could, she'd stay dancing forever. But her happiness never lasted. No, it was always temporary, and now she had to meet up with her husband, smile for reporters at the gala, and most likely endure *"celebration"* sex which involved her husband rutting on top of her as she pretended to enjoy his small, lackluster penis.

At least when he gave her to one of his debtors for a night, they usually had a bigger package. Jane had to look on the bright side of being a toy for men to use and abuse. It was the only way she survived it. And his debtors weren't *that* cruel to her. None of them cared about her pleasure, but at least most of them didn't hit her—some were even gentle. Her husband was neither kind nor gentle. He seemed to like painting her body with bruises.

The icy midwinter air sliced along her skin as she exited the back of the Ballet and headed first to bathe and then to the gala. Another bitterly cold night in a string of them. It didn't help that the streets of the Gold Quarter were literally made of metal. Not only were they slippery, they were also freezing.

The sweat-soaked strand of hair dangling from her bun hardened into an icicle within moments of being outside.

Not again. Jane groaned.

But her groan was quickly turned into a muffled scream as a man in a balaclava and gloves jumped out at her and covered her mouth with a slightly sweet-tasting rag.

Jane's knees buckled first before her eyes fluttered shut, and darkness enveloped her.

Chapter Two

Age 21.

Pain.

All Jane knew was pain.

It clung to her skin and soaked into her hair. But the worst of it felt like it was coming from her wrists. She swallowed, trying to get her bearings, but the world was all black.

A flash of wet coldness hit her.

She tried to blink her eyes open, but it was difficult; they appeared to be swollen shut. From drugs or abuse? She didn't know. She didn't remember anything past the ballet.

"Welcome back, little whore." The words echoed through her brain, but she didn't understand them or their origin.

Water hit her face again and dripped from her eyelashes as she desperately tried to pry open her lids. With considerable effort, she eventually managed to do it. She blinked open her drugged and droopy eyes.

Everywhere she looked was grey concrete and silver chains, and she was hanging from metal cuffs and chains with her hands stretched up above her.

Her shoulder ached. No, scrap that, everything hurt, and she felt the blood draining further and further from her fingers and arms.

A black haze stepped in front of her, and she blinked again, trying to focus.

"What do you want from me?" Jane croaked, her mouth dry.

"Oh, we don't want anything from you," a man who had finally come into her vision said, as he grasped her chin. "You are the payment. We are going to torture you until you die, and then we are going to hang your mangled body from the ceiling in your husband's living room."

Jane sucked in a breath. She'd known she would die young, but she never imagined it would be because of her horrible husband. The idea made her livid.

"He won't care," Jane said through gritted teeth.

"We shall see."

Then the torture began.

~

A high-pitched ringing sounded in Jane's ears as she blinked and tried to open her eyes again. One of them was swollen shut and leaking blood.

The disorientation hit her in waves. Jane knew she should remember where she was, how she'd gotten there, and why her wrists felt like they were burning. But she didn't, at least not at first.

So, she tried to take in her surroundings. The room was pitch black, or at least she thought it was because she couldn't see anything, and she was pretty sure she managed to get one of her eyes open. *Pretty sure.*

Jane didn't mind the darkness as much as the sound.

Drip, drop. Drip, drop. Drip drop.

A sound that would haunt her nightmares for years to come.

Drip, drop. Drip, drop.

She shuddered and tried to pull her hands up to inspect her

wounds, but her wrists chafed against the ropes that stopped her from moving more than an inch or two.

She was trapped, tied to a chair, and hurt... badly.

It was then that the world came crashing in. She'd been kidnapped and endured three nights? Four days? Seven? Jane's nose bunched as she tried to remember, the movement shooting pain through her cheeks. She moaned. Everything fucking hurt, and she didn't know how long she'd been in this room, and whether it was a blessing or a curse not to remember.

She vaguely remembered being hung from the ceiling, so the chair was a relief at least.

The one thing she knew for sure was that they had a healer. After she'd passed out from the beatings and carvings, she'd wake up, and someone would come and fix her flesh just enough for her to take it all again.

Again and again and again.

Jane sat in the darkness and silence for what felt like an age, and in that time, her memories seeped back in. Fear and anticipation were her constant companions. They sat on her chest like a heavy weight. She didn't want to die. She'd just become the prima ballerina. She had too much to live for, and she refused to let this end her. But how could she get out of it?

These men wanted her to pay for her husband stealing from them. Was there anything she could offer to fix it?

Eventually, three men entered the room and turned on the light. It took her too long to acclimate, and she blinked several times to do it, each movement causing a rippling of pain through her.

When she was able to see again, she noticed that one of the men was burly, another was average in build, and the third was muscular, but dressed in a sharp suit and cravat.

"Please stop." The words came out as a low, husky whimper. Her throat was raw, too. Had she been screaming? "Please, I'll do whatever you want."

The burly man stepped forward. "Unless you have a magic

pussy that can grant us the 100,000 siennas your husband stole from us, there is nothing you can give us."

100,000 siennas? What? That was the fortune of several men combined. What a fucking fool. Her husband would never learn.

"Unfortunately, deary, you are the lesson," said the one in the sharp suit. "We're going to kill you and leave you for your husband to find."

"Then why torture me first?" Jane said with a sarcastic lilt. Sometimes, her tongue was a bit too barbed for her own good. Usually, she chose to respond to situations with calmness, but on occasion, she just couldn't hold herself back.

The sharp one's eyes flared—clearly the leader. "Because we enjoy it."

Jane clenched her teeth. Where was the honor in beating a woman? These men were just as bad as her husband.

Acid frothed in Jane's esophagus. She hated these men. No, more than hated them. If she could, one day, she was going to make them pay. But first, she had to survive, and if it was money that they wanted, then she'd get it.

She only had to Bargain with a Mirror God.

Easy...

The punishment for getting caught bargaining underage was high. However, how could it be worse than this?

She'd have to do it.

In New Swansea, the country was run by Mirror Gods, also known as Bargainers, who traded magic, wealth, and knowledge for a cost... often a wretched one. However, people couldn't bargain with them until they reached the age of majority, twenty-three. However, that often didn't matter because there were entire markets and businesses devoted to making mirror bargains, so people didn't have to. They would get mirror objects and then sell them to the public. That was how Jane could easily buy Mirror Cosmetics to cover her bruises.

At twenty-three, every citizen had to do their Mirror Rite—bargain at least once with a god—or receive seven years of bad luck. Gangs, businesses, and markets took advantage of this fact and paid those performing the rite to bargain on their behalf.

Jane hadn't thought much about her rite yet; she still had two years before she was of age, and she figured she'd take one of the businesses up on their offer. She'd make a low-level bargain with a harmless mirror and get some money out of it.

But now, if she wanted to live, she'd have to bargain for seven fortunes' worth of money, and lower-level, harmless mirrors would never, *ever* make that deal. Jane wasn't even sure if they could. There seemed to be a hierarchy of Mirror Gods, but they were never made public.

One thing for sure was that the Looking Glass—also known as the Mirror of Nightmares—was the most powerful god in the country. He was one of the only gods whose deals and magic extended outside of his mirror cage. But there was no way in all the heavens and earth that she would bargain with him.

So, who else?

Midnight was powerful but known for being unhinged.

Beautiful Decay was powerful but cruel.

Chaos had been dormant for years, but she would have been a good option. She was a psychopath, but she enjoyed making good deals with pretty women. She especially enjoyed talented women. Jane was both beautiful and talented, but sadly, Chaos hadn't let anyone inside her prison in thirty-nine years.

Jane was pulled out of her thoughts by a young brunette woman, possibly Jane's age or a bit older, who approached her and murmured, "I am sorry, miss, but it's time to heal you."

Jane flinched. This woman's healing hurt just as much as the beatings, which was precisely why every time the brunette came to heal, she apologized for it.

"Wait, wait," Jane said a little frantically. "Before you do all this again, perhaps we could make a deal."

The leader raised an eyebrow.

"I might not have a magic pussy, but I can make a mirror bargain for the money you need."

The leader narrowed his eyes. "A bargain that size would come with a steep price."

Well, considering you're going to murder me, a steep price seems far better cost than that, Jane thought, but instead, she said, "I'm willing to pay it."

"I want an endless supply of riches."

Jane swallowed. That was an impossible deal.

"And I want it from Nightmare."

Jane gasped. He was playing with her. No one got a good deal from Nightmare. No one. This was just another means to torture Jane. What the fuck had her husband done for them to hate him —and by association, her—so much?

"Why not Beautiful Decay?" Jane dug her fingernails into her wooden armrests.

"Only Nightmare will do."

Chapter Three

Age 21.

What would a Den of Nightmares look like?

Not this.

Or perhaps this was precisely what nightmares looked like: grand, luxurious palaces with turrets scraping against the sky and stained-glass windows allowing rose-honey light to illuminate gilded walls and enchanting halls.

It was a fairytale come to life, and Jane Whitfield-Klein hated fairytales.

She hated damsels in distress and Prince Charmings fighting great beasts to save them. But, most importantly, Jane hated happy endings. They didn't exist—no prince was coming to save her, and none ever would. Because princes were daydreams, and Jane lived in a world of night terrors.

How fitting that this is where she had ended up.

A snake of nerves coiled up her arm. If Jane didn't bargain with the Mirror of Nightmares for enough riches to satisfy both the Cobra Lilies and her horrible husband, then the gang would kill her. And she wasn't particularly fond of the idea of dying.

17

So, she squared her shoulders and swallowed hard, causing her mouth to purse and her split lip to sting.

Just another reminder of the gang and their price. At least they'd had a healer patch her up a little before forcing her into the mirror. It was the small niceties Jane had taught herself to cherish. It didn't matter how pathetic that might make her

Jane was used to being pathetic.

But right now, she had a goal to accomplish: find the biggest villain in the world and somehow convince him to bargain with her for an impossible amount of money with no lasting consequences.

Easy.

So fucking easy, right?

The sound of her heels clicked against the ornate marble floors as she walked further into the opulent lair. The Mirror God had to know she was inside his domain. Yet, he hadn't appeared.

Because he was toying with her.

Building up the anticipation and drama. Wanting fear to soak into her soul.

But Jane wouldn't be scared. Her life was horrific outside the mirror glass, so no matter what happened next, it wouldn't matter.

Death and abuse were her options out there. But hope existed inside the glass—even if that hope was also horrible.

Jane knew the legends, and she knew the Looking Glass was evil, but the depths of his evil was unknown. This made her hopeful in a strange way.

So, no matter how hard the Bargainer tried to unsettle or break her, it wouldn't work. Nothing broke Jane Whitfield. Not her parents' deaths, not losing her sister and being abandoned by her uncle, not marrying an abusive, disgusting man thirty years older than her. Not being tortured by a gang, and definitely not a Mirror God.

Because Jane's strength was unbeatable. Unbreakable.

As if on cue, a string quartet began playing an off-key melody in a three-four time signature—a rotten waltz.

The god was trying to unsettle her. He had chosen the wrong trick for the wrong girl, because music could never harm Jane. Music was her comfort. Even the creepy kind. *Especially* the creepy kind.

Jane pinched her eyes closed and let the chords hit her as if they were a physical force, visualizing them as ballet ribbons floating and pulsating through the air. The silk caressed her arms, legs, and face like a lover after a long round of lovemaking—not that she knew what that feeling was like.

With her eyes shut, her other senses took over, and the scent of lavender, mixed with hints of basil and jasmine, wafted toward her as if mingling with the music and ribbons.

And it was casting a calming spell.

A deep sense of peace settled into Jane's bones. It was probably the opposite of what the god intended. Even though it was utterly ridiculous and unadvisable, Jane felt safer in the mirror with a devil she didn't know than the ones living in the outside world.

If she could bottle this moment and keep it forever, she would.

But moments never lasted.

Opening her eyes, she walked to the edge of a balcony overlooking a massive ballroom lit by hundreds of red bayberry candles in elaborate gilded sconces. In the corner were four translucent ghostlike string players—two violins, a viola, and a cello—and across the floor were translucent couples dancing a waltz. Floating through the air were aerialists and acrobats.

A ghost ball.

The hairs on Jane's arms rose, and her heart pounded in her ears, ticking like a broken grandfather clock.

"Beautiful," she whispered so low only a vampire would hear it.

All the candles flickered at the sound of her voice, and time slowed.

Jane sucked in a breath, and time crashed into her, and so did a man. She choked on her breath as a forceful gust of wind hit her in the chest. Her body was thrown off its axis, and her back hit the wall opposite the balcony railing with a loud thud.

Before she could orient herself, a large hand clutched her jaw hard.

"Witch," a man hissed with the low, dark tones of a bass singer.

Jane blinked twice, trying to get her eyes to focus, and when they did, all the air in her lungs was knocked out of her once again. Because there was no question who was pinning her to the wall. The Lord of Nightmares. And, oh, was this man—god—the most attractive person she'd ever seen. So stunning, her eyes instinctively flicked away in shame.

Her heart drummed in her ears because she was not worthy to look upon such a being.

Yet she also couldn't help but look at him. Because he was fucking beauty and fury made manifest.

He was tall, muscular in frame, but it wasn't just that. His demeanor and being were so striking that no words could do him justice, not even the word "divine." If Jane had to try, she'd say it was like his body had been carved out of the rarest diamonds in the world, which then morphed into unblemished, unwilling flesh.

His eyes were also indescribable. The color was the deepest azure she'd ever seen, laced with sparkling silver. But even that description didn't do them justice. They were simply magic.

Every part of this man was enchanted. Inhuman.

Impossible.

His hair looked like it had been dipped in melted silver, one black streak remaining. It was almost as if the mirror prison were slowly taking over him. The strands of silver were pure magic, they glowed and shimmered like liquified metal, like mercury.

Jane imagined that, like mercury, this god was also toxic to the touch.

As she took him in, he did the same. His gaze tracked up her body, pausing as he moved. Oh, so slowly tracking over her skin. Jane shivered from the phantom contact, his stare a physical force touching her in the most indecent yet alluring ways.

Her breath hitched as he finally made his way up to her face and hair.

"Cinnamon red," he said, seething, anger pouring out of him like paint dripping off a canvas.

What was happening? This response wasn't normal... at all. This wasn't the anger of trespassing. It was something else. Something darker.

"Witch," he growled again.

Jane swallowed. "I'm not a witch."

"You reek of witch." The vein in his jaw ticked, and his finger-pads dug deeper into her neck.

"I am not."

His eyes sparked and grew distant, as if lost in a memory. "She said you'd come."

"Who?"

He blinked, and his gaze moved to hers. "Two thousand years, witch. Two thousand years I've been waiting."

Acid crawled up her throat, and she didn't know what to do or say. This Bargainer was crazed. Beautiful but unhinged.

"Why have you come? To destroy me?" His voice was a cobra readying to strike.

"Destroy you?" Jane placed a palm against the wall to steady herself. "I just want to bargain, Mr. Nightmares."

The god cocked his head. "Mr. Nightmares." He twirled one of her curls between his fingers with his free hand, as if enchanted by it. "Red, that's not my name."

Jane's chest heaved, matching her frantic heart and breath rate. Yet she kept her voice steady. "What is your name?"

"Lord Gavriil Alexei Dimitris Draven Hawthorne Wrixon Wryte, the Count of Draculei."

"That's quite a mouthful."

His lips twitched. Unclear if in amusement or worsening anger. He twirled a curl again, fixated on it. "You are far prettier than she ever was, and that truly is dangerous."

"Who is she?"

"Do not ask questions," he snapped, his grip growing tighter on her throat. "Now, tell me why I shouldn't simply snap your neck right now, prophecies be damned."

Prophecies?

Jane swallowed past the lump in her throat. "I—"

Fuck. This was going much worse than she had ever imagined. But then, she should have known better. Nothing ever went well for her. Ever.

Her fingers clutched the wall, digging in as if she could escape behind it. She looked for a way out, but there wasn't any. This man was a god and far, *far* stronger than her.

"I just want to bargain with you," she whispered.

Nightmare's gaze turned up to the ceiling as if in thought. His movements were slow, like a snake stalking its prey. So irritatingly slow. It felt like it took hours between each thought. And maybe it did. What was time in a mirror?

"I think I will kill you."

Jane shuddered. But she held her resolve. "If you want to kill me, you really must get in line. The men waiting outside your mirror also want to kill me, and will if I don't get them what they want."

His eyes snapped back to her. "Only I get to kill you." Nightmare leaned in closer, and his thumb tracked across her split lip as if he were noticing it for the first time. "You are a fragile little thing, aren't you?"

Jane's nose flared, and she felt the tiny grooves of the wallpaper for comfort. This Bargainer wanted to kill her. The men outside wanted to kill her. Half of the time, her husband threatened to kill her.

Did anyone want her alive? Or even *want* her at all?

Of course not.

"Will you at least do it quickly?" she asked, the corners of her eyes stinging.

At this, he blinked again, and with his free hand, he caressed her cheek. "So fragile. So weak."

"Yes."

"You are mine." His thumb caressed her lips again.

Jane's eyebrows creased. "What?"

He nodded, as if answering someone else's question. "Yes, you'll be mine..."

The god definitely wasn't talking to her. It was as if he were talking to a ghost or a long-lost memory.

The candles flickered again, and the music got louder.

How long had it been since someone had come to this mirror god's domain? He seemed to be going crazy from all the isolation.

"I—" Jane bit the inside of her cheek. "Nightmare, what—"

"*Do not* call me that."

Jane shivered. "What should I call you?"

"I have many names. Choose one."

"Lord Wryte... umm Count of Draculei, Lord Draculei?"—she cleared her throat—"I would like to make a deal with you for—"

His hand moved over her mouth, silencing her.

"Shh, pretty one." He leaned in and closed his eyes, his mouth resting on her neck as he inhaled deeply. "Tasty."

His teeth—fangs—grazed her neck.

What the fuck was happening? Was Lord Draculei a vampire? No, she would not call him that, not in her head. He was Nightmare, because he was her nightmare right now.

But he didn't bite down. Instead, he trailed a kiss down her throat, and her toes curled in her shoes as she clutched the wall tighter for support.

The Mirror of Nightmares was smelling her, touching her, and she liked it. She was getting... Jane didn't even know what was happening to her body. It was like a spark bursting through her center. It pulsed with anticipation, and she absentmindedly glanced down to his pants to where his cock was hardening against her. She sucked in a deep breath. It seemed... very large. Fear and excitement skittered up her back. What that must feel like...

What the fuck was she doing? Jane never enjoyed that act. Ever. Yet now she was staring at a man's legs, imagining his member... Possibly inside her.

Stop it.

You hate penises. All they'd ever brought was pain and a pounding discomfort.

"Mine." His hot breath caressed her earlobe as his fingers raked through her hair, and he tilted her chin up as if he were going to feed on her.

And Jane both wanted to be fed on by this god-vampire and to be his. Whatever that meant. Even as she also hated him.

Jane's breath hitched, wanting, needing him to... to do something, anything, but at that precise moment, in a blink, he was gone.

"What?" she breathed, her weak knees only standing with the support from the wall.

"Your bargain," he said, matter-of-factly, leaning against the balcony railing, his demeanor utterly shifted. Strong, coherent, and powerful. "What is it that you came for?"

Jane bit her lip and stared at him. Her chest rose in passion-filled breaths.

What the fuck was going on?

"Your bargain, witch?"

"I am not a witch."

"So you say." The corner of his lips rose. "To the point, why are you here?"

Her brow furrowed. "To bargain with you for an unending supply of money."

"For the men outside?"

So he was listening. Interesting.

Jane nodded. Everything about this man was baffling. "Yes, and my husband."

For her husband, so he wouldn't have another reason to hit her after this was all over.

"Husband." He chewed on the word and spit it out, and the room temperature dropped. "And they'll kill you if you don't get them the money?"

"Yes."

Unease burrowed into Jane's stomach.

"Well, as I said before, only I get to kill you." He crossed his arms and smirked. "And I've decided not to do that yet. I'd rather play with you first."

"Play..." Jane drew out the word. What did he mean by that?

"Yes." His eyes twinkled. "So I guess I'll have to give you that unending money supply."

He wasn't serious, was he? That easy?

"But there is only one deal I will accept from you."

An anchor dropped in Jane's heart. She knew his next words would change her life forever and ruin her all at once.

"And what is that?"

"You."

"Me?"

His wicked smile widened. "You will become my bride and anchor. I will own your soul, mind, and body, and you will do everything I command."

Every muscle in Jane's body froze.

"No." The word came out as a broken whisper. *Absolutely not.*

The only thing Jane had was her mind... And soul. Everyone had already taken everything else. Her husband owned her body. As did the ballet. But her mind, her soul, that was hers and hers alone.

"You are afraid."

Yes. She swallowed.

"Do not worry." He took a gentle step toward her. "I treat my brides well... for the most part."

That didn't matter, even if she believed him, which she didn't. Because if she gave him this. It would be everything. Life would have stolen everything from her.

"I cannot be your bride. I am already married." It wasn't the protest she wanted to make, but it was the one that came out of her mouth. "See?" Jane held up her left hand, showing off her hideous ring.

Nightmare seemed to have a visceral reaction to it, tensing and shifting away. But she couldn't tell if the response was from the ugly nature of the ring, or the mere fact that she was married, or both.

"I will keep your loving husband alive for now."

Please don't.

"When he dies, you will become my bride fully, in all ways,"— he took another step toward her—"but for now, I will give you a reprieve. You will be my bride in all but name. And when he dies, I will have all of you."

"I can't." Her knuckles turned white from digging into the wall.

"By all means, leave my mirror." He motioned to the exit portal, knowing her options were him or death. This wasn't a choice at all.

Nightmare was a true villain. A monster. But was he the better monster?

Yes.

"Alright." Her nose flared, and tears grew at the edges of her eyes.

"You understand you will not be able to deny me?" He took another step toward her. "You will attend to all of my demands, always."

A tear fell down her face, and his gaze tracked it as it went.

He took the last step to meet her, reached out, and wiped away the tear with his knuckle. "I will be mostly good to you." *Unless you disobey me*, hung between them, unspoken.

Jane inhaled sharply, more tears meeting the first one. But even as she cried, she wouldn't let him, or anyone, break her. She rolled her shoulders back and met his gaze.

He smiled at her resolve. "You're going to be so much fun." He stroked her jaw with his thumb. "You don't break."

"No, I don't."

He waggled an eyebrow. "Good. Do you understand what you are agreeing to?" he asked gently.

Jane nodded. "Yes."

He lit up like a thousand beeswax candles. "Then the deal is set. You will have an unending supply of riches in exchange for being my bride and anchor, and you will obey my every command."

"Yes," she said harshly.

"Then we seal it as all weddings do, with a kiss." And before she could respond or protest, he cupped her face, tipped her head back, and touched his lips to hers.

The kiss was gentle and sweet. Barely any pressure at all, like he didn't want to intrude. It was respectful.

From his lips, magic poured out and into her, seeping into every ounce of her bloodstream. Coating her. Claiming her. Changing her.

Externally nothing looked different, but inside, she felt his bond, his control. Like he was now a part of her, welding them together forever. It was an unbreakable bond that not even death could break.

His lips left her swiftly, but his hand reached out and clutched hers. He turned it over and placed a metal object in her palm.

It was a ring, and she gasped when she saw it—a rare, ancient red diamond ring. But it wasn't just any ring. "Is this the Heart Diamond?"

Nightmare raised an eyebrow. "Yes."

"But it's been missing for thousands of—" She stopped mid-sentence, remembering who and what he was.

"Keep it on you always."

The command physically washed over her, her blood spiking with heat. Even if she didn't want to, Jane had to do what he said.

She'd have to do what he said for the rest of her life, and he could ask for anything.

Anything.

She'd traded one monster for something far, far worse. She should have just let the gang kill her.

"Well, bride,"—he stroked her face—"I am going to have such fun with you... Until you break."

"Nothing can break me." She sucked in an icy breath. "Not even you."

"Then I will enjoy trying."

Chapter Four

Age 21.

"Dinner," he commanded, turning on his heel and expecting her to follow. And as if her shoes were tied to strings which were latched to him, she was forced to walk in his shadow.

Her heart pounded in her chest, defiant, resistant, but her footfalls were light and cooperative.

As they walked, Jane took in his domain. It was a gothic-style mansion harking back to the Middle Ages, except it wasn't just any castle. It was alive, the walls whispering and watching. Invisible eyes followed her as she moved, and she felt them on her skin like a haunted caress. A shiver ran up her spine.

The rooms they passed were not typical. They were like portals to other dimensions. One room shone with the moon's light, another was covered in dancing shadows, and a third was simply empty save for the rotting wood of the walls and floor.

But the room that caught her eye the most was a ballroom made from briars. It had likely once been a magical, lush forest, but it was now a vacant, twisted, and cursed place.

Almost like the man walking her to her doom.

Mirror-blessed buildings often took on the personalities of the mirror that created them; perhaps this castle was a peek into Nightmare's soul.

Jane shuddered. That was a terrifying idea.

They reached their destination, the Dining Hall, with a long wooden table stretching across a room filled with portraits and nature landscapes.

Nightmare motioned for her to sit in the chair at the head of the table, across from him. The distance was both uncomfortable and a relief. On the one hand, it was awkward and cold, but on the other, she didn't really want to be anywhere near this monster.

Jane slid into her seat quietly. Waiting and watching.

And he said nothing. Did nothing. He simply stared.

Jane sucked in a breath and held it. She wanted to look away, to hide, but she didn't. She rolled her shoulders back and caught his glare.

The seconds ticked by, feeling like hours, an eternity that bent and distorted, like paint melting into a grey-black sludge. And perhaps Nightmare could mess with time, at least in his realm.

Letting out her breath, Jane ran her fingers along the rich wooden table, over the intricately carved grooves. All the while, his eyes never left her, and the longer they sat there in the unbearable silence, the darker his gaze turned.

And Jane didn't know what to do. What was there to do? She had no idea of the level of his monstrousness, nor did she know what he even wanted from her.

Was it sex? Like all the rest? Was he going to shove her against the table and have his way with her?

Jane bit her lip. If that were his plan, she'd survive it. She'd always had. She just turned her mind off. Her brain was like a light switch. When it was on, she was kind, present, and empathetic, but when she turned it off, she became distant, ruthless, and dead inside.

But nothing happened. He didn't move to hurt her, nor did

he try to make her feel at ease. Just nothing... Nothing but a glower.

Nightmare was the master of glaring. Something he must have perfected over centuries.

Ice radiated from him. His fury burned so hot it was cold, and his mood changed the room's temperature. Goosebumps rose on Jane's arms, and she shivered, her breath becoming visible. It was like an arctic wind had blown through.

His stare was literally turning her into an icicle.

Jane curled her toes in her shoes and curled her napkin between her fingers to feel more present in the room, but also to have something to occupy her hands. Because she would not give in to his intimidation, he'd made this deal with her. He wanted her to be his bride and anchor... whatever that meant. Jane had no clue what it meant, but one thing was certain: He needed her for a purpose.

So, she would not fear him. Not yet, at least.

"I should have killed you." His voice caused the hair on her arms to rise.

Jane's nostrils flared. Why? What had she done to him? But that's not how she responded. He would not break her so instead, she said, "Perhaps you should have." She shivered again and rubbed her arms. She might be able to resist him with her words, but her body felt the cold seeping between them.

"Since I seem to have made a terrible mistake, we will have rules. Guidelines for how I expect you to behave," he said authoritatively.

Jane nodded. It was best to keep quiet and measure the god. Let him set the game they were playing.

"Because you have a despicable husband"—he had no idea how true that statement was—"I will have to share you... For now." He said the last bit through his teeth.

Jane opened her mouth to respond, but only a sound came out, much like a gasp. She didn't want to go back to her husband. She didn't want to be shared.

When Nightmare's eyes darkened, a shadow coating them, Jane knew he'd misinterpreted her noise. He thought she didn't want to be shared *with* him. Not that she wished quite the opposite, but she couldn't get herself to say it.

It would give him too much power.

"Honor compels me to share, despite having no interest in doing so." He placed his hands firmly down on the table. "So here is how it will be. You will be mine every other week for the whole week. During that time, I will do it with you as I please. On the other weeks, he can have you and do whatever he pleases."

Jane pinched her lips together. Had she no say in it? By either man? Was she to be a toy to be played with and tossed around until she was used and broken?

"On the weeks you will be with me, I expect you in my realm nightly. You will have dinner with me and sleep in my bed every night. When I have need of you, I will command you to do whatever I want."

Jane wrung her hands in her lap, her eyes stinging at the corners, yet still she said nothing. It was easier to avoid wicked men's wrath if she didn't provoke them in any way.

"Do you understand me?"

Jane inhaled sharply. "Yes, my lord."

He nodded, flashing her a look that said, *This is too easy*, before continuing. "You may have free rein of my realm when you are here, except you may not enter the Shadow Wing."

"Shadow Wing?"

His glower spoke volumes. "The wing coated in shadows."

"Right."

He moved on as if she'd said nothing. "There will be times when I command you with the magic, and you will be incapable of resisting me, and there will be times I simply tell you to do something without the compulsion. I expect you to obey me either way."

Jane's eyebrows crinkled together. "So you'll be testing me?"

"Yes." His voice was liquid darkness. "I expect that you will never lie to me." Jane waited to feel the pull of the compulsion—the unbeatable urge to comply, but nothing happened. She felt nothing. "That was a command without the force of magic, yet I expect you to comply regardless."

He lifted an eyebrow as if challenging her.

"Why not force me always to tell you the truth?" she asked. Trusting her not to lie to him was rather foolish. Of course, she *would* lie to him. Cruel men often didn't like the truth.

"Because I want you to choose to obey me. Always. Do you understand?"

"Yes. My Lord." And Jane wasn't sure if it was a lie or not. She'd rather not lie to him, but if necessary, she absolutely would.

Chapter Five

Age 21.

When Jane made her deal, this was not at all what she expected. She expected pain, torture, and trauma. Not silence, awkward tension, and lingering confusion. After dinner, he escorted her to his bedroom with a massive four-poster bed in it. He left the room to change and then slid under his sheets. No words. No commands, just silence.

Jane stood, her lips slightly parted, staring at him, her heart roaring in her ears. What was she supposed to do? Get in bed, and if she did, would he... How cruel was he going to be? Was he going to be at the level of her husband, or would he be like the debtors—bad but not horrible? Or would he be a new level of brokenness?

She swallowed. There was no way to know which was worse. But she could survive anything.

She already had.

"There are nightgowns in the wardrobe." Nightmare pointed to the side of the room.

Jane's fingernails bit at the palm of her hand, and she sucked in a tight breath as she slowly, as if not wanting to wake a sleeping tiger, walked to the wardrobe. She felt his eyes following her every movement.

She selected a nightgown, and then, button by button, she undid first her jacket, then her ruffled undershirt, then her top skirt. It wasn't until the petticoats and corset that Jane paused. Anxiety stroked the lining of her stomach. His gaze was on her the whole time, as if he were assessing his prize.

What would he do when she got down to her chemise? Would he ask her to take it off?

But he didn't say a word. Jane untied her petticoats and stepped out of them, then pulled the strings of her corset, loosened and removed it. She had gotten down to her last items of clothing and nothing.

It was infuriatingly silent, so much so that it took on its own life. He was as quiet as a shattered porcelain doll. It was creepy and haunting.

But Jane wouldn't bend or break. He had made the deal. He had bought her soul and body. Why not show it all to him? Show him what he bought. So, glaring directly into his eyes, Jane slowly, torturously removed one button of her combination chemise. Taunting him.

Her breast fell free, and she slid her drawers down her legs and stepped out of them. Naked, save for her socks and shoes.

He didn't move, but his intense, midnight gaze took in first her breasts and then her pussy, and finally the curves of her hips and legs. His only reaction was a bob of his Adam's apple.

Jane couldn't even tell if he liked what he saw. The man—the god—was unreadable.

And she was strangely disappointed. She wanted him to... Want her? Like her? She didn't even know. But not this. Not indifference.

Jane turned, grabbed her chosen nightgown off the hanger, and pulled it over her head. Then, she slid under the covers next to him.

Their bodies were mere inches apart, but he didn't move to decrease the distance. Instead, he snapped his fingers, and every beeswax candle in the room faded into darkness.

And then... Nothing. Absolutely nothing.

Jane expected him to pounce on her. To mount her and roughly stick his cock inside of her—like all the rest. But still, nothing. And somehow, it was infuriating.

The anticipation felt like its own nightmare, and that may have been the point.

Or maybe she just wasn't enough for him.

Did he regret his choice?

Did she want him to?

She bit her lip, inhaled sharply, and stared up at the darkness, counting his breaths until she drifted off to sleep. She could not want her captor.

He only said fifteen words in the morning before kicking her out of his mirror. "Go home, tell your husband of our deal, and meet me again tonight at sundown."

And Jane was reasonably confident he would be the one to break her—with his silence, if nothing else.

Leaving the mirror had been far worse than entering it. First, Jane was forced to deal with her husband's debtors, and then, finally, her despicable husband. When she had finally arrived home after days of torture and one night in a mirror, he'd hit her. Slapped her across the face, pulled her by her hair, and slammed her head into the wall. She had crumpled to the floor, at which point he kicked her twice before leaving the room.

And that was before Jane even had a chance to tell him about her deal with Nightmare and the money. He left her with two black eyes, a bruised side, and possibly a broken rib. Thankfully, she managed to get through telling him without any more injuries

—because she lied. She told her husband that if he hurt her again, Nightmare would come after him.

It wasn't true. Of course, it wasn't. Nightmare didn't care about her. He wouldn't do anything to her husband, but he was still a villain, and Jane would use all within her power to gain some semblance of control over the situation. Even lie.

And, oh, did Jane lie. Because she didn't stop at telling her husband not to abuse her, no, she told him that the deal with Nightmare was for three weeks of the month, not the two the deal promised.

She'd get a whole week to herself.

Jane didn't know where she would stay and what she would do with the week alone, but at least she would have it.

Amazingly, the lies worked. Her husband hadn't touched her. Instead, he popped a bottle of sparkling wine and celebrated his new endless supply of money, saying, "Well, if you have to fuck a mirror for my wealth, so be it. How rough is he? You know what, don't tell me. I'd like to imagine all the ways he tries to break you."

A charmer.

But that was her husband, and Jane was so glad Nightmare had commanded her to return.

But returning wasn't easy with all the bruises. So, after using Mirror Cosmetics and Mirror Balm—a medicine that helped reduce swelling and increased healing speeds—Jane took a streetcar back to the Grand Library that housed the Mirror of Nightmares and stepped right back into his mirror.

Entering the mirror felt like promises kept and gentle comfort, like a hug from a parent who loved her, or even a lover who'd never let her go. But that was the insidious part of the Mirror of Nightmares. His realm felt safe... But there was no way it could ever be.

Jane hadn't made it two feet into the realm before Nightmare appeared from the shadows in front of her and said, "Turn around. We're leaving."

"Leaving?" Jane's eyebrows flew up. "The mirror? Is that even possible?"

"With you, it is. You're my anchor." At her continued baffled look, he explained, "When you made your deal, you agreed to be my bride and anchor. As long as you are wearing this,"—he stepped closer, and with one finger, he slowly pulled the chain with the wedding ring out from beneath her blouse and between her breasts—"I can leave my mirror whenever I want."

What? Jane gasped. That was not good. The mirror was a prison; it kept him inside, and she had given him everything he needed to escape it and wreak havoc on the city.

Fuck.

What had she done?

A wicked smile crept onto his cheeks. "Yes, precisely. Now let's go."

"Why did you want me to return? Couldn't you have left yourself? Why am I needed?"

Jane may have given him the ammunition for his gun, but she didn't need to see him use it. Perhaps that was a cowardly thought, and maybe she *was* a coward, but Jane didn't want to see him slaughter people.

Nightmare's smile fell flat.

So, he needed her with him for a reason, but he refused to say. Interesting. One day, she would find a way to use that against him.

They left the way she had come, and when his body left the portal, he somehow... changed. He was still impossibly beautiful, still god-like, yet somehow also more human. Was that possible?

Did his magic change outside of his realm? Jane truly hoped so. If he were less powerful outside of the mirror, he might be unable to destroy the city. She could hope.

As usual, Nightmare was utterly silent, not saying a single word to her the entire time. He simply walked ahead of her, got on a streetcar, and headed towards the Estate District. But his lack of words didn't keep his attention off her—no, she was his puzzle he was putting together with his eyes.

Jane swallowed and tried not to stare back, but that was an utterly useless endeavor because, somehow, she liked staring at him too, although she'd never admit that out loud.

The trip from the Art Sector to the Estate District was not very long, considering they bordered each other. So, after about ten minutes in the car, they disembarked in a neighborhood full of massive mansions.

Acid filled Jane's throat. She didn't like being around rich people, especially after living in an orphanage for six years. Granted, she wasn't poor—her husband had once dripped in jewels before bad deals and wasteful spending—and she hadn't been poor before her parents died. The Ashelles were an exceedingly wealthy family. However, unfortunately, neither Jane nor her younger sister, Quinnevere, received any of that wealth until they both turned twenty-five. So Jane had to wait until her sister, six years her junior, turned twenty-five, in ten years. There was still no guarantee that Jane would see any of the money, as the lawyers would inform Quinn on her 25th birthday. The problem was that Quinn didn't know she even had a sister.

When their parents died, their uncle could only take in one child. He wanted to take in Jane because she was ten and Quinn was four, but the only thing Jane cared about was keeping her younger sister safe, so she begged her uncle to take Quinn instead. Her uncle only agreed to do it as long as Jane would never be in Quinn's life. Unfortunately, the trauma from witnessing their parents' horrific murders had stripped all of Quinn's memories away.

It was painful that Quinn didn't remember, but it was ultimately better for both of them.

So, it wasn't that Jane was poor, but wealth reminded her of her pain, all its layers. From her husband to her parents to her uncle, wealth was a symbol of her trauma.

So she hated being in the Estate District, because it was where the wealthiest people in the city lived.

But it turns out Jane shouldn't have been worried about wealth. What she really should've been worried about was the monster standing beside her.

Nightmare found the mansion he was looking for and immediately broke down the door with zero effort—the man had superhuman strength outside his mirror. Not a good sign. He then marched into the dining room, picked a man up by his throat, and slammed him against the wall, causing the fine china to rattle.

The man's family sat in stunned silence, watching the scene unfold.

"Where is the diary?" Nightmare's voice was dark and full of twisted cobwebs.

"I... I don't know what you mean," the man stammered.

"Yes, you do."

A shiver stroked up Jane's arm, leaving gooseflesh in its wake.

"Helene's diary, where is it?" His voice pitched low, growing darker and deadlier. "Your family are the keepers of the Ash Witch secrets."

Ash Witch?

"Yes, we are, but—"

"But?"

The man's face grew ashen. "It would have been the Ashelles who knew."

"Ah, so you want to blame a dead family for your lack of knowledge?"

"There is one Ashelle left. The redhead girl who works at the morgue."

"No—" The word left Jane's lips in a wailing plea.

Nightmare's gaze cut to her.

"Please, she wouldn't know anything." Jane stepped toward him and reached out her arm.

Nightmare's nostrils flared, and he turned his eyes back to his victim. "You will stay here."

And as if in response to his words, ropes of light burst into the room and wrapped not just around the man's body, but all of his family, too.

Nightmare was a light bender. Jane had only heard stories of few vampires of old who could do that. But vampires were extinct.

Right?

Nightmare turned on his heel, grabbed her by the upper arm, and walked her into a parlor off the dining room. "Explain."

His voice was laced with compulsion, but she didn't know what he wanted her to explain. "What?"

"The girl…"

Jane gritted her teeth tightly, but she couldn't resist his magic. "She's my sister, and she doesn't know anything about Ash witches or diaries. She was four years old when our parents died, and if my parents knew, they never told me."

Jane had told him everything that she thought he might want to know because she didn't want to prolong the heat of his stare, which was burning into her like he might end her.

"So, you are an Ashelle?"

"I was… but I don't have that name anymore." It was part of the agreement with her uncle to keep Quinn safe.

"But you have their magic dormant in your veins."

"I don't know what that means."

"But you will."

"Please don't hurt my sister."

His dark eyes flared. "I won't… for now, since you were telling me the truth."

As Nightmare returned to the dining room, Jane grasped a cabinet to help hold the weight of her body. Her knees wobbled, and she gulped. Nightmare knew about Quinn.

The only thing she cared about. Now he could use that knowledge for leverage.

Jane listened to the click of her footfalls as she re-entered the room, trying to calm herself. She knew what she was about to see would be as bad as any nightmare the man with the same name could create.

And she wasn't wrong. As her foot hit the landing, she watched Nightmare break the man's neck and turn on the rest of the family.

"You hold the Ash Witch secrets." His attention was directed at the man's oldest son, who had to be about nineteen. "The next time I return, you'd better have more information for me."

That was the first time Jane watched Nightmare kill someone in front of her, but it would not be the last.

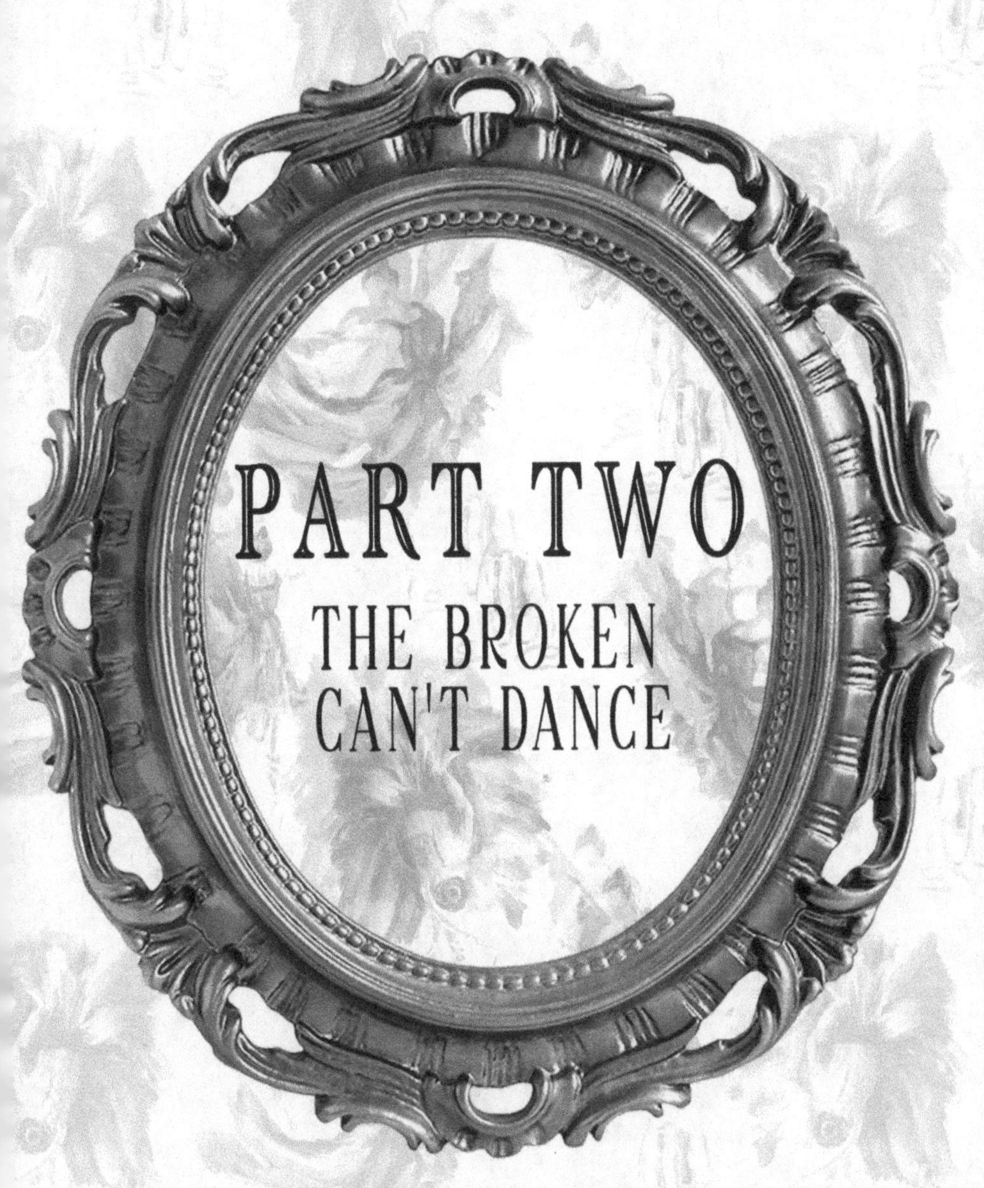
PART TWO
THE BROKEN
CAN'T DANCE

Chapter Six

AGE 23.

Murder had become far too mundane. In the past two years, Nightmare had murdered so many people in his quest to find Helene's journal that Jane had lost count.

She still had little idea why the diary was essential, or who Helene even was. From the tiny parcels of information Jane had stitched together, she'd gathered that Helene was an Ash Witch—a being as mythical as a vampire. Ash Witches were ancient, and they had created vampires, who in turn created mirrors... which trapped ancient gods. That second bit, Jane wasn't so sure about. The one fact she did know for sure—since it was taught in history classes—was that seven hundred years ago, when vampires were exterminated by humans, only mirrors remained, left to control the city through wicked bargains.

Ones like hers...

Although, apart for being complicit in evil acts and being Nightmare's minion, the deal hadn't been too bad. Nightmare never touched her; he hardly even commanded her. And, quite frankly, he barely spoke.

And the silence was... Soothing?

She didn't need words anymore. Nightmare never told her of his feelings or machinations, but his house sang to her. She could tell when he was in a good mood by the blossoming of flowers, the brightening of the paintings on the walls, or even the tone of the whispers coating the halls. The house liked her. It aided her, consoled her, and kept her safe. So, while Nightmare gave her nothing to work with, his house conspired against him to tell her his secrets.

Nightmare was in a good mood tonight. The wallpaper was brighter, and the blood roses were tight and freshly cut, with no hint of wilting or decay. Even the ghost servants who removed the cloches for their dinner had smiles on their faces.

Nightmare's good mood often coincided with making strides in his revenge quest.

He was close to finding the diary. Jane felt it in her soul. Nightmare affirmed her suspicions when he said, "Tonight, we are returning to the Estate District to visit the last remnants of the Harwood witches."

Jane simply nodded. The Harwoods were part of the Wood Witches, which were, in ancient times, weaker witch clans.

"The Harwoods have often been the Ashwood lackeys throughout the millennia." He slowly cut a piece of his steak, then continued. "According to records, their family line had died out, but the records have lied. In hindsight, I probably should have realized this sooner, but paying attention to human dramas is quite... tedious."

"Yes, *tedious*." Jane smiled. He thought most things were tedious.

He raised a silver-manicured eyebrow at her tone but said nothing.

"Do I require anything special for our mission tonight?" she asked.

He rubbed his chin slowly, his gaze fixed on her, roaming over her black lace blouse that dipped low at her cleavage. "No, not particularly. Although you may want to change into something slightly more conservative."

Jane played with her fork and met his gaze. He hated it when she wore low-cut blouses outside of his realm. She wasn't sure if he liked them much in his realm, either, because he always became more tense when she wore them—which was precisely why she did.

Small resistances.

But in truth, when she was forced to spend her week every month with her terrible husband, she never wore anything remotely attractive. She often tried to wear things with as much padding as possible. Because a year into Jane's deal, her husband had hit her again, and since Nightmare hadn't come to stop him, he continued to do it, although typically, he did much less damage now.

Small victories. She bit her lip and responded to Nightmare, "And what would you have me wear, Dimitris?"

Nightmare hated when she called him Nightmare, but that was his name to her. He had always been the Mirror of Nightmares—her nightmare bringer. It was hard not to think of him that way. But when she did refer to him out loud, she called him by one of his many names, except his first name—Gavriil. She never used that, and she never would.

Captors didn't deserve their true names.

But Dimitris was the name she used when being sassy. That, and sometimes, *my lord*. Though that was also used in much more serious moments.

A hint of a smile played on Nightmare's face—or at least his jaw ticked in an amused way, not an annoyed one. "I shall pick out an outfit for you."

The edge of Jane's lips rose. "By all means, *my lord*." She pulled out his title like sweet taffy, and his jaw ticked again. But even more telling, the wallpaper grew crisper and the roses redder.

Jane enjoyed forcing him to show emotions, even if only through his house, in how it morphed around him. He seemed to lack complete control over it, and she loved it.

Thirty minutes later, she walked her to their room, where an outfit lay on the bed. It was dark riding gear, the kind of clothing she would have worn on a bicycle or a hike. It consisted of over-sized black bloomers cuffed at the calf, a dark blouse that reached her neckline, and a black jacket that covered the top.

"Will I be fighting someone?" Jane asked as she began to unbutton her blouse.

She didn't always change in front of him, but she enjoyed watching the subtle shifts of his body when she did. It was hard to tell if he enjoyed it, because unfortunately, in their room, the house was of little help. It was the one place that never changed.

"It's not outside the realm of possibility, not that I would ever let anyone get close to you." He slid his gloved hands into his pockets. "But on the off chance they did, it would be good for you to have more mobility."

"And how many people are we planning on murdering tonight?"

Nightmare shrugged. "It depends on how useful they are to me."

"Ah, useful..." Jane released her petticoats, but she didn't need to undress fully this time because she still wore undergarments under athletic wear.

~

It took them twenty minutes to arrive at the Harwood Manor, and only five seconds for Nightmare to start killing people.

As soon as they walked inside, it was a bloodbath. The Harwoods were expecting them, and chaos erupted. But it was the sound that Jane would remember forever. Loud blasts mixed with the sound of crinkling glass and screams. So many screams—the timbre of which created an evocative symphony of blood, guts, and heartbreak.

Jane blinked, and more glass shattered as bullets flew everywhere. One so close to her face, she was fairly certain it grazed her ear.

Jane's heart hiccupped, and dread twisted her stomach. Blood gushed down walls, the world blurred together, and she was all alone. Nightmare had disappeared into smoke, moving as fast as lightning. Outside of the mirror, he was a vampire, ripping people's throats open with his fangs. He was a monster wrapped in coiled muscles and tipped with sharp metal claws.

A scream bubbled in Jane's throat as more guns were pointed in her direction.

Then, a force slammed her painfully into the wall.

Nightmare.

He pulled her into his chest and shielded her body from the bullets, soaking them into his flesh seemingly without harm.

A cloud of red hair fell in front of Jane's face as she tilted her chin up and caught Nightmare's silver-laced sapphire eyes.

Jane's teeth chattered as she tried to open her mouth and thank him. But nothing came out.

"No one kills you, save me," he said, stroking her hair behind her ear.

Jane's stomach dropped out as her feet left the ground and, in a moment, she was pulled through space as if at the speed of light. Nausea climbed up her throat. *What the fuck was that?* Had Nightmare moved her with his superhuman speed?

"Now, stay put until I come back for you." Nightmare set her down in a hallway closet as if she were a rag doll, before closing the door in her face and leaving her in darkness.

Her limbs grew tight and heavy with compulsion. It was an order she couldn't disobey, even if she wanted to. The blood rushed to her head, and she tried to swallow around the knot in her throat. He so rarely commanded her that she'd forgotten what it felt like. Typically, she followed his orders to the letter without magic forcing her, so he no longer bothered with it.

But the reminder rankled.

Because she wasn't free, she was owned by two monsters. Her life was split between villains. The villain of the day and the villain of the night. And she couldn't figure out which one was worse. At least her villain of the night didn't hit her. He only made her bones uneasy and commanded her to hide in closets in the middle of gunfights.

What felt like hours later, but was probably only around twenty minutes, the door creaked open. She expected to see Nightmare, but instead it was something far worse—a man with a twisted smile on his face.

"What do we have here?" The man stepped closer, shadows sliding over his grin as he did.

Jane gulped but didn't even try to move because she couldn't. The command's unfortunate consequence was that she wasn't able to move at all. Nightmare had said to "Stay put".

It was far too broad a command, and the result left her stuck.

"What is a pretty thing like you doing in my closet?" he asked.

Jane smiled through her teeth. "I rather like closets. They're very peaceful. No?"

"Oh, yes." A sickening chuckle left his chest. "Are you Nightmare's?"

Jane pinched her lips together. She would not answer that. Where was Nightmare? He couldn't die, could he? Jane had never even seen him get injured. He'd just taken thirty bullets for her and walked away like it was nothing.

He couldn't die. Could he?

"Where is he?"

"Oh, I have a ghost taking care of him."

Jane's brow furrowed. What did that mean?

"Why don't you join us out here in the light?"

Jane bit the inside of her cheek. Even if she wanted to, she couldn't. "I think I'd rather stay here."

"And I'd rather you come out."

"No."

Without saying another word, he reached in and yanked her out, nearly pulling her arm out of the socket as he did. Then he slammed her against the wall, his hand around her neck.

"Why does he want the diary?"

"I don't know," she croaked. *And even if I did, I wouldn't tell you.*

Jane was loyal to Nightmare. Despite everything, because in the two years that he possessed her, he had never crossed her boundaries, never hit her, and never even once raised his voice at her.

He wasn't her protector because he barely cared for her. But he was her keeper, and while he didn't always deserve her respect, she would give him her loyalty until he proved unworthy of it.

The man tightened his hand around her throat, obstructing her airway.

Nightmare, help. Help me. The words played in her mind on repeat. Over and over again because she couldn't do anything. She couldn't fight—she couldn't even move.

"I'll give you one more chance until I kill you. What does Nightmare want with the diary?"

"One more chance than I'm offering you!" Nightmare roared, slamming into the man. "I don't give people who touch my things any chances."

And he ripped the man's throat out with his teeth, causing blood to splatter on Jane's face and her dinner to nearly climb up her esophagus.

"Why didn't you fight back?" His furious glare landed on her.

"You commanded me to stay put." Her voice was raspy. "A command that is still active, by the way. I couldn't do anything. You left me defenseless." The last cracked.

"Oh,"—his eyebrows shot up, and something unreadable crossed his features—"move freely."

Then he turned and began to walk out. "Come with me." His

voice was low, but not cruel; it was more imploring than anything else. "I want you to see something."

It wasn't a compulsion this time. She could deny the request. But she didn't. Instead, she followed Nightmare down the stairs.

A soft light poured from the basement, haloing the door. The glow was unnatural, but it didn't seem evil. However, it did call to Jane, feeling like a mosaic of dreams, thoughts, and fleeting ideas. Behind the door wafted a soft melody played on the piano.

One of Nightmare's strong hands pressed the door slowly open, revealing a striking image. A translucent woman, coated in a white, glowing light, sat at a piano, her fingers light and delicate on the keys.

Nightmare held open the door for Jane to enter, and because she didn't believe he would intentionally put her in harm's way—after all, he needed her as his anchor—Jane slowly stepped inside.

But her voice felt clogged. She wanted to say something, but she couldn't.

"Jane, this is Charlotte. She's a—"

"A ghost trapped in this basement," Charlotte said, her eyes snapping to Jane, and the force of it made Jane want to take a step back. "I am like a Mirror-Echo."

Mirror-echo?

Nightmare must have sensed her confusion because he clarified, "Like the mirrors at the foot of the Ruins. I think you humans might call it Trapped Souls Row. Those aren't mirrors. They are echoes of souls who control the mirrors in the city."

"They're echoes," Charlotte added.

"And that's what you are?" Jane asked.

"Not precisely." Charlotte's fingers stilled on the piano keys. "My soul is trapped here, while my body is long dead."

"Why?" Jane breathed.

"Because I angered my mother's minions, and this is how they punished me."

There was so much information wrapped in that statement,

but Jane barely had any information, so it just caused her to have twenty more questions. The one that came out was, "Mother?"

"Helene Ashwood."

Helene, like Helene's diary?

"Ah, I see you recognize the name."

"Barely," Jane admitted, but pointed to Nightmare with her thumb. "He's mentioned it a few times."

"From what I hear, he's been on a rampage for the last two years to find her diary."

Jane let out a laugh and then immediately tried to stifle it. "Apologies."

Charlotte laughed, too. "He is a monster. More so now than ever, since my mother cursed him, but once, he was my friend. Perhaps there still might be some softness left within him."

Nightmare let out a growl as he hovered behind Jane's left shoulder.

Jane wasn't sure if Charlotte was delivering a warning, but the way she spoke suggested that there was a lot of subtext beneath the words.

"It is with that hope that I give you this." Out of a pocket in her skirt, she pulled out a leather-bound journal that looked ancient and fragile.

Nightmare sidestepped Jane, stepped up to the ghost, towering above her, and held out his hand. Charlotte handed over the diary, and her face grew even more ashen—if possible.

"I am so sick of this, Gavri."

"I know." He kneeled beside the ghost, and in that moment, he had never looked more human. At the very least, it was the first time he showed any form of empathy.

"I'm trapped." A white tear rolled down her face. "Do you know how to help me, old friend?"

Nightmare placed a large hand on either side of her face and kissed her on the forehead. As he pulled back, he nodded his head at Jane. "Do you know who she is?"

The ghost's gaze once again landed on Jane. "Is she a lost Ashelle?"

"Precisely that."

"Why are you keeping her?" Concern dripped from Charlotte's face. "She's supposed to—"

But she never finished the sentence because Nightmare silenced her with, "Yes, she is, but that's my problem to deal with."

Charlotte nodded. "Be careful, Gavri."

"I always am." He dropped his hands from her cheeks. "If anyone could break your curse, it would be an Ashelle."

Charlotte's nose flared, and more tears fell down her face, but it was now painted with hope.

"Jane, please join us. Kneel beside me and take her hands," he said, and Jane complied.

Charlotte's hands were cold, like touching a corpse, but they felt solid.

"I'm not sure what I can do. I'm not a witch. I'm not anything."

"A witch without magic is still a witch." Charlotte's voice was airy and coated in faith. "You wouldn't even be able to touch me if you didn't have magic within you, girl."

Jane's face grew tight with confusion. For two years, Nightmare had been calling her a witch, but she had never believed him. Yet, if what Charlotte was saying was true and only those who possessed magic could touch a ghost, then... Was she?

Nightmare leaned into her, his body framing her and his lips touching her ear. His breath was hot on her neck. "Close your eyes, Jane, and feel. Feel the temperature in the room, hear the humming of streetlamps outside, and hear the calls of owls in the distant trees. Sense the world around you and feel its magic."

At first, it felt like a fruitless task. What would listening to her surroundings truly do? Jane had spent twenty-three years listening to her surroundings, but nothing was ever special or different.

"Be still," he said, his lips on her.

Jane was, and she tried, but everything felt normal. Because she wasn't special, she never had been, and she never would be.

"My realm speaks to you, Jane. It sings to you, and sometimes it even bends to your will." He slid an arm around her waist and pulled her closer to him. "Humans cannot bend a god's realm."

Jane gulped because his realm did sing to her.

"Listen. Feel," he whispered into her hair.

Jane did, and nothing happened until... Vibrations. She felt them first in her hands, warm like firelight. But then she felt them everywhere. The ground, the electricity, the warmth of the god holding her. Everything had a pulse, an energy.

"Good," his voice was smooth whiskey. "Now pull the string. Absorb the curse's magic."

Jane didn't know what that meant, but instinctively, she felt the pull of a tainted enchantment. She felt its edges and heard its rhymes, and she pulled and pulled and pulled. Unlocking, unshaping, undoing. Absorbing.

The whole time she worked, she also felt him holding her, supporting her.

"Goodbye." Charlotte's voice was a faraway ring.

Throughout the process, she kept her eyes closed until the very last moment, when it was too late to stop what she had done.

When she opened her eyes, she saw the white light, the edges of what once was Charlotte, fold into Jane's skin.

She'd consumed the magic, everything, including the ghost.

"I absorbed her." Jane jumped back and tried to get to her feet, but she couldn't get away. Horror licked at her bones. She'd just consumed a soul.

She was a monster.

"Calm down." Nightmare was on his feet quickly, and he pulled her into a tight embrace, cocooning her body. "You didn't consume her. You untethered her. You released her soul."

"I *ate* it."

Her body shook uncontrollably.

"No, shhh," he said into her hair. "You ate the magic. Trust me, witches can't eat souls."

The shaking didn't stop. She wanted to believe Nightmare. She wanted to believe that she wasn't a monster, but she felt the magic in her veins—pulsing and alive.

Chapter Seven

Age 23.

Nothing felt the same after she ate the ghost. Technically, Jane believed Nightmare when he said she'd only devoured the magic, but she couldn't unsee or unfeel what had happened that night.

When they returned to his realm, Nightmare took the diary and placed it in the Shadow Wing—the one place she was forbidden to go to—and Jane hadn't seen it since.

It had been three months since then, and every day, Jane felt stranger and stranger things as if the magic inside of her was stirring and begging for a release, yet nothing had happened. Not until her husband tried to kill her.

The first time she went invisible was when her husband was choking her. His sausage fingers were wrapped around her neck when suddenly her throat wasn't visible any longer. Unfortunately, one didn't need to see the person they were strangling to finish the job, but fortunately the incident confused him enough to let go.

Her husband had reached the tipping point where he no longer wanted to share Jane with a Mirror, and if it were up to him, she'd never visit Nightmare again, but it wasn't up to him, and he knew it. But regrettably, he had figured out that Nightmare wouldn't come to Jane's aid, and his abuse was escalating again.

But the one thing that kept him from killing her was the money. His endless supply of wealth would run out if she died, so he kept her around like his little golden goose.

This meant she was forced to endure dinners with him seven days a month.

Dinners like tonight, where he sat inches from her with a possessive hand on her leg.

Jane swallowed and tried to empty her mind because when he got this way, it usually meant he would force her down and painfully take her. Sometimes on the kitchen floor, sometimes on the dining room table, and on good nights, he actually made it to their bed. But when he was in this mood, it was always rough and was always accompanied by excruciating pain. Sometimes, he punched her or slammed her head into things: the table, the wall, once a grandfather clock, anything really. He wasn't very inventive.

"You're getting fat," he said, squeezing her upper thigh.

She was not. Jane couldn't get fat with her diet and exercise routines. Especially with her body type. She was tall but had a thin frame. It took her considerable effort to gain any weight at all.

But Jane knew better than to talk back to her husband. She was his little rag doll, which he tossed around and manipulated like a puppet on strings.

She simply smiled sweetly at him, and he scooted closer.

Fuck.

Jane sucked in a rattling breath as the lights flickered in the wall sconces, singing an off-key harmony of dread.

"I want you to eat this." Her husband held out a small white worm the size of a sienna coin.

Jane instinctively leaned backward. "What is that?"

"It doesn't matter. Open your mouth, and I am going to feed it to you."

"No." Jane scooted her chair away from him. "Absolutely not."

His fingers dug into her thigh and kept her from moving any further. "You are my wife, and you will do as I will."

"No," Jane breathed, "no."

"What did you say to me?"

It was the first time she had ever said the word to him.

"No?" He seethed. "Did you just say no?"

"I will not eat that worm." Jane clenched her jaw tightly. She wouldn't allow it. Whatever it was, it was not going into her mouth.

Never.

Besides the fact that it was disgusting, there was no telling how it would affect her dancing.

It all happened before she could comprehend it. In a flash, her husband was slamming into the floor, breaking apart her chair in the process as he straddled her and forced open her jaw, slamming the white slimy worm into her mouth.

"Swallow."

"No," she mumbled.

"Swallow." When she didn't, he punched her in the face.

Magic tingled in her veins, just out of reach, and she didn't know how to pull on it to help herself.

Her husband punched her again, repeating the process until she was fairly certain she had swallowed the worm, but it was unclear because, after a while, she had lost consciousness completely.

There was a part of her that begged the darkness to stay—begged the world to just be done with her.

But it wasn't.

At least not yet.

Chapter Eight

Age 23.

Jane was out of her Mirror Cosmetics and Balm.

Without them, her face looked pale, sallow, sour, and sick. Mirror bargains had consequences—even if she wasn't the one who bargained for the goods—and unfortunately, the consequence of the makeup was that she would always look dim without it. She had lost all her shine.

But she had to use it. If she didn't, she would all be one big mass of bruises.

Jane swallowed hard past the lump in her throat. She didn't have time to go and buy more makeup. Nightmare had summoned her, and if she didn't show up soon, he'd pull her into his mirror with or without her consent.

Not that consent really existed with him. She had traded *herself*, and he could technically do whatever he wanted.

But Jane hated being torn through space and into his mirror realm—Jane called the experience going through the travel void. It made her queasy and messed with her balance. Neither of these would be suitable for a prima ballerina.

He had done it three times before when she hadn't arrived on time. And every time, it made her vomit and feel nauseous for days.

Jane's head and face hurt. Not just from the bruises her husband had left there, but also because of the emotions pooling behind her taut cheeks.

She didn't want Nightmare to see her like this. The only time she'd let him see her with bruises was the first time. Every other time, she was prepared.

But not now.

And the bruises were bad.

Fuck. Jane rubbed her face. What was she going to do?

She scrambled through her bottles and pills, losing all sense of order to them. She knew the search was in vain. Jane wasn't a super clean person per se, but she always knew where everything was. It was organized chaos.

So she knew she wouldn't find any hidden makeup anywhere.

But her fingers curled around a bottle, and she pinched her eyes shut. Fuck. Oh, she hated it. Jane didn't use Mirror-Poppy much because she hated how it made her feel. Yes, it healed her wounds quickly, but it slowed her reactions, made her mind loopy and elated. It made her high, and she hated being high—hated losing control.

But it was the only option. It was the only thing that might make her face look reasonably presentable.

Jane turned the lid, and she poured out the pills, taking one and swallowing it dry.

The effects were almost immediate. Ecstasy surged through her blood. Hot and cold all at once, but oh, so good. Everything felt so wonderful and peaceful. Nothing could go wrong. Her mind was filled with bright pink bubbles and glitter dust. She no longer cared about anything at all. Why would she? She was whole and right. It was enthralling and so intoxicating, and she almost forgot... hmmm, what? She was supposed to do something. Wasn't she?

Before she knew it, her body was pulled taut like a tightrope, and she was launched through space, the blackness sparkling around her like diamonds. Teleportation always felt weird. But when she was high, it felt fuzzy and warm, as if she were cuddling with a life-size bunny.

The thought made her giggle. High and bright. And that was what she was doing as Nightmare's lair appeared before her. She sat cross-legged on the floor, pretending to hug a massive bunny while she giggled.

Sober Jane would have been horrified. But alas, she was very much not sober.

"Get up." The words were harsh, dark, and filled with magic. Like any order Nightmare gave, Jane had to comply.

So, she did, the laughter still falling from her lips, cut off only by a massive hand that touched her skin. At his touch, she sucked in her giggles.

Nightmare clutched her chin tightly, cruelly, and stared into her eyes, emanating disgust.

His skin sizzled on hers, and she knew she should feel afraid or ashamed, but all she felt was lust and longing.

Her heart beat outrageously fast in her chest. It felt like she was driving one of those new automobiles at a thousand miles an hour. Not only from the drugs, but from him.

He made her high, too. He made far too many sensations stir inside her, and while she would normally deny all of them, right now, she couldn't. Her mind wasn't capable of lying.

Not now.

All she wanted to do was strip this man bare and fuck him like she'd never been fucked before. She'd heard from other women it could be pleasurable.

With him, she thought it might be.

"You're high." His voice was a hot iron, and his nose flared.

"No, I am not." She let out a high, soft, feminine squeak, nothing like her usual sultry tones.

Nightmare winced at the sound. "Sober up now."

Jane's eyebrows drew together. One did not just sober up

because they wanted to... Except... *She was.* His words had stolen all the drugs from her system.

How?

She blinked, and she finally—soberly—saw him in all his glory and all his fury.

The excitement and energy left her body, and she returned to her typical self. Rock solid, yet soft. Stable yet broken. Quiet, yet fiery.

"You can just demand things like that without a deal, and it works?"

"With you, I can. You're my bride." He said it like it explained everything. It didn't, but she knew he wouldn't elaborate.

Jane bit the inside of her cheek and stared into his sapphire-blue eyes. They still twinkled, but with his disgust-laced fury.

"Why were you high?" Nightmare still hadn't let go of her chin.

Jane inhaled slowly through her nose. She didn't want to tell him.

Apparently, she didn't need to. "Because of these bruises?"

Jane gave him a minuscule nod, and his fingers tightened around her chin.

"How did you get them?" he seethed, and the flash of fire in his sapphire eyes caused a shiver to skate up her spine. "You always have so many bruises."

He had seen them?

Jane's breasts lifted with her tight, tense breaths. In this, she couldn't be truthful. She just wouldn't. Jane wasn't weak, but this... It made her feel pathetic. But lying was his line. It was his rule—the only rule he'd given she could freely break.

And to lie to him would break his trust—if he ever found out.

Every muscle in her body tensed, and her heart raged in her ears. So loud she couldn't hear anything else.

She couldn't lie to him. It would ruin everything, but she also wouldn't—she couldn't tell the truth. Yes, he was a god and could probably fix all her problems. But there was no guarantee that he would and more importantly Jane couldn't say the truth.

She just couldn't.

So, she let the lie roll off her tongue. "I got them at dance practice. I fell, and my face hit the bar." *Lie, lie. Lie.* She held her breath. Could he see it?

Internally, she winced but tried not to show it on the outside. She'd promised never to lie to him. And she hadn't really, thus far. He barely asked questions of her, so she barely had to speak about the one thing she'd want to lie about.

The lie must have been believable enough. After all, she was still in her tights and flowing ballerina dress. However, she wasn't in ballet slippers. She'd worn Mary Janes.

He gritted his teeth. "Then you're done with dance. I forbid you from doing it again." His hand dropped from her face, and he turned around and began walking towards dinner.

What?

What?

What had he just said?

When her brain caught up to the words, she let out a wail, and her hands flew up to her mouth, horror twisting in her stomach. "No, you can't do this, Alexei."

"I can." He didn't even turn around.

"No!" she howled. "Please don't do this. *Please.* I beg you. Anything but dance."

Anything but dance.

Nothing. He said nothing. He didn't turn. He didn't acknowledge her pain. Just nothing. Instead, he continued to walk away, only coldness following in his wake. He didn't care. He'd just caused pure and total devastation.

Why would he? He didn't have a heart.

Jane fell to her knees. Tears stormed down her face like rough, deadly rain. She didn't have to try to do a pirouette to know it was gone. She felt it ripped from her soul like a physical force. And it felt like dying. She clutched her heart. The pain unbearable. Her chest burned, and her throat was raw from all the screaming because she didn't stop. The pleas flew from her lips. Over and over and over again. She'd never begged like this. Never. Jane didn't beg. She endured. She was a fierce mountain, taking on the wilds of winter, taking on a tsunami. She didn't bend. She didn't break.

Until now.

Jane thought she'd had nothing else to lose, but she was so utterly wrong.

This was the one thing she had left. The one thing that hadn't been stolen from her before.

Jane had wanted to ask Nightmare how to reach her magic and control it so she could protect herself from her husband, but now Jane couldn't stomach even looking at the monster.

He was worse than any abuser she had ever had... because he took away the one thing she loved.

And she would never forgive him for it.

"Get up and come to dinner," Nightmare said harshly.

Jane didn't know how long she had stayed on the marble floor of Nightmare's Castle entranceway, but it must have been a long time because her knees were getting sore, and her voice was nearly gone from all the wailing.

"Get up, put yourself together, and come to dinner," he said again, this time as a command before he once more disappeared into his dining room.

Jane was forced to comply. It took her about fifteen minutes to accomplish the task, though, because getting herself together was not easy.

Her heels clicked as she entered the room and slid into her seat across the table from him like the Queen of his castle.

"I see you have calmed down," Nightmare said, his voice cold and empty of all understanding.

Jane swallowed, hatred coating the lining of her stomach. She glowered at him, but if he noticed, he didn't show it. He simply ate his dinner.

One of his ghost servants served her the same soup he was devouring. Jane picked up the spoon rather too harshly, the metal digging into her palm.

But she sucked in a deep breath and let it go, trying to steady herself and the next words that were to leave her mouth.

"Lord Draculei,"—he liked to be called Lord the most—"please don't take dance away from me."

He simply grunted and refused to look up from his meal.

"It's how I make my living," Jane said, a creak in her voice. "It's my life."

"I have more money than you will ever need."

"Lord Draculei, please."

"Enough," he glared up at her.

"Alexei, please, if you ever do one thing for me. If you only give me one thing in life, please let it be dance. Don't take this away from me. It's all I ha—"

"Enough; I don't want to hear more on this topic." He cut her off and held up his hand. "Only I get to hurt you, witch."

No, she opened her mouth to scream, but nothing came out.

Another tear stroked down her face.

He had silenced her forever on this topic. She'd never be able to beg him to give it back now. She'd never be able to convince him he was wrong. And even if she wanted to, she'd never be able to tell him the truth. Dance never hurt her. It wasn't dance that left the bruises on her body.

It was men.

Jane's fingernails bit into her tights so hard she put holes in them. She'd never dance again. Not even her husband was cruel enough to take that away from her.

"I hate you."

Chapter Nine

Age 23.

Breathing felt like dying, and getting out of bed was next to impossible. Without dance, Jane had no hope. She was a useless blob of human flesh. She was nothing—a girl controlled by two evil monsters.

She was a shattered mirror. Dead and filled with horrible luck.

Somehow, she had managed to inform the Royalle Ballet Director that she had sustained a career-ending injury and that she would no longer be able to perform. Saying the words aloud was the hardest thing she'd ever done, but somehow she had managed.

And now she lay in the fetal position in her bed, which she hadn't left in two days save to drink water and relieve herself.

It was her week to herself. The week she didn't have to stay with her husband or see Nightmare, she rented a room at the Viridian Nightclub.

The Courtesan Club and Cabaret was one of the seventeen known Mirror-Blessed buildings in the city. Kordelia, the owner of the Viridian, made a deal with a mirror to create a club that was alive, always moving, and always changing with enchantment. It gave the attendees their heart's desires, conjuring up any and all fantasies one might have. It was a den of pleasure and sin.

Most importantly, it was a refuge for the lost and broken, and it was the place Jane turned to for the week she was alone.

A soft pattering sounded at the door. Jane mumbled and smashed her pillow over her face. She wanted nothing to do with whatever was beyond her room.

"Janey?" A soft, feminine voice floated through the crack in the door.

Another soft knock.

"Move aside, Constance. She won't hear you if you knock like a hummingbird." Kordelia's harsh tone pierced through the wood.

"I am trying to be gentle," the softer voice said.

Kordelia scoffed. "She doesn't need gentle."

And with that, the door flung open, and light slapped Jane across the face. She groaned and slammed her face further into her pillow.

"It's time to stop sulking, girl." Kordelia's formidable footsteps sounded like thunderclouds as she moved closer. "Get up."

The pillow was ripped out of Jane's hands, and that horrible light surged through her skin and into her bones.

"No," she moaned.

"You need to get up and move on with your life." Kordelia crossed her arms and glared at Jane.

"It's only been three days. She can sulk for at least four more." Constance was generally the nicer of the two, but she was even more so now, since she was also a dancer. The Viridian's star cabaret dancer.

Jane was semi-friendly with both women, but she didn't truly have any close friends because her husband never wanted her to have relationships beyond him. When she was with Nightmare, they were focused on his machinations, and Jane didn't have time to connect with people.

Kordelia clicked her tongue. "The longer she sulks, the harder it will be. She needs to push through it."

"No, she doesn't." Constance's voice sounded as light as birdsong despite being firm.

Kordelia stepped closer and put a gentle hand on Jane's shoulder. Then she knelt to eye level. "I do not possess a heart any longer, but this one"—she motioned to Constance with her thumb—"is trying to teach me empathy. And here is what I have gathered. You are a young, broken girl with an unfair life and unfair circumstances. You have experienced far more than most will in their entire lives. You are hurting, and you don't know how to live past your most recent setback. But I also see you, girl. You are strong, talented, and resilient. You can get through this, too. The Viridian is a safe haven for girls like you, and you can sulk for years if need be. Constance and I are immortals; We're not going anywhere, so if you want to be a pile of pathetic human flesh taking up one of the beds in my nightclub, by all means..."

"Kordelia—" Constance chided.

"But I think you are too driven and too full of life to waste your youth away sulking. So you can't dance anymore—it's awful, but it's not *who you are*. So, who are you? A girl who gives up?"

No. Never.

The words must have played on Jane's face because Kordelia said, "I didn't think so." Then, she turned back to her lover and business partner. "I think I did brilliantly, don't you?"

Constance shook her head but smiled. "You didn't do terribly. Jane, there is a position available teaching at the Royalle Ballet School if you're interested. I know it might be hard considering your... injury, but it might help give you a purpose."

No one actually believed Jane was injured. Not after the Cobra Lilies kidnapped her and forced her to make a mirror deal. Apparently, the Mirror Mafia loved to spread rumors. And the ongoing rumor was that she had lost her dancing ability because she had made a bad deal with a mirror, and this was her unintended consequence.

In a way, they weren't wrong.

~

Five days later, Jane stood at the front of the juniors' ballet class. The class was for advanced dancers ages fourteen and up—the dancers who would go on to audition for the Royalle Ballet's apprenticeships.

Jane arrived at the Royalle Ballet Dance School thirty minutes early to meet with the Artistic Assistant Director and prepare for the class. She'd never taught anyone anything before, and she had no idea what she was doing, but she wasn't going to be late on her first day.

So she was there when all of the dancers arrived. They came in pairs and groups, and as they walked in, the Artistic Assistant Director introduced her to them. Upon the arrival of the third group, Jane saw a glimmer of crimson hair, and immediately, all of the breath left her body.

Jane was not prepared; she probably never could have been. Pain blossomed in her chest, and every muscle in her body grew as tight as a harp string.

Quinnevere.

The redheaded girl, who must have been about seventeen years old, was Jane's little sister. She was shorter than Jane by about four inches, and her hair was slightly darker—more cinnamon than Jane's ginger—but Jane would have known her anywhere.

She wore a soft pink flowing ballet dress, and with her foot-falls, a blood-red necklace bounced around her neck. Jane sucked in a breath. The necklace hummed a smooth tune that only Jane seemed to hear. She cocked her head; it emitted a similar frequency as the invisible mirror in the Royalle Ballet.

Strange.

Jane's gaze slid back to her sister's face, and their eyes caught. It was too much. Jane mumbled something unintelligible to the

Artistic Assistant and rushed to the powder room. It was too much. Jane had only seen glimpses of her sister for the past thirteen years. It was part of her promise to her uncle that she would stay away. And for the safety and well-being of her sister, she had.

A harsh sob rocked Jane's shoulders, and she smashed a hand over her lips to try to cover her mouth. The pain was a hoarse echo rattling through her bones. A pounding war drum. A rotting bouquet of roses.

A clock ticked somewhere in the distance, and Jane knew she had to pull herself together. She had to get up and act like nothing was wrong. It was her duty to the Ballet Director. But she also needed to patch herself together, because this was her chance to see her sister, and maybe even get to know her, too.

Jane pinched her eyes shut for one moment, and she let the tears ricochet down her face and tinkle to the marble floors. Then she stood up, turned on the faucet, and threw water on her face before returning to the room and making her apologies, saying she was nauseous.

People might assume she was pregnant, which may be why, in their minds, she quit ballet and began teaching.

The entire class was now present, and as soon as she was introduced, they started warming up and going through their positions. Once they ended their warm-ups with the grand battement, Jane and the Artistic Assistant began teaching them the choreography to "Winter's Eve" and the corps parts.

It was an advanced class, so the corrections were minor. There were slight redirections to positions, postures, and the lines of their arms. Jane tried to keep her eyes off her sister, but they found her anyways. Over and over and over again. She was surprisingly talented, but she also had a lot of work to do if she were going to make the Royalle Ballet.

The first class was tough, much harder than Jane had ever imagined. Still, she got through it, and would get through it again and again until teaching became easy. Although, she suspected that teaching her little sister, who had no idea they were even related, would never get easier.

~

Months passed as Jane taught at the Ballet School. During that time, she still had to split her time between her husband, Nightmare, and her week at the Viridian, but Constance was right: Teaching gave her purpose and small hints of happiness.

But she was still grieving the loss of her dancing.

So much so that Jane hadn't spoken to Nightmare in months. Not even her curiosity about her dormant magic could bulldoze through her anger. She hated him now. So they ate in silence. When he gave her commands, she merely nodded her head and did as he wanted. During the time she spent with him each month, she'd sleep in his bed and never say a word. She was punishing him, but he didn't even seem to notice.

He never mentioned the silence, nor did he compel her to speak to him. He was simply okay with it, which made her all the angrier. She wanted to punish him for stealing dance from her, but the god had no feelings. He didn't care about anything or anyone. So how could she punish someone like that?

It wasn't possible.

It was like trying to weave with invisible thread or paint a portrait with a blindfold. One could do it, but it wouldn't turn out very well.

So, instead of focusing on her hatred for him, she turned her eyes to her sister. It took Jane six months to build a meaningful relationship with Quinnevere. At first, it was too hard to talk to her for any period without wanting to break down completely. But slowly, Jane let her sister in—let her sister see pieces of her that others didn't. They started by chatting after classes, but when Constance decided to join the ballet class, they would grab lunch and dinner together and slowly began building a friendship.

Constance was different outside of the Viridian. Almost

more... free? As if away from Kordelia, the girl was more alive, bubbly, and energetic. Almost like Kordelia sucked the energy out of Constance. It wasn't Jane's place to judge—after all, her husband was abusive, and her soul belonged to a mirror—but something was off about the girl's relationship with the Viridian and its owner.

Jane enjoyed both versions of the girl, but it was rather interesting to see how different she could be when away from her responsibilities. It made Jane wonder if she was the same. Probably, considering she felt like two different people when she was with her husband and when she was around everyone else.

She was a meek, pathetic, quiet doll when she was with her husband, and with Nightmare and her friends, she was both lighter and stronger, like a dragonfly—able to metaphorically lift twice her body weight.

But the strangest thing was that she could say she had friends; and incredibly, her friendships didn't end with Quinnevere and Constance, because their trio was soon joined by two more. Jevon, a quiet, astute but messy young man, and Giselle, a vibrant, colorful acrobat who worked at the Viridian alongside Constance. There was something about Jevon's mess that comforted Jane. His suits were always wrinkled, and his cravat was tied loose and off-center, but there was beauty in it. Jane wasn't remotely interested in him romantically, and he never once made any advances toward her.

He was the first safe man she'd ever been in a relationship with, and it meant all the more that it was so platonic. Giselle and Constance also came to mean the world to Jane. They both had vibrant energies that twisted together, got knotted, and clashed, but there was something magical about it all.

But of course, it was Quinnevere who truly meant everything to her. It was remarkable getting to know her, getting to see the fruit of Jane's sacrifice. Quinn was brilliant and talented, although her closed-off nature and unwillingness to feel emotions hindered her dancing skills. Technically, the girl's dancing was perfect; she just lacked acting and artistry, but with time, Jane was convinced she'd get better and that, maybe one day, she would grow to be a better dancer than Jane had ever been. But it was Quinnevere's mind that Jane was most proud of. The girl was a genius. She was the youngest apprentice medical examiner in the history of University Square.

Jane had only watched Quinnevere do one autopsy, but it was the most fascinating thing she'd ever seen.

And all of it warmed Jane's soul. Before she had often wondered if her sacrifices—the orphanage, her husband, the abuse—were worth it, but after spending only a moment with her sister, she'd do it all over again—a million times.

Quinnevere was imperfectly-perfect. And so were the rest of Jane's friends, and Jane loved them more than she knew was possible.

The group was like a tree. Giselle and Constance were orange and yellow leaves that had fallen off the tree and were violently dancing in the wind, while Jevon was a breakable branch attached to the tree. Quinn was the trunk, stubborn but fierce in her loyalty and personality. And Jane was the roots, digging into the ground and anchoring them all down.

It was a beautiful group of friends, and for the first time in her life, Jane was truly happy.

The only problem was that her husband was beginning to get jealous, which never boded well.

CHAPTER TEN

AGE 24.

Dying felt worse than she imagined, and, unfortunately, by the very nature of her existence, Jane had imagined dying many, many times.

Every time her husband assaulted her with his hands, feet, and dick, every time her husband's debt collectors cashed in her body as their price, and every day since Nightmare stole dance from her.

She imagined dying.

Jane didn't *want* to die. She simply imagined it. Sometimes, it was the only thing that gave her comfort. Jane knew, one day, all of this would be over. She knew she had a future with safety and peace—that this was only temporary.

She didn't know how she'd escape her horrific circumstances, but she knew eventually she would. Because men could take everything from her, but they would never take her fight, and they'd never steal her happiness.

She could have joy amid chaos. She could find happiness in a sea of pain.

She could find peace in dying. Because somehow, she knew

she would die young. It was a feeling that clawed at the back of her neck—a knowing.

Yet knowing still never truly prepared her for it. The shock, the pain, the hurt. Knowing it would happen only made the process harder.

Because Jane was dying, and her husband was murdering her.

She reached her hand up to the necklace holding Nightmare's ring and screamed in her head. *Help. Help me, Alexei.*

Jane didn't want to die. She wanted Nightmare to save her. She wanted a knight in shining armor. A hero in ancient poems. A prince to swoop in to rescue her from her pain. She wanted to live—to survive the night.

She *had* to survive this final assault. And it would be finally, because she was leaving him after this. She'd never return to his house, and she didn't care what the consequences were.

Bring them on. She'd take on anything to be rid of this wretched man.

Jane knew she shouldn't have stayed with him. Of course she knew. She should never have gone back to her monster after she lost the ballet—honestly, she should never have gone back to him after she'd met Nightmare.

But she had, and she hated herself for it.

Other women stayed in terrible situations because they loved their abusers, they had children to protect, or for a multitude of different reasons. Jane stayed simply because she hated change. After all, there was safety in what she knew. She stayed because it was easier than leaving, than facing a world with no money and nowhere to go. Kordelia wouldn't let her continue to live in the Viridian without paying rent, and her husband controlled the pot of gold Nightmare had created. He controlled everything.

And now Jane didn't have dance to fall back on. She had nothing. So, staying was easier. But she was now realizing that staying would be her end. Ever since Jane met her friends and found some happiness, her husband had been escalating.

More broken bones. More black eyes. More burns, cuts, and scars. Just more.

Yet she still stayed, and she hated herself for it.

But what were her other options? Jane's life was split between two villains. The one she knew and the god who gave the city nightmares. The god who was known above all else for his cruelty. The god who had stolen the job she had loved from her.

Nightmare was evil, too. But at least he didn't hit her. Not like Jane's husband, who currently clawed at her shoulders, trying to get his hands around her throat, but she couldn't let that happen because if he succeeded, she'd only have seconds to live. So, she kicked her knee up hard, hitting him in the balls.

Jane tried to run as he fell, but he reached out and grasped her ankle, bringing her to the ground with him. She hit with a thud, all her air rushing from her body.

His dirty nails dug into her shin, and she screamed, kicking her leg out, trying to free herself.

It worked—barely. Jane scrambled up, begging her body to move so she could get away before he managed to get up again.

But Jane was slow. This attack had started with her husband throwing her onto the kitchen counter, and she hit her head on the sharp corner. She probably had a concussion. Blood gushed from her scalp, and she painted her white cotton dress in a sea of crimson.

Every muscle hurt, but she wouldn't let that stop her. She was six feet from the door, and if she could make it outside, she could scream and hopefully get help.

Nightmare's red diamond ring, which was placed on a chain, bounced between her breasts with her footfalls. Its movement was a reminder of why she was in this predicament to begin with. Her husband didn't want to share anymore.

He had demanded she move back in every day of the month, and when she told him the money would run out if she did that, he had become vicious.

But now Jane was almost to freedom. Reaching out her hand

for the front door knob, Jane sucked in a breath... that was immediately torn from her.

A pain screamed through her scalp as her husband grabbed her by the hair, red pooling between his fingers. She was hauled backward and slammed against the entry hall, her shoulder hitting hard.

"No," a whimper left her lips. "No." She'd been inches from freedom and escape.

Inches.

"Please, don't do this," Jane begged.

He towered above her and pushed her down onto the floor. Her shoulder made a wretched popping sound as it crashed into the marble. Her husband jumped down on her. His legs were straddling her and pinning her down. "You've been fucking another man."

He slapped her across the face. "Wearing his ring, like his little whore." Technically, wearing his ring wouldn't make her a whore; just his wife. But, semantics.

Instinctively, Jane's fingers brushed the ring sitting on the necklace chain. She pinched her eyes shut and screamed in her head. *Please, please, I don't want to die.*

Jane's husband squeezed her breast hard as if he wanted to tear it from her body before slapping her hand away and taking the chain with Nightmare's ring into his hand.

"Whore." He slammed her head into the floor, the vein in his forehead bulging. "Only I fuck you. You and then the men I sell you to."

Please, she screamed into her mind again, as if Nightmare could hear her. A tear leaked down Jane's face.

"What the point of your dirty, defiled cunt now?" He seethed. "You can't even do your job and give me heirs." He'd been trying to impregnate her with his tiny, disgusting cock almost nightly when she was forced to be in his house, but it'd never work because she was secretly on prevention.

"Useless cunt."

With the ring still in his fingers, Jane's husband curled his hands around her neck and squeezed.

"You're worthless now."

His fingers pressed harder, and Jane knew she was dead. She tried to scratch his hands and face, but the fight was to no avail.

Jane couldn't scream, she couldn't breathe, and she could barely lift her arms to fight. Her head was tight, an intense pressure building behind her eye sockets, so intense she thought her head might explode.

She felt like she was drowning in liquid fire.

A loud pop sounded in her ears before a chorus of rings burst out, roaring like a train.

Panic churned in her stomach, and she tried to hit him or do anything to free herself. But it was all in vain.

Jane's vision blurred, and another tear streaked down her face. She was so mad that she was going to die before experiencing life, before enjoying sex and having her first orgasm. It was a stupid thought to have before death.

But death wasn't rational.

If she could scream, she'd scream for *him*. Draculei might have been a villain, but he was *her* villain. Her Nightmare.

Jane's eyelids grew heavy, and she let them flutter shut. But it was then that she felt the magic in her veins fighting back. It bubbled in her blood, and a rush of air burst from her—she acted on instinct. She shoved against her husband's chest.

The next thing she knew, the weight left her neck, and she fell limply to the floor.

She sucked in a slow, torturous breath and blinked. Did she do that? Was it her magic? Not quite. With the world tilted to the side, she watched as Nightmare plunged his thumb into her husband's left eye.

Jane blinked again, wondering if that was what she had actually seen or if it was all a dream. But her vision cleared as Nightmare pulled his finger out of the eye socket and licked the blood from his nail before he looked into her husband's only remaining eye and compelled him. "Do not move from this spot."

Then, as fast as lightning, Nightmare's hands were on her, inspecting her injuries. His gaze caught the wound on her head, and he leaned down and licked it, tasting her.

Jane trembled. Was he going to eat her? But just as the thought came, it was replaced by amazement. The wound was healing.

Did vampire saliva have healing properties?

"Breathe." Nightmare's voice was cloaked in shadows, the tone so villainous she flinched. But it was a command, and as he said it again, "Breathe," she felt her lungs fill with air and a warm sensation coat her throat. He was healing her with his words.

Jane really shouldn't have been surprised. He had taken away her drug high with a couple of words before. But she still was.

None of this was normal.

"You're going to be okay." Nightmare kissed the top of her head before he shifted his body and took in the wailing man beside them.

In a blink, he was on the man. Nightmare's nails, which had turned into claws, pierced into her husband's shoulders as a pained cry left his lips.

"You hurt something that belongs to me," Nightmare growled. "No one hurts things that belong to me."

Jane wanted to be insulted by the use of *thing*—and she was—but she was also curious to see what Nightmare would do next. So, she lifted herself onto her palms, and with wobbly legs, she tried to get up in order to watch. So she could tower over her attacker for once.

But she was too weak.

Nightmare turned his gaze to her, and in a gentle tone, he said, "Stay down."

She gave him a look that said, *Is it a command?*

He seemed to understand the unspoken question because he softly said, "No."

Jane pinched her lips together. She couldn't get herself to ask him for help—or truly speak to him. It had still been months since she'd deigned to talk to him. But he seemed to understand what she wanted—needed—and he stepped away from his prey to lift her up and help steady her.

Jane swallowed hard and tried to convey her thanks with her expression.

Nightmare cupped her head in his hands, and his silver eyes tore through every protection and wall she'd put into place. "You're mine, little witch. You're safe." A sob rocked her shoulders, and he pulled her into his chest. "I will never let anything happen to you. Only I get to kill you, remember?"

She nodded into his chest, his masculine scent filling her senses. Cedar, chai, and musk. She listened for a heartbeat, but it never came. Nothing. Just an echoing emptiness. Jane wanted to knock on his chest and see if it was actually hollow. Maybe Vampire-Gods didn't have hearts? Either way, it didn't matter. She appreciated his comfort, especially when she knew he didn't care about anyone.

Nightmare sat with her like that for a long moment. Nightmare rocked her body back and forth, and he sang a somber melody in an ancient, long-forgotten language. Jane closed her eyes, sank into his comfort, and curled into his body.

Eventually, he pulled away and asked, "Are you okay now?"

She nodded.

Nightmare turned back to his prey and smiled widely, his fangs sliding down. He leaned over and pierced into the flesh of her husband's neck.

Jane's breath hitched, fascinated. She'd never seen a vampire feed before, and it was... exhilarating. Jane wanted to watch as he drained every last drop of blood from her true monster, but Nightmare stopped. She didn't know why, but she hated it. She wanted her husband gone. She wanted vengeance.

Nightmare froze, hovering above his meal like an animal on alert. He was listening for something, feeling for something.

But what?

He didn't turn his head, but she saw his gaze lock on her out of the corner of his eye.

Was he asking for permission? Did he think she didn't want this?

"Alexei," she whispered in a raspy, broken voice. Nightmare's head slowly turned to her, his demeanor a pit of black cruelty. "Please, kill him for me."

It was fitting that these were the first words she'd spoken to him in months. A request that might help mend their broken relationship.

His lips curled into a slow smile. "It would be my greatest pleasure."

Draculei, Lord of Nightmares, placed a hand on either side of her husband's face and squeezed. Like popping a grape, her husband's head burst. Blood, brain, and skull fragments exploded into the room, covering both Jane and Nightmare in a waterfall of death.

She inhaled sharply, tasting her husband on her tongue. She had never enjoyed tasting him, but tonight was the exception.

Chapter Eleven

Age 24.

Shock coiled around her body, and it felt like she was swimming in a sea of snakes. Reaching a hand up, she wiped her face. Chunks of flesh and blood came off, and she doubled over and vomited onto the floor. Then everything rushed back into her. The pain from the attack, the truth of her husband's death, and a weariness that she couldn't escape.

Her knees buckled, and she hit the ground hard. But within moments, she was no longer on the floor. She was in his arms. Warm. Safe. Gently, he set her on the couch as he knelt beside her, taking in all of her injuries and emotions.

He let out a low sound that might have been a hiss or maybe even a growl. It was hard to tell with him, and then he ran a thumb along her jaw and the bruises forming there from her husband's fingers.

Jane sucked in breath at his touch, from pain and something else she couldn't quite put a word to.

"I should kill you." He ran his thumb along her jaw again as his second hand laced into her hair, both caressing and assessing.

Jane chewed her cheek for a long moment, matching his intensity. "You should."

But he wouldn't. They both knew it. He hadn't saved her life just to take it now. Jane believed he would kill her one day, but she also thought it would be a long time from now. Because now, he needed her as his anchor. He had a plan that needed to be seen through. She would worry for her life when he finally got what he wanted.

And what he wanted was still maddeningly unclear.

"Heal," Nightmare's low voice commanded.

Jane's skin, muscles, and bones tingled, stitching themselves back together. One command, and her body was better than ever. It was unsettling. But what came out of Nightmare's mouth next was even more unsettling.

"How many men has he sold you to?"

Jane merely stared and swallowed. How had he known? Did he overhear what her husband had yelled while he was trying to kill her? He must have. But there was no way in all the heavens and hells that Jane was going to admit to the answer.

"How many men have violated you?"

A thick tear rolled down her face.

His voice turned soft. "How many, Jane?"

She swallowed past the lump in her throat, her chest tight and full of pain. "Seven."

His eyes flashed. "Names."

"No," she breathed. "You'll kill them."

"Yes." He ground his teeth together.

"They aren't all bad men."

His nostrils flared. "Any man who rapes a woman as payment for another man's debt is a bad man."

"Please don't say that word." She closed her eyes for a brief moment, her cheeks stinging from holding back her pain.

"That's what they did, Jane."

"Please." More tears streamed down her face, and he wiped them away with his knuckles.

"Have you ever been with any man by choice?"

No. "Please."

Nightmare stared at her, his glare burning into her skin. It was too intense, and she averted her gaze. Then he did something she never expected: He pulled her into a hug, his chin resting on her head. "You're safe now. I'll never let anyone touch you unless you want it." He paused for a long time, just holding her. "Not even me. I'll never do anything to hurt you."

"You already have." Her voice was raw and filled with emotion. Nightmare didn't react to the words, almost like they were meaningless to him. Jane swallowed. Of course, he wouldn't care that he hurt her—that he stole the one thing she loved from her. Dance.

Her fingernails bit into her palm, and she looked down at her headless husband. She shook with both rage and pain.

"Alexei, I don't want to keep his last name." The last part came out as a sob, and she didn't know why she said it. Now, or at all.

But she didn't. Jane couldn't keep that horrible man's name any longer.

"Come with me." He held his hand out for her to take.

Chapter Twelve

Age 24.

Ten minutes later, they were walking to the entrance of the Russet and into the Grand Casino.

The Russet was one of the seventeen sentient structures in the city, meaning it was a building controlled by a mirror and was a living, breathing, and moving entity. Keeping with its peculiar theme, the casino's entrance was at the back of a shadow-coated alley, beneath mahogany cellar doors that opened onto lightless stairs. Claustrophobic, yet exciting. At the bottom of the stairs was the bouncer.

A girl who looked to be only seventeen with bouncy blue curls and a sing-song voice. Jane was fairly certain the girl had made a deal with a mirror for eternal youth or something, because she hadn't aged a day since the first time Jane had come to the casino at seventeen years old.

"Why is a bullet like a tender caress?" the blue-haired bouncer asked. The only way into the Russet was to answer a riddle.

"Because both bullets and love pierce through hearts," Jane responded before Nightmare could.

He glanced at her and nodded in approval before pulling her

through the doors and onto the wooden platforms that made up the gambling den. The place was a cave with beautiful lagoons that sparkled with the shades of a sunset. Stalactites formed stakes of crystals from the ceiling, and glow worms and enchanted fire-flies lit up the rooms.

The place was gorgeous.

Nightmare marched up to a private table where five people sat playing poker, Jane still clinging to his arm.

The first and most shocking member of the table was the Playboy Prince, Emrys. Jane immediately wanted to curtsy to him out of respect, but she wasn't sure if it was the appropriate thing to do, considering... everything. So, she gave a slight and awkward bounce that was certainly not missed by anyone watching.

Jane had met Emrys three different times at the Royalle Ballet. He was a fan of the arts. Surprisingly, considering his proclivities towards bedding women, he had never flirted with Jane.

Tonight, he sat in a midnight suit spun from spider silk with purple accents. The man sitting to his direct right—François— was also impeccably dressed in a burgundy, pinstriped suit. The color made his russet-brown skin and dark eyes stand out. The two of them looked like the wealthiest men in the room, and they probably were. François was the leader of the Fantômes gang and the most powerful man in New Swansea's underworld.

On the other side of Emrys was a gorgeous woman with golden-brown hair. She wore a low-cut dark pink dress that sparkled under the shine of the Russet's glowworms.

Two other men filled out the table and seemed to be members of the Fantômes gang.

"A meeting. Now," Nightmare demanded.

"Well, it's nice to see you too, Gavriil." Prince Emrys drew out the name, almost tauntingly.

"It seems you two have been having quite a fun night," François said with a rather amused smile on his face.

"And who did you kill?" the girl with golden-brown hair and two different colored eyes—one pink and one blue—asked in a bored tone. She ran her hand along the felt of the table, her long nails stroking the fabric almost like claws. "I think you still have their brains in your hair."

Jane shuddered. Disgusting. She didn't even want to think about that.

As the brunette's eyes slid over Jane, they sparkled—literally sparkled. Her face was young and soft, but underneath was an iron temperament. So beautiful and so fierce. A woman Jane never wanted to anger.

"Her husband," Nightmare finally answered the question in an equally flat tone.

"Ah, I see you finally wanted her all to yourself," Prince Emrys said, raising a suggestive eyebrow before turning to François. "You owe me 20,000 Siennas."

François sighed. "You had to go and kill him." He shook his head.

Jane's mouth nearly fell open. Not only did Nightmare know two of the most influential men in the entire country, but they also knew about her and *him*. Which meant they went into Nightmare's mirror prison, right? And frequently?

"So, what do we owe this pleasure?" Emrys asked. "I know it's not covering up a mirror since New Swansea's laws don't apply to you."

Nightmare growled. Deeply. "I have multiple demands."

"Of course you do." Emrys slid his hands into his pockets and leaned back in his chair.

"Firstly,"—Nightmare looked to Emrys—"I need you to write up a marriage certificate and change her name,"—his eyes shifted to François—"and I want you to take Jane into your gang and give her a job..."—after a moment of hesitation—"a good one. You will protect her like one of your own."

What? Nerves flew up Jane's throat like a flutter of butterflies.

François's brow furrowed, but it was Emrys who said, "And what name precisely do you want me to change her name to?"

"She'll take my name as my wife." Nightmare's jaw tensed; he was clearly annoyed at being questioned.

"Her husband's body isn't even cold yet, and you're already stealing his wife." A smirk climbed up Emrys's lips. "And they say I'm a rogue."

Nightmare ignored the comment. "She'll become Jane Wryte."

"No, Jane Ashelle Whitfield-Wryte," Jane said far too meekly, like a mouse. She cleared her throat and tried again. "I want to keep Ashelle and Whitfield."

Jane didn't know why she wanted to keep the name Whitfield, which had been given to her at the orphanage, but she did. It was the name she danced under, her public name, and perhaps even the name that represented resilience. Ashelle was her identity, but Whitfield was her strength, and Wryte would become her hope.

Hope that, for once, her life would be lived without facing violence.

Nightmare waved his hand. "As she says."

"Just to be clear, you are marrying her tonight?" Emrys asked.

"Yes."

"Should we have a ceremony?"

Nightmare's eyes darkened. "The paperwork will do."

"How romantic," the brunette woman said under her breath. She leaned in closer to Emrys, and he ran a very suggestive hand up her thigh.

Jane gulped and glanced away.

Then the prince looked first at Jane, who was wringing her hands, and then at Nightmare, who looked like he was a shadow made of stone. And with a mischievous glint in his eye, Emrys said, "I will marry you two, but it would be such a shame not to have a ceremony." Nightmare growled, but Emrys simply shrugged. "It's my condition, Gavriil."

"I would remind you of the Gilded Alliance and the extremely lenient deal I gave you for protection from prosecution by the police."

Jane would later learn that the Gilded Alliance was an agreement to work together with the most significant mirrors in the city, the Fantômes, Kordelia, and the Prince. Apparently, the Fantômes made a deal with Nightmare to counterbalance the deal that the police had made with him. The police had made a deal that every crime against a non-mirror-blessed person would be instantly solved. Completely fucking over all the underground factions of the city.

Emrys tapped the table. "I never made that deal with you."

"Yet you benefit from it, as the de facto leader of the Fantômes."

François let out a low snarl. He didn't like the insinuation that he wasn't in control of his gang.

"We are allies, nothing less." Emrys held up a placating hand. "Nightmare, darling, just marry the girl properly."

Darling. Oh, Nightmare was going to kill him.

Yet he didn't.

He simply nodded.

"Please, clean her up and find her something to wear." Emrys turned to the brunette, whose glare could have cooked a steak. Emrys leaned in closer, whispering into her lips. "Please, do it for me, Harlowe." He closed the distance and passionately kissed her while everyone looked away, pretending not to watch.

Jane wanted to burst out of her skin. It was too... carnal. Too heated. Too much. But mostly, Jane was jealous that no one had ever kissed her like that.

Like they wanted to consume her.

Granted, it was this moment that Jane would look back on when this foolish Prince turned his eyes to her sister. It was at this moment that Jane would probably never approve of him.

Not for *her*, Quinny.

"Yes, fine," Harlowe said before standing and motioning for Jane to follow.

Harlowe took her first to a pool, where she helped her clean up and then gave her a glittering silver gown.

"Do you have something more..." Jane didn't quite know what she wanted, but she didn't want a white gown or a white adjacent gown, not for her second marriage and not to marry a monster cloaked in shadows.

The silver wasn't fitting.

"Black or blood red?" Jane finally finished the question.

The corner of Harlowe's lips lifted. "Something more monstrous?"

Jane nodded.

"Fitting, I guess." Harlowe pulled out a black velvet hoop-skirt dress with deep crimson embroidery and lace, mixed with black lace and red velvet sleeves that doubled as gloves.

The sweetheart neckline was cut low and exposed ample cleavage. In the dress, Jane's red hair looked darker, almost black. Almost as if the dress were adapting to her, and her to it.

It was the perfect dress to marry Nightmare in, and ten minutes later, she was walking down the aisle for her second wedding, just hours after her groom had murdered her first husband.

The ceremony was quick and beautiful. It was held in an underground cave overlooking a lava pool and a tranquil waterfall. There was little sound apart from the steaming hiss when the cold water met the lava.

It was beautiful, but all Jane could focus on was her heart, ticking away in her chest. *Beat, beat, boom, tick, tick, crack.*

Nerves coated the lining of her stomach, and her knees shook beneath the massive skirts of her dress.

Only François, Harlowe, and Emrys witnessed the nuptials as the words of the ceremony blended together, as she looked up into Nightmare's sculpted face—a face so beautiful a mortal dared not stare too long. Outside the mirror, his hair was more white than silver, and his eyes had more blue cutting through—but he still didn't look human.

Godly was the only word that could ever match his radiance.

His throat bobbed as he looked down at her. He, too, seemed

to ignore the prince's words, his focus tearing into her and devouring her.

"I now pronounce you husband and wife. You may kiss your bride."

Nothing happened. Nightmare didn't move his lips to hers. He didn't do anything save glare at her.

Emrys cleared his throat. "Umm, you are supposed to kiss."

"Can I?" Nightmare whispered so only she could hear him.

"Yes."

Nightmare stepped in, lifted Jane's chin possessively, and whispered into her lips. "I really should kill you before you destroy me."

Then his lips met hers.

At first, the kiss was a hard press of lips against one another. No softness, no giving in from either side. Jane expected him to pull away after a moment, but he didn't. He grunted and laced his fingers into her hair, pulling her in closer as he opened his mouth and let her in.

At first, Jane didn't know what to do. Of course, she had been kissed before, but never with passion and never of her own choosing. She had always just been a toy.

But at this moment, she didn't want to be. So she opened her mouth to him, and he slipped his tongue in.

Jane's breath hitched, and her heart pounded in her ears. She was kissing the God of Nightmares... at their wedding. He tasted like black tea and darkness.

Jane's hands trembled, but she ran them up his chest, holding on to his suit coat for stability.

And he did keep her stable. He was a wall of solid muscle, and surprisingly, a source of desire.

He growled as he plundered deeper, one of his hands moving down her waist and pulling her closer to him. Passion sparked, and tension between them pooled at her core. She wanted to feel more of him—to feel all of him. But they were far too clothed for that. Her hand drew into his coat and under his dress shirt, trying unsuccessfully to pull it off. She wanted to feel his skin touching hers. His mouth was not enough.

It wasn't enough.

Because a beast was growing inside of her, and it was like nothing she had ever felt.

Jane whimpered as his fingers stroked her waist, exploring and learning her body like a violinist tuning his instrument.

The sensations he coaxed and the way his hands moved thrilled her and made her oh-so curious.

Jane wanted more. But she wasn't going to get it.

François cleared his throat. "We have rooms if you prefer to consummate immediately."

Without warning, Nightmare pulled away and stepped three feet backward, leaving Jane cold and listless. Her knees were weak, and she no longer had anything—or anyone—holding her up. When Jane's eyes caught Nightmare's, acid singed her throat.

Because Nightmare was painted from wisps of rotting fury, everything about his posture was suddenly off... something dark and twisted lingered behind his eyes. Then, without another word, he disappeared in a cloud of iridescent light.

He'd married her, kissed her with the most passion she'd ever felt in life, and then he just left her in a den full of vipers.

"Well, that was certainly entertaining," Emrys said, perhaps to break the tension pulsing through the cavern, or maybe he just said it because he never took anything seriously.

"I assume you will probably follow him to his mirror to *celebrate* your marriage. But when you return, you will start your new job." François slid his hands into his pockets before turning on his heel to leave.

"Job?" Jane asked, trying to keep her voice steady.

"Gavriil made it clear you are now a member of Les Fantômes. I hope you love paperwork."

Chapter Thirteen

Age 24.

Jane held her breath, her heart raging in her chest and her core pulsing with... with a feeling she didn't recognize. They were in their bedchamber after officially marrying, and the marriage needed consummation.

Jane knew what that meant.

She'd done it before... horrifically.

Swallowing hard, anticipation rolled in her stomach like a mixture of butterfly wings and rotten tomatoes. She desperately wanted to know what his touch might feel like, especially after that kiss.

Her fingers grazed her lips, and it kept everything in her to hold back a moan at the memory.

His kisses were consuming. But sex?

Would he be soft or demanding? Gentle or rough? And what did she want him to be?

Jane had no idea.

She craved it, yet also dreaded it.

Would it hurt as much as it did all the other times?

Jane had never had sex without pain. Not once. She heard from the other ballerinas that sex could be pleasurable. They used to speak in hushed whispers to their friends about the glorious things their partners would do to them. Often involving tongues and inventive positions. Once, Jane even heard about the use of blindfolds and chains.

She found it frightening and tantalizing. What if she could trust a man enough to chain her up? What could it be like?

Nightmare sat underneath the covers with his shirt off and chest exposed. His chiseled pectorals and abs were on full display.

Jane gulped and walked to the wardrobe.

Jane tried to grab the laces of her corset at the back. But as she did, she got an idea. "I—" she started and then stopped. "Will you help me?" She turned her back to him and motioned to her laces.

She didn't need his help, but she wanted it.

Jane bit her lip. Waiting. When nothing happened, she closed her eyes. Defeated, but then...

The bed creaked, the springs bouncing as he stood up. With every step closer, her heart beat like a war drum.

Anticipation ate away at her. One step. Another. Another. Jane sucked in a breath.

His large fingertips grazed the center of her back, and she desperately wanted to lean into the touch. But she didn't.

The last thing she wanted was for Nightmare to know that she wanted him. It just couldn't happen.

She held her breath.

His fingers brushed her red curls across her back and over her shoulder, his fingertips skimming the nape of her neck.

A shudder ran through her body, and her core tightened.

Slowly, Nightmare dug his fingers into her laces as he loosened them. Tension turned in her stomach. If it were a noise, it would be a string quartet playing, plucking the strings faster and faster as the unease rose before the climax of a ballet.

When Nightmare finished with the laces, his hands came up

to both her shoulders, running across them as he lowered her sleeves. Once her arms were free, he skimmed his hands down her stomach and off her thighs, letting the garment pool at her feet.

Jane stepped out of it as Nightmare turned his attention to her petticoats and then to her chemise. One by one, he removed her clothing from her body until she was naked, still standing with her back toward him.

Jane gulped, swallowing past the lump in her throat. Then she slowly turned, and as she did, her breasts grazed his chest, her nipples hardening. Her eyes dipped down, and disappointment whispered through her. She wanted to see his penis, but Nightmare still wore his trousers.

"Thank you for saving my life." Jane's gaze tracked up and met his piercing silver eyes. From this close, she saw the streaks of blue in them—the streaks of his mortal form remaining.

Nightmare grunted and stepped back. Then he turned on his heel and returned to bed, slipping back under the covers.

Jane's eyebrows bunched. He'd just gotten back into bed and closed his eyes.

Closed. His. Eyes.

What?

Jane followed him and lay down. Waiting and still hoping.

But nothing happened.

After a while, her eyes drooped closed, and darkness consumed her.

And that was when the nightmares started. She dreamed of all the men who abused her. Over and over and over again. Every night for the next four years.

Villains never took care of their messes. Jane was good at handling crime scenes, and even covering them up at this point. While it was true that the police had made a deal with Nightmare to be able to solve any murder instantly, there were a lot of loopholes. First, the deal didn't work on Mirror-Blessed, but second, it didn't work on anyone who had a bargain to subvert it. So, of course, the police's bargain wouldn't work on Nightmare. However, it didn't keep them from investigating.

So, Jane often had to clean up crime scenes before the police arrived. She wasn't sure what they would do if they found out that an ancient Mirror God was out in the wild, murdering people whenever he wanted. However, she didn't want to know

But if there was one skill Jane had, it was cleaning up other people's messes.

Unfortunately, getting married last night had kept her from getting to the crime scene in a reasonable time, so her husband's body had already been discovered, and she was suspect number one—especially after immediately remarrying, which seemed highly unjust because in what world would she have the strength to smash her husband's skull in?

Well... in this world, because anyone could bargain with a mirror for magic. But she hadn't, and she wasn't Mirror-Blessed. No, she'd just sold her soul and body to a monster—a monster who crushed men's skulls.

Although technically, Jane was guilty. She had asked her monster to kill her husband. Did that make her a murderer? Probably. The problem was that she didn't care. That man deserved to die, and Jane wouldn't have her life ruined because of it.

The problem was that his body had already been moved to the morgue. A terrible thing, except that her sister and new closest friend worked there. Jane could get in and tamper with the evidence, erasing anything that might lead back to her. But Jane couldn't stomach getting her sister in trouble.

Prince Emrys Avalon had no such compunctions. In fact, he seemed to enjoy it.

Jane ran into him, walking through the concrete decor-less halls on the way to the lab, where her first husband's corpse was to be found.

At seeing Emrys, her eyes went wide, and the muscles in her back coiled. "Why are you here?" Jane whispered out of the corner of her mouth.

"Your husband requested I bury this for you." Emrys plucked an invisible piece of lint from his jacket and smiled like a wicked witch. "Shall we?" Emrys motioned forward to the lab.

Jane rubbed her temples and shook her head. This was not going to go well. Jane felt it in her sinews and connective tissues. Handsome, arrogant princes never helped with anything. Usually, they just got in the way.

But he held power so Jane would take his help.

Emrys reached the doorknob first, twisted it, and held open the heavy wooden door, all the while his eyes mischievous and locked on Jane. But the real trouble started when Jane stepped into the doorway next to him. His gaze swept into the morgue and clocked Quinnevere, following her movements like the chalk outline around a corpse, and as he watched, a darkness swirled in his irises—literally—and seeped out of his suit coat. They seemed to buzz with some sort of excitement.

"Emrys—" Jane started, but the prince seemed lost in his thoughts. "Hey, playboy," Jane gently tapped his face, pulling him out of his trance—"focus?"

"Why yes, of course." Emrys dropped the door nearly on Jane and walked into the room like a preening peacock.

Well, this was fucking perfect.

At this, Quinnevere's gaze shot up—she had been so absorbed in the body she was dissecting that she completely blocked out both Jane and Emrys entering the room. The scents of decomposition and formalin hovered like a fog in the room. It stung Jane's nostrils and surrounded her .

A snake of nerves slithered up her insides, coiling into the rungs of her ribcage as Jane's gaze took in the pale white corpse of her headless first husband. The snake coiled tighter, moving around the edges of her heart. Jane wanted to feel bad, but all she felt was relief, accompanied by a hint of guilt.

"Oh, Janey, what are you—" Quinn cut herself off when her gaze latched onto the prince. She stammered, opening and closing her mouth a couple of times before she took her hands out of the corpse and smiled. "Uh, hello, Mr. Prince, sir?" she said it all like a question. "None of that seemed right."

"Technically, you should refer to me as Your Royal Highness, but you can call me Emrys." Emrys strolled over to Quinnevere and stopped inches from her, sliding his hands into his pockets. His voice was laced with pure seduction, and Jane wanted to vomit a little bit in her mouth.

She was going to kill him before he touched her sister.

"Oh, uh, Your Royal Highness, Emrys." Quinnevere's eyebrows drew together like she was still questioning if she had done it right, and then she made an awkward curtsy-bob-like movement.

He chuckled. "Perfect."

Jane walked to the edge of the table to get a better view of them.

"Sorry," Quinnevere said. "One does not often meet the prince with their hands inside a body."

"I'd say you are the first person I've ever met with their hands inside a body." He paused, cocking his head. "At least in this context."

Eww. Jane could not unhear that, but naive Quinnevere only asked, "What other context could there be..."

Emrys raised a suggestive eyebrow.

It took Quinnevere a moment to grasp the meaning. "Oh." She nodded, her eyes dipping to her core as if she were imagining it. "Well, probably less bloody."

"Possibly."

Her eyebrows crinkled, but she was far too focused on the prince. Studying him in a way that Jane *did not* like. It was probably time to step in, so Jane cleared her throat, and both sets of eyes landed on her.

"Oh, right, Janey. What brings you here?" Quinnevere asked.

"Seems obvious, no?" Emrys asked. "We're here to bury your investigation. I have already told the police that they are not allowed to investigate this murder, and since no one in this pathetic man's life even cared about him, no one will bat an eye at his unsolved murder."

Quinnevere returned to the body, her gaze measuring the corpse, before flicking to Jane. "Did you kill him?"

Jane sucked in a breath. She didn't want to lie to her sister. It wouldn't be good for their relationship, but how would her sister, who worked every day to get justice for the dead, think about the fact that one of her closest friends was a murderer? "Not technically."

Quinnevere sucked her bottom lip into her mouth. She paused for a long minute in thought. Then she nodded and said, "Alright." She picked the intestines, which she had been studying, and she shoved them back inside the corpse. "I have to close him so that he might be able to be placed in a coffin. Not that it will be an open-coffin funeral. Not with no head."

Emrys chucked. "I'd say not."

Quinnevere nodded again, before taking a needle and thread and very methodically sewing shut the flesh. Jane wasn't squeamish, but this was, in fact, disgusting. Yet neither the prince nor her sister seemed to mind the sight at all.

As they watched, Emrys turned back to Jane and said, "Don't you look forward to one day being on that table?"

Jane protectively hugged her arms around her center. "What is that supposed to mean?"

"We all end up in the morgue, Jane." Emrys winked, far too amused by the entire situation.

"Not you," she whispered through her teeth. Not vampire princes. After their meeting at the Russet, Nightmare had filled her in about his involvement with the gang and the prince and that, in fact, Prince Emrys was the King Emrys who had led humans in the war seven hundred years ago against the last remaining vampires. Unfortunately, before the war was over, Emrys had been turned. After the war, he established a secret society called the Blood Council and Accords, which bound the remaining vampires to secrecy and prevented them from killing and becoming tyrants again.

It was a long and complicated history, but the most critical piece of information Jane learned was that her blood-painting tattoo was actually a symbol of the secret society and that her parents had been key members before their deaths. Jane very much intended to reopen the investigation into their murders.

But first, she needed to survive this one.

"Well, when I do end up at this table, I hope it's a much better atmosphere than this. How sad would it be for no one to care about your death?" Jane said, loud enough for both of them to hear.

"If you die, I will make sure people care." Emrys's voice dropped an octave, expression growing serious.

When I die, Jane felt it coming... Jane swallowed and tried to let that thought fly away. She hated it when she got that feeling.

"You're not going to die, Jane," Quinnevere said, not looking up from her task.

Jane forced a smile on her lips. "Of course not."

Fifteen minutes later, after Quinnevere returned the corpse to a cold chamber and threw away all of her findings, Jane and Emrys left. As soon as they were in the hallway, Jane turned on the Playboy Prince. "Please don't fuck her." Jane crossed her arms and glared at him.

"She's too young for me."

Thank god. "Yes, she is, and you're going to stay far away from her."

"Now, where is the fun in that?" Emrys's eyes twinkled maliciously.

"Stay away, Emrys."

"I think I've just gained a massive interest in crime." He winked. "One really must solve murders."

"Emrys," Jane warned, but the prince simply strode away from her, whistling an annoying tune.

Well fuck.

~

"You will move in with me completely, now." Nightmare ambushed her as she entered, as if he had been lying in wait for her to return.

An anchor dropped in her stomach. She enjoyed living at the Viridian and having a week of freedom. But she knew arguing wouldn't do her any good. Nightmare was not reasonable. He did not make compromises or hear people out.

"Alright." When Nightmare didn't move and continued to stand before her like a wall of muscle, Jane added, "Was there something else?"

A low rumble sounded in his chest. "Yes, you will no longer ignore your magic. You will learn how to control it and protect yourself."

"I wasn't ignoring my magic—" At his violent glower, Jane stopped talking. *I was ignoring you.*

He crossed his arms, his biceps bulging. "We start now."

"Could you just order me to learn how to use my magic and we could skip all of this?"

"Magic doesn't like being commanded."

Jane wouldn't understand what he meant by that until much, much later.

It took Jane nine and a half months to get any semblance of control over her powers. At first, it felt there was no rhyme or reason to control them. Ancient witches had been born with their powers and had intuitive control over them, but since Jane hadn't grown up learning to bend and move magic, it was difficult. It was as if she were a baby learning to crawl, walk, run, and speak for the first time.

It was irritating because Mirror-Blessed never had this level of difficulty using their magic, and when Jane had complained about this to Nightmare he merely said, "Of course, they are using a tool. You *are* the tool. They tap into magic. You are its source. The magic needs to trust you, because what you can become is far beyond anything I or a Mirror-Blessed can ever do."

Nightmare often spoke as if magic were sentient and had its own personality. And it seemed to. It was like coaxing and seducing a ghost or the wind. One couldn't see or grab the source, but one could feel it and hear it—sometimes.

Magic was like emotions. Not in the sense that it worked with emotions. It was like emotions themselves. Moving and rolling and flipping through moods, often pausing on one for a long time. One day, it might be big and hot like anger, but the next day, it could feel lethargic and low like sadness.

Half of learning magic was learning how to regulate it, just as one should with emotions. That was precisely the reason it took her so long even to get a grasp on it.

So far, Jane appeared to be a Wind Witch, but Nightmare was convinced she would become more. There were five types of witches. Wind, Water, Fire, Earth, and Chiaroscuro—Often referred to as Light or Shadow Witches.

Wind Witches controlled more than just the wind; they took on all the properties of wind and bent any type of magic relating to it. So, a Wind Witch would become invisible, move objects, and do things like morph their bodies into air, making it so they could slip through cracks in walls, almost like they could walk through them. But it didn't start there. They could often hear voices on the wind, or even read people's hidden thoughts or intentions—that last bit only the most skilled Wind Witches could accomplish.

When witches existed, there were many different levels, just like humans had various levels of intelligence. The most powerful were nearly unstoppable.

Nightmare was convinced Jane would become one of the most powerful witches of all time. Jane was less sure, since she could barely stay invisible. She'd managed five-minute stints, and that took nine months to accomplish.

But Nightmare was certain, and often said, "A pathetic witch wouldn't be prophesied to destroy me."

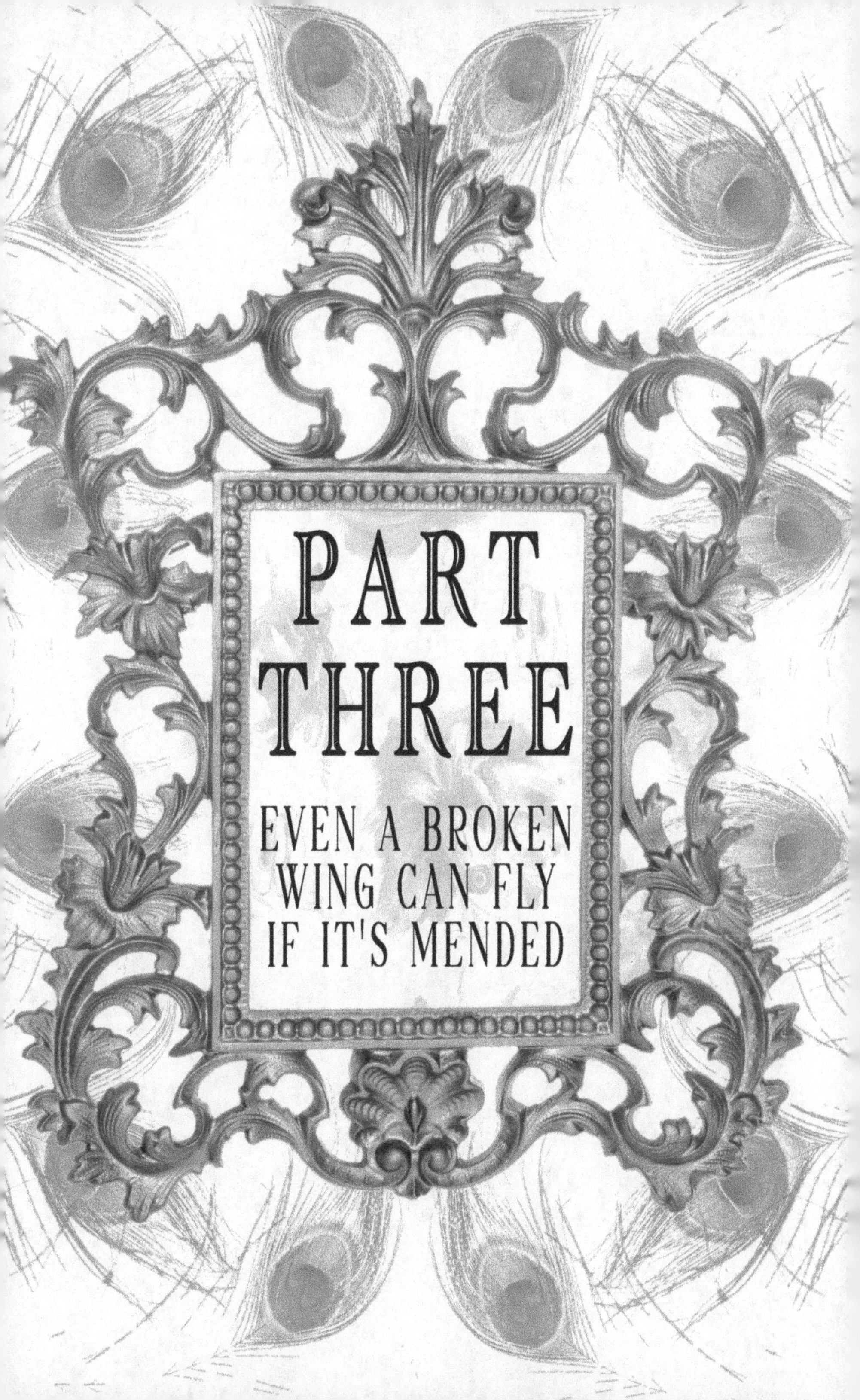

PART
THREE
EVEN A BROKEN
WING CAN FLY
IF IT'S MENDED

Chapter Fourteen

Age 26.

The walls were bleeding. Spilling down the sides like thick crimson paint. The smell was suffocating, coiling into her nostrils and sticking to her skin.

With one hand, she held her little sister's mouth shut and squeezed her to keep her from screaming—he couldn't hear them, he couldn't find them—and with her other hand, she pressed her fingertips into the marble floor to ground herself and kept herself from screaming.

Glass flew through the air, and Jane screamed in her mind, or maybe she screamed out loud.

It was hard to tell anymore.

She thrashed and cried and fought, and then she was pinned down. He was going to kill her.

"Shhh," a soft baritone melody sang into her hair and held her like a straitjacket. "Shhh, you're alright, little doe. You're alright."

Jane blinked and then blinked again, a fuzzy world beginning to focus, but her body could not move. Nightmare clutched her chin tightly, staring into her eyes and pinning her torso and legs to the bed.

"Breathe." It was a command. Magic filled her lungs, and Jane complied. "Breathe," Nightmare said again, still clutching her jaw hard.

Jane closed her eyes and sank into the feel of him encasing her, and she breathed in one, two, three, four counts and held her breath for another count of four before releasing it to a count of four. She opened her eyes again when she had finished that cycle three times.

"Tell me their names." His voice wasn't hard, but it wasn't soft either.

For the last two years after Jane's first husband's death, she had night terrors. Dreams of his hands around her neck that sometimes felt so real she swore she woke up with white finger indents in her skin. It didn't happen every night—at least not anymore—but the dreams were extreme and felt so real when they did. Sometimes, they included her first husband's deputies, but often not. But every time Jane woke up from one of these terrors, it was in Nightmare's arms.

So it wasn't surprising that he thought she was dreaming about them again.

"It wasn't them." Her voice was hoarse. She must have been screaming. "It was my parents."

"Your parents?" His eyes darkened.

Jane's eyebrows scrunched. "Oh, no, they didn't do anything to me." Jane gulped. "They died... They were murdered."

Nightmare's chest rumbled, and the only remaining black strand of hair fell in front of his liquid silver eyes.

"It happened when I was ten years old." Jane squeezed his shoulder, almost as if she were the one comforting him. "I am not sure if the dream was a memory or a distortion."

Jane needed to find out. It wasn't the first time she'd had a night terror about it. In fact, it was overtaking the ones about her abusers, almost like her subconscious was trying to tell her something. She knew the dreams wouldn't stop until she addressed them.

She also wanted to look into it for herself. Jane didn't remember that night. Her brain was locked, and the key had been thrown away a long time ago.

But maybe it was time to revisit it—time to learn the truth about her parents' murders.

"I want to find out," she said. "I want to know what happened to them."

Nightmare only grunted in response and slightly shifted his body.

Jane's breath hitched as she suddenly became very aware that Nightmare was still pinning her to her bed and still had his hands all over her. But even more disconcerting was that he had a massive hard-on, and it was digging into her pelvis.

Jane wiggled, and she felt the friction against her clit. She bit her lip and closed her eyes, sucking in the moan of pleasure.

Their game of tension had two rules: never let the other see and never ever mention it.

At least those were her rules, because Jane was very uncertain whether he even wanted her. Although his hard cock might suggest he did. But he never acted on it and never mentioned it.

It was infuriating.

Two years of tension pooled in her stomach. Two years waiting for him to fuck her—to touch her sexually.

But he didn't.

He never did. But his eyes possessed her. In everything they did, his gaze followed her, caressing her, punishing her, holding her, fucking her.

But never—never his hands, or mouth, or penis, and it was beginning to make her mad. In every definition of the word.

"Why don't you fuck me?" Damnit. She broke the second rule of tension—never mention it. "Are you not attracted to me?" And she broke first—never let him see. That last bit came out far too desperate, and Jane snapped her lips closed. Mortified. *Fuck, get control of yourself.*

Nightmare ran his thumb along her jaw and then over her

lips. His gaze latched onto her soul. "Because you never gave me permission."

"I—" Her mouth fell open, and his thumb entered, continuing his caressing. "What?"

"I will fuck you in all ways. Gentle, rough, possessive, demanding, lovingly. I will own and destroy you, but first, you must be ready."

"I am—" but she couldn't finish the sentence and say the word *ready*. Because was she?

"You've only ever been raped, Jane." He took his thumb out of her mouth and tipped her chin up. "You have nightmares almost every night of how those men touched and abused you. You are not ready."

No. The nightly nightmares were about her parents, but she didn't feel like correcting him.

Then he leaned in and gently pressed his lips to hers, kissing her like he'd done it a million times, before quickly pulling away and standing up off the bed.

Confusion licked at her core. He was only soft to her, and only her, and it rattled her.

"Go get ready for work. You have a gangster to turn in for stealing, and possibly to get murdered." Nightmare winked and disappeared into the midst.

Jane had long since given up asking how he knew *everything*.

Thirty minutes later, Jane was dressed and at the Russet casino, waiting outside her new boss's bedroom. He was currently fucking someone—a girl this time, from the sounds of it. François didn't have a gender preference. Not that he took many people to bed. He was a playboy, but not quite like the prince.

Emrys was a king among playboys. He had a new girl in his bed weekly, if not nightly, which was precisely why he'd never touch Jane's sister. She wouldn't allow it. She'd castrate him first.

Which Emrys seemed to understand because Quinn was still a naive, innocent girl.

Probably not for long, but Jane would protect her for as long as possible.

Especially from the men she worked with. All of them were playboys—every single one—although none were married or committed to anyone. So, in comparison, François was a saint because he barely partook in carnal pleasures. Maybe three times a year.

Still, it wasn't fun to wait and listen to the sexual activities, particularly because she was so starved for touch and pleasure.

Fucking Nightmare.

Jane considered fucking a random patron of the club, but she couldn't. Nightmare would kill them, and while Jane had become fairly okay with murder, she didn't want to be responsible for an innocent man's death.

Not in any area of her life. Because all of her bosses were dangerous and deadly and killed without hesitation. Jane technically had three bosses: François, Emrys, and Nightmare. Everyone pretended Emrys wasn't the boss of all Mirror Mafias, but he was. In small ways, Emrys was the boss of everyone in the city, and it was the Mirror Mafias, specifically the Fantômes, who enforced his rule—because technically, the man couldn't murder anyone himself as a result of the Blood Accords that bound vampires seven hundred years ago.

Jane adjusted the lapels of her pinstriped suit dress as she tried not to hear the moans coming from inside François's room. She leaned against the wall, her hair tight, and pulled back. At the Russet, Jane was all business. She was in charge of all of the finances of their many businesses, and Jane took the job very seriously.

She needed to bring three reports to François's attention as soon as possible: unusual losses at the tables, an employee embezzling money, and a large offer for the gang to bargain for a Black Market mirror object.

The Fantômes ran an infamous Black Market, and if someone couldn't find what they wanted there, they often asked the gang to make a deal with a mirror for them to receive it. The Fantômes had many members whose sole job was to mirror bargain, but the most infamous of them all was Harlowe Merriwether—New Swansea's Monster Girl. She had made over ninety mirror bargains in her life and had at least three visible mirror consequences.

Her irises were sculpted from diamonds, one pink and one periwinkle blue. Her hair was enchanted and dangerous, causing severe frostbite to anyone who touched it. Her skin shimmered in pure darkness, like a night-light.

Harlowe mostly hated Jane, but she wasn't entirely sure why. Probably because Jane had so quickly gained the trust and favor of both Emrys and François —mostly due to Nightmare's threats, but also because Jane was good at almost everything she found interesting.

Sounds of flesh slapping and moans finally stopped—thank God—but Jane still didn't want to enter. Emrys Avalon seemed to have no qualms, though, because he nodded at Jane as he walked to the door.

"He's fuckin—" Jane wasn't able to finish the sentence before Emrys shrugged and opened the door anyway.

"Then it shall be a show."

The girl shrieked, and Jane rested her head against the wall again, closing her eyes with a frustrated huff. But if she were forced to wait even longer because of Emrys's schemes, then at least she could practice her magic.

So she did, focusing all of her energy and spirit into becoming one with the wind. Into seducing her magic to make herself invisible. All the while, Jane listened in.

"Oh, did I interrupt something?" Emrys asked in a far-too-satisfied tone. The dick. "I see you had a fun night and morning, François, but I have business to discuss."

"Get out." François's tone was harsh, and at first, Jane

thought he was talking to Emrys, but then the girl almost whimpered, and it was clear that François was throwing her out like trash. "There is some money on the table."

"I am not a courtesan."

"Perhaps you should be. You're very talented with your—" A crashing noise and glass smashing shook the wall behind Jane's head.

Emrys let out a deep chuckle. "Oh, this is very entertaining."

"Fuck you."

Another smash and a bunch of clumsy sounds floated out into the hallway, as if someone was hurrying to get dressed.

"Get out and don't come back." François's voice was dark and dripping with fury.

The girl scoffed. "François Jules Visage. Mark my words, I will break you." Then the girl—a brunette in her early twenties—marched out of the room, holding a sheet to cover her breasts, her head held high but tears lacing her eyes.

Jane had to stifle a gasp when she saw her face. It was Giselle Reyes-Vega, a close friend of Jane and her sister. She must not have been successful at covering up the gasp because Giselle looked in her direction but blinked a couple of times in confusion when she didn't find a source for the noise.

Jane had done it. She was invisible.

Before returning to solid form, Jane cracked her neck and shook out her arms. As she reappeared, Giselle squealed but immediately slapped a hand over her mouth. She clearly didn't want the gentlemen in the next room to know she was still out there.

"You're Mirror-Blessed?" Giselle breathed.

No. But Jane said, "Yes."

"Invisible, huh?"

Jane nodded. "Are you okay, G?"

Giselle's throat bobbed. "Yes, of course." The words were a show, and neither girl believed it, but they still pretended all the same.

The candles flickered in the cave hallway. They clearly didn't believe her either. It was then that Jane's gaze caught the red on the sheet. Giselle had been a virgin, and she'd given her first time to a man who didn't deserve it. Jane knew what that felt like.

Giselle followed Jane's gaze, and when she saw the blood, she let out a sob. Giselle was the emotional one. Her feelings were like waves crashing on a sandy beach. They were always there, always coming, but usually stable—even when large. But sometimes, the waves grew and crashed into more than just the sand. Sometimes, they destroyed everything in their path.

One of those waves was coming, and Jane knew she had to comfort her friend. So she gave her a big, warm hug.

"He doesn't deserve you," Jane said into Giselle's hair. A sob shook the brunette's body, but she still tried to make no sounds.

Giselle hiccupped and said, "I am going to destroy him."

"I would prefer that you not." Jane squeezed tighter. "He is my boss. Albeit a dick."

"You work for him? Why?" Giselle asked.

"It's too long a story for right now."

Giselle nodded into her friend's chest. "Yeah, now might not be the best time for stories."

Jane laughed. "Probably not."

Clapping sounded within François's room, and both girls' attention drew back to the doorway, and they stepped apart.

"Well, that might be some of the best entertainment I've had all week, and that's saying a lot because I dropped by the morgue to torture the little redhead ballerina again."

Jane gritted her teeth. She was going to kill him.

"If you wanted to torture a redheaded ballerina, we do have one on staff."

"Yes, but Jane is so... serious."

"Your little ballerina never smiles and always scowls at you."

"Isn't it great?"

"So when are you going to fuck her?"

Jane flashed Giselle a, *Sorry, I have to handle this* look before stepping through the doorway and saying, "Touch her, and I will kill you."

"I would enjoy watching you try."

Emrys stood with his hands in his pockets, leaning against one of the four-poster banisters, his body pointing at François, who was sitting at the table next to his bed where he typically took his breakfast and did his morning job tasks. As his room was in the Russet, the walls and ceilings were still formed from rock crystals.

"Ah, Jane, just the person I wanted to see," François said. "I believe there is a fiery brunette storming through the casino at the moment. Will you handle that?"

Jane's eyes flew to the ceiling. Men. Always so dramatic. "There is no need."

"So you have already handled it?"

"I don't need to. She is not going to break anything at your casino." Jane rubbed her face, exasperated. "If I know her well—and I do—she will go home and plan a long and torturous way of getting her revenge on you, which you will deserve. A virgin, François? You're better than that."

François sat back in the chair next to his bed. "And how do you know all that?"

"She's my sister's best friend. The sister"—she glared at Emrys—"who you are going to stay away from."

Emrys's eyebrows wiggled, and he flashed a taunting smile. "Maybe I will, maybe I won't. I do love to fuck..."

"He has no qualms about deflowering virgins, either." François tapped his fingers on his table. "That's the difference between him and me. I don't fuck virgins—save the mistake that just walked out of my room—and I don't sleep with a new person every night. She was the first one I've been with in nine months."

"If you're superior to me, then why toss her out? Half naked, I might add."

François dragged his finger along the wooden edge of his table. "Because while she was fascinating, she was also the most tempting piece I've had in a long time. She's a distraction and not worthy of my time. She's not…"

Emrys crossed his arms across his chest. "For often being the smartest man in the room, you can be very obtuse."

"You're saying I'm smarter than you?"

Emrys let out a deep chuckle. "On many occasions, yes. Today, you were not. You were cruel."

"No more than you are or anyone else here. I am a businessman. I run nine immensely successful enterprises. Some legal, some illegal, I don't have time to deal with the emotions of a girl I fucked, no matter how good it was."

"Seems wasteful." Emrys shook his head. "If she's a good fuck, you should have kept her around for a while. But you wouldn't do that because then you might grow attached."

"I've only been attached to two people in my life." François's voice darkened. "One's in prison, and the other one is dead. I have no interest in attachments now."

"Your loss."

Jane stepped into the room closer. "If you two are done. I have some business to address."

François pitched his chin down slightly and motioned for her to go on. So Jane gave her fully practiced speech, going over all three issues she needed to address.

François moved quickly on her information, particularly about the traitor in their organization. An hour later, Jane stood next to him in the deepest parts of the Casino, beneath the water pools and gorgeous sights—in the pits of despair—as he tortured his underling, who was tied to a chair, into a full confession. The whole time, Jane stood stoically by her boss's side, even handing him tools when he needed them.

It only took ten minutes for him to start saying everything. Apparently, he preferred keeping his fingernails and teeth on his body.

"Jane, shoot him in the head." François removed his gun from its holster and held it out to her.

Jane swallowed and stared first at her boss and then at the gun dangling from his hand. "Are you sure?"

"Yes."

Without any more hesitation, she grasped the gun from François, cocked it, pointed at the man's head, and pulled the trigger. He should have known better. Everyone knew stealing from a gang was punishable by death.

"Good." François dipped his chin in approval. "You will take over the Black Market." With that, François turned on his heel and walked out. Not cleaning up his mess or saying another word.

Jane gulped and looked at her murder victim, but dread didn't slide over her body. She didn't feel anything. But goosebumps rose on her flesh. Not because she was a killer, but because the honor that François had just bestowed on her was massive.

It was a symbol of his deepening trust for her. It would also piss off Harlowe Merriwether, which was why bile climbed up her throat.

Harlowe was a vicious monster. But maybe Jane might become one just as frightening.

Chapter Fifteen

AGE 27.

Jane's life was one of service. Serving and servicing powerful men. Working for the Mirror Mafia was no different. She didn't have to touch any of these men, but she did follow their every command.

Tonight was no different, except it was a Gilded Alliance meeting. This gathering of the most influential people discussed top-secret issues, including vampires, Blood Mirrors, and long-dead evils that were brewing. It was a meeting of rivals, enemies, and forced allies.

The list of attendees tonight included three powerful mirrors: Nightmare, Nightshade, and Midnight. Names that were far too close and far too confusing for their good. Why did the three most powerful mirrors all have the word night in their nicknames? That was just silly. But try telling them that.

Also in attendance were François, Emrys, Constance, Kordelia, and the leaders of the other four gangs in the city.

Jane, surprisingly, was the newest member of their group, and she was fairly certain she was only invited because she was Nightmare's wife.

The meeting took place in one of the curtained alcoves of the Viridian Nightclub. A sentient building that catered to one's greatest desires. A club of sin and nighttime pleasures. The place was decorated with peacock colors and decor, and everything about the building caused one's heart to race and other regions to become hot and bothered.

"We have many things to discuss tonight. Shall we get started?" Emrys cut through the group's side chatter. But as soon as he spoke, Nightshade, an extremely tall Mirror God formed from muscles, growled and glared like he might cut the prince's head off.

Nightmare was intentionally placed in between them to keep the peace. "Darcy," Nightmare reprimanded.

Nightshade—also known as the Mirror of Beautiful Decay—aka Darcy's deadly glare flashed toward Nightmare, who simply shrugged it off.

Emrys ignored the outburst. "I would like to discuss the last two remaining Blood Mirrors. I am becoming more and more convinced that whoever killed the Ashelles and destroyed the first Blood Mirror is out there creating vampires and preying on the weak."

Every muscle in Jane's body went tense like a harp string, and she inhaled sharply. Nightmare, out of protective instinct, ran a possessive hand down her thigh and squeezed.

"You have no evidence of that," said the leader of the Cobra Lilies—another Mirror Mafia, and rival to the Fantômes. Thankfully, he was not a member of the gang that had tortured and kidnapped Jane. If he had been, his life would not be safe from Nightmare.

"If I had solid evidence, I wouldn't be asking for the Gilded Alliance's help. I would just handle the matter myself." Emrys crossed his muscular arms across his chest.

"What does your pretty little ballerina know? Wasn't she there when her parents were murdered?" Kordelia leaned forward and stroked the arm of her chair like a jungle cat.

Emrys's mouth fell into a flat line. "Nothing, she was four when her parents were murdered."

"Perhaps you could dig around in her mind and find out?"

Jane sat forward, reading to attack or do something, but she didn't need to because, for the first time ever, Emrys and her were aligned on the topic.

"I will not." Emrys's tone was riddled with rotting shadows as he picked up a glass of whiskey and took a sip.

Kordelia clicked her tongue. "Then what would you have us do? If you can't even do the one thing that might give you the answers you seek?"

"I would have you protect our city. Evil is brewing, and it's going after the second two Blood Mirrors, and since we so brilliantly stripped their locations from everyone's memories, I have no way of protecting them and their contents."

"That is not my problem," Kordelia said.

Emrys's knuckles went white from how hard he was clutching his glass. "If the villain gets hold of the contents of those mirrors, it's everyone's problem."

"Why not go to your precious Blood Council for help?"

"You and I both know that the Blood Council is a farce. A body that thinks they hold power in this city but don't," Emrys said harshly. "The people in this room are the ones who truly control the city, so I am asking you for help."

Jane bit the inside of her cheek and tried not to intrude, resisting the urge to interrupt the flow of information—a flow of information that was directly related to herself.

The Mirror of Midnight sat forward, her bubblegum-pink hair bouncing with her movement. "It is a quandary. How does one find something that cannot be found?" Midnight—also called Periwinkle—spoke with the voice of an eerie child, and had the face of a seventeen-year-old while being over a thousand.

"If anyone knew the answer to that question, it would be you." The leader of the Rose Vipers played with his pocket square, but his gaze cut directly to the Mirror God.

"Perhaps," she said brightly, "Perhaps not. It is a puzzle."

Nightmare leaned forward, his hand still protectively on Jane's exposed thigh. The slit in her dress was probably far too indecent for polite company, but they were in the den of sins. If she were going to dress provocatively, why not do it here? "While all of this talk of Blood Mirrors is illuminating, we have a much deeper problem. More and more tremors have been felt stemming from the Lake of Mirrors and the tomb of the Seven Wicked Witches. If an evil is stirring, it would be there."

"The Lake of Mirrors has been dormant for over a thousand years," Darcy said. "Not even Chaos has been seen for the last eight hundred years. This city sits in the heart of an earthquake country. If the tremors mean anything, it's that."

"Are you willing to take that chance? Are you willing to do nothing and let Helene rise again?"

Darcy visibly shivered at this.

Who the hell was Helene, that she could make the two most powerful and terrifying Mirror Gods wary?

"So, in summary, two dark evils threaten the city." François's tone was light but also deeply concerned. "Wonderful. Does anyone have any plans on how we handle these stirring evils?"

Nightmare's gaze flashed to the prince. "Where are the two Primordial Relics I left in your care?"

Emrys's face blanched, and his body grew stiff, as did François beside him.

Fuck. This wasn't going to go well. No matter what happened next and what came out of the men's mouths, there would be disaster. Jane felt it bubbling in her blood, like foresight.

As Emrys said, "We currently don't know," Jane stood up and put her body between them just in time to be slammed between the Vampire Prince and the ancient god. At the impact, Nightmare's hands wrapped around her waist, steadying her.

Periwinkle giggled and said, "The little witch seer." At the same time, Emrys held his hands up defensively and put his body in front of François, shielding him. "We gave the location of the relics to one man, and he's unfortunately now unreachable and locked in Pelican Bay."

Nightmare let out a low, wicked growl. The whites of his eyes bleeding red, fury painted on every curve of his body, his fangs and metal nails bared. Ready to kill every mortal in the room if Jane didn't do something quickly.

~

"Everyone get out now," Jane said, her hand on Nightmare's chest and her voice wavering. Her eyes never left Nightmare. "Thorne, my monster. Keep your eyes on me." She dug her hand into his shirt while he tightened his hold around her waist. At the same time, she heard movement from all around them. Everyone else, leaving them alone in the room.

When he still hadn't calmed down, and his eyes hadn't lost any of the red, Jane asked, "How can I help you settle down?" Jane flattened her palm once more over where his heart should beat—but it never did. "What do you need?"

"I need to feed." Nightmare's eyes flashed, and he darted around, presumably searching for an unsuspecting human he could eat.

"Are you going to kill your food?" she breathed.

"Yes."

"Do you have to?"

Nightmare blinked, his black, well-manicured eyebrows creasing together.

"Are you able to control yourself?" she asked.

"Yes," he said slowly, cocking his head, his eyes fixating on her neck.

"Then feed on me." She cocked her head to the side, giving him permission to take her blood.

"You may hate it."

"It's fine. I am not afraid of you."

An unreadable sound vibrated in his chest, and then, without warning, he pushed her fiercely up against the wall, pinning her in and biting down on her neck.

At first, it hurt, his fangs piercing her skin and claiming her. It was a sharp pain, but then the wound began to tingle and turn... the feeling becoming something hot and pleasurable.

Every nerve ending in her body lit up with an intense feeling that she'd never felt before. Her pussy grew wet and oh so needy. A moan escaped her lips, and she suddenly needed to be closer to him, to be touching him, one with him. Fucking him. She needed him inside her, bringing her ecstasy.

She ground into him, and just the friction of her body against him was enough to send a wave of pleasure through her body. Her toes curled, and she let out a soft cry as her body shook in his arms.

Confusion licked at her neck. What was that? What was that feeling?

But when the wave ended, she needed more, and she became possessed by an unstoppable lust. Her hands trailed down to his pants, and fast and clumsily, she unbuttoned them, freeing his massive cock to the world.

Instinctively, she curled one of her hands around it and began to stroke. Up and down. Feeling him. It was thick and smooth, like wonderful velvet.

He let out a rough sound. Somewhere between pain and pleasure, he pulled his teeth out of her neck, licking the puncture wounds before grasping her hand, stilling her movements, and pinning her hands to the wall on either side of her head.

A mix of doubt and hurt danced in her belly. "Did I do it wrong? Do you not like it?"

"Oh, fuck Jane." He leaned his forehead against hers, blood still dripping from his mouth. "I liked it. But if you continue down that road, I will fuck you on this loveseat. Rough, hard, and unforgiving."

"Please do." A desperate need clung to her voice.

"I will help you with your carnal desires—if that is what

you want—after you calm down." It was like he forced the words out of his mouth. "I do not take advantage of women."

"I am calm," she begged, her eyes flashing down to his still-hard cock.

"I told you never to lie to me," he snapped. "Never, Jane."

She panted and leaned her head against the wall, her arms still trapped by his strong, large hands.

Sucking in a shaky breath, she tried to calm herself and let go of the cloud of lust plaguing her brain.

"Vampire bites can elicit many reactions. Fear, peace, even lust." He sighed as if the sentence pained him. "It would seem you are the latter."

Only for you. And somehow, she knew that to be true. Emrys could bite her, and she'd feel nothing like that.

"It's not real."

It was. Too real. But she didn't have control of her voice yet to say it. Anything she tried to say would just come out as begging. Because she still very much wanted him to fuck her on that loveseat.

A sigh mixed with a whine came out of her mouth. And she pinched her eyes shut in embarrassment. How was he always so cold, so unbothered, and she was a fucking mess?

It wasn't fair.

"What was that?" She blurted out because she needed to say something.

"What?"

"That, um," oh gods, how did she phrase it? "That trembling. What was that? Another vampire thing?"

He coughed. "Do you mean pleasure?"

Yes, she nodded, her eyes still shut.

"The orgasm?"

"Orgasm?" she parroted back.

"Oh gods," his voice was a dark baritone. "You don't know what an orgasm is?"

"I..." She shuddered and opened her eyes, her gaze locking on his molten silver irises.

"You're saying not a single one of those bastards gave you an orgasm?"

"Sex has always been painful and unpleasant."

"Painful? Do they not get you ready?"

Jane scrunched her nose. "Ready?"

Anger painted across his face. "What are their names, Jane? I'm going to kill them."

"No, you aren't." She should have let him know, but she couldn't, and she didn't know why. It wasn't like she was against violence. The gang murdered people frequently.

"I am a villain, yet I still treat my women well," he growled. "Men who don't treat women well deserve to die.

"Please, Alexei, don't."

"Sex isn't even good without your partner experiencing pleasure. Not to mention, it's atrociously boring." He shook his head. "For that alone, they deserve death."

"Perhaps we could solve some problems without murder."

The glower he gave her was twisted like a tree branch in a forest of rotting trees.

Completely ignoring what she said, he asked, "Red, my little doe, have you ever even been kissed?"

"Of course. You kissed me on our wedding night."

"Truly kissed?"

A flash of hurt heated her chest. Did he not consider that a true kiss? Was it that bad? That unremarkable to him?

"Would you like to be?"

"I—what?"

"Would you like to be passionately kissed?"

"I thought," she stammered, "I thought you didn't want to be passionate with me tonight."

"I changed my mind. But I still won't fuck you."

With that, he dropped her arms, clasped her face tightly, and brought her mouth to his. It was dominant and powerful and left no room for argument. His tongue plunged inside and danced with hers like a passionate tango.

Quick, quick, slow, twist, pleasure. They were dance partners in lust and delight.

His fingers laced into her hair, and he tilted her chin back so that he could have more access to her.

He let out a rough breath, and then he bit her lip, and a drop of blood mingled into their passion. An iron scent combined with the whiskey on his breath and the black tea and musk of his cologne.

He kissed her like he was building a castle, and she kissed him like she was losing a war.

It was an exploration, a scientific study of one another. Constant discoveries, from the way she curled her fingers into his back as she whimpered, to the way he softened only for her.

A new heaviness dropped between Jane's legs, her core once more becoming slick, wet, and ready for something.

Is that what he meant by ready?

Nightmare picked her up like he was about to carry her over a marital threshold, but he didn't move far. He gently laid her down, but his lips never left hers the whole time. His talented tongue never stopped its ministrations until she was fully lying on the couch.

When his lips left hers, she whimpered, but he moved south, exploring her body. First, playing with her breasts and then moving even further south to her core, which demanded friction.

Nightmare dragged his hand up her leg, bunching her skirts as he caressed her. He kissed the inside of her knee before continuing to pull up her skirt, petticoats, and chemise. He licked a trail up the inside of her thigh, and she shivered, another moan escaping her ruby mouth.

But when his mouth touched her folds, she jolted, tensing up like a turtle retreating into its shell. He ran his tongue along her clit, and Jane tensed again, a cloud of tears tracking down her face. Nightmare stopped, his head appearing above her skirts.

"No, please don't stop." Her voice cracked. "I'm fine."

"You're not." He sat on the chaise and pulled her into his lap, kissing the top of her head. "You're not ready."

"I am," she sobbed.

"No, little doe, you're not." Then, without warning, he disappeared into smoke, leaving her reeling in his absence.

She reached a hand out to thin air like she could catch him and keep him near—but of course, it didn't work. It would never work.

Jane stood up and lowered her skirts back to the ground. Then, she began to fix her hair.

Jane tried to process everything that had happened, but it was too much. Blood Mirrors, wicked witches, and an orgasm. It was too much. Yet she knew she would have to look into all of it when the storm calmed.

She needed to find out what happened to her parents and who Helene was. Somehow, she knew both things were vital.

Jane let out a squeak as Periwinkle appeared behind her. Oh gods, had she seen what had just happened? Had she heard?

"Gosh, you scared me." Jane placed a hand on her chest.

"The information you seek lies in the rooms you cannot find."

"What?" Jane's brow furrowed as Periwinkle once again disappeared.

Fucking vampires and Mirror Gods. Were they all the same? Utterly confusing.

Chapter Sixteen

The Russet sparkled, a night formed from daydreams, tension, and seductive mysteries. Every night at the casino was an experience, glittering with sin and magic, but tonight was special. It was like the place hummed with sparks.

Like most nights, Jane was overseeing the casino floor, ensuring that no one was stealing, cheating, or causing fights. Jane, Gabriel, or Alexandre typically acted as the Pit Boss. They took turns doing it, with Gabriel being the main Pit Boss, especially since Jane was given rule over the Mirror Black Market. However, Jane had full command tonight.

There were no events, no special singer or even a tournament, yet the floor felt different. Two of Jane's closest friends were at a table, but that still didn't explain the energy. Patrons were louder, cheering as people won, and even gossip and chatter increased.

Jane walked over to her friends, Constance and Jevon. At this point, Jane felt terrible that her sister was the only one from their group who didn't know Jane also worked at the casino. But Jane didn't want her sister near the city's underbelly.

Unfortunately, she couldn't keep her other friends from

discovering it. Giselle hadn't returned since being caught in François's bed, but Jevon and Constance were regulars at the Russet. Interesting, considering how connected Constance was to the Viridian.

But the girl loved a party.

"Do you sense something strange in the air tonight?" Jane asked her friends. "Something seems weird, but I often have those feelings."

Jevon rubbed his chin. "You should listen to those feelings. You are typically right."

Warmth spread in Jane's chest. "Thank you." She smiled

Jevon always had a way of making her feel better about herself. She loved all her friends—including that silly prince and François—but Jevon was a calm and warming presence that none of the others were. Constance was a firestorm, Giselle a tidal wave, and Quinn a blizzard. If Jevon were a storm, he would be a windstorm. All great and terrible in their own ways.

"Your scary, intense blond boyfriend is staring at you again." Constance narrowed her eyes before waving across the room.

Jane's gaze followed her movements and landed on Nightmare. "He's not my boyfriend... And don't draw his attention," Jane moaned. The last thing Jane needed was Nightmare to ruin her night. He was both far too possessive and totally unconcerned.

It was too late. He had noticed and was stalking over to his prey. Stalking, and preening, like a peacock showing its feathers.

That was the thing about Nightmare. He was never just one thing. He was a multitude, and it was impossible to know all of him at one moment.

"Hello..." The word was said as if it were a delicious candy. Nightmare stopped his prowl at the edge of their table, towering above them, and sliding his hands into his damask silk suit pockets. The pattern was woven together from black and crimson spider silk.

Prince Emrys and Nightmare didn't have much in common

—other than both being powerful vampires—but the two men loved to dress like they were in competition for who could look the richest and deadliest.

Jane crossed in front of Nightmare, shielding her friends. "Hello." Her voice was too bright and coated with little lies.

Nightmare's countenance immediately grew darker.

Fuck.

Jane grabbed the curve of his elbow, her eyes flicking down to the gondola boats floating through the lagoon. "Would you ride with me?"

Jevon coughed behind her, suppressing a laugh, but Constance didn't even bother. Her laugh was bright and a little bit wicked. Jane wanted to kill them. They were not making this easier. Did they not know how close they both were to getting their heads ripped off?

A slice of silver hair fell in front of his eyes as he cocked his head to glower at them.

"Thorne,"—the name she used when he was at his most monstrous—"please, I'll even let you decide how we do it."

Both of her friends laughed as she led him away. His muscles coiled underneath her petite fingers, and his frame was solid stone, yet he let her lead him to an enchanted gondola.

"Please don't kill my friends."

"I don't trust him."

"You don't trust anyone." Jane pinched her lips together. "Don't be jealous and possessive."

A thunderstorm rumbled in his chest. "I'm not."

No. Perhaps you're not because it would require you to care. "He's harmless. Please don't kill him."

Jane was only met with a growl.

"Thorne, promise me you won't."

The boat rocked underneath them, the wood creaking as she tilted her chin up so she could see the depths of his irises. Sometimes, the only way to communicate with him was to read the twisted thoughts in his molten silver eyes. They flickered with puzzle pieces that were nearly impossible to decipher. But she was becoming a Nightmare whisperer. A deep-seated fury danced in the blue-swirling silver, but there was also something else.

Almost like lust.

The boat floated into a dark cave, the Cave of Sinful Desires. It lasted long enough for a couple to fuck if they would like. That, of course, was not on the table for her, but...

She wondered. What if?

Without convincing herself out of it, Jane stood, the boat wobbling beneath her feet. She straddled him, and his hands circled her waist to steady her and the boat. Moving in closer, she straddled his lap, her eyes never leaving his the whole time, measuring his reactions.

"You are not going to distract me with your wiles, Jane." His hands slid up her torso, directly opposing his words.

"I know," she whispered into his lips. "Trying to seduce you will never work, because you'll never give me what I want."

"And what is it that you want?"

"You know."

"Do I?" he raised a black eyebrow. "Why don't you say it?"

Jane answered by placing her lips on his. Soft and gentle, she kept her eyes open, her focus still fully on him. A cloud of red hair fell around them, framing both of their faces.

"Jane," he grunted a dark warning.

"Wryte." She played with the name. It was the first time using that particular one with him. Alexei was what she called him most of the time, and Thorne was what she called him in his monster form. She used one of his honorifics when she was being sassy or actually adding respect to his name. Dimitris was for when she was being playful or light-hearted. She didn't have a name for him when she *wanted him*—wanted him to rip her clothing off and take her.

One of his strong hands drifted south while the other one stayed on her waist. He was fighting a battle and losing. She smiled into his lips and deepened the kiss, opening her mouth and pressing her body deeper into his.

The action caused her hips to grind against his stiff erection. He groaned but allowed the kiss to deepen. The friction felt like heaven, so she ground into him again, wishing there were no clothing between them, but she also wasn't going to fuck him for the first time on a gondola boat while she was working.

She sighed into him and bit his bottom lip before sliding her tongue into his mouth. With a violent rock from the boat, he lifted her by her waist and slammed her back into the bottom of the boat, pinning her there.

She panted, a wordless plea escaping her lips.

Slowly, tauntingly, he slid her skirts up her legs, his palms spreading heat and desperation as he worked his way up. Goosebumps painting her legs. She moaned, and he let out a dark chuckle.

"Is this what you want?" Lust dripped from his dark voice.

She nodded, and his hand reached her pussy, sliding a finger through her folds. Her breath hitched, and she clawed at the wood beneath her.

"Like this?" he asked again, circling her clit.

She whimpered and nodded again.

"Your words, little doe."

"Yes," it came out as all breath. "Please, that."

He chuckled again and dipped one finger inside her, curling it. But then something terrible happened. Her inner walls tensed, and a sharp pain rippled through her. She pinched her eyes shut against the pain. He removed his fingers, and she whimpered. It hurt, but she didn't want it to stop. Flashing her eyes open, she begged him to continue.

"I am not going to hurt you."

"You didn't."

"Liar."

Her finger dug deeper into the wood, this time out of anger and desperation. "Please."

Nightmare didn't return his fingers to the entrance, but he did something almost better. He dipped his head down and blew against her clitoris.

She shivered and moaned. "Yes, please." This time, she didn't tense or revolt against him as his head dipped to her core, and he ran a long, luxurious lick to her folds. "Oh god, Wryte, just like—"

Her words were stolen from her as she easily fell apart, shaking beneath him and letting out a scream. But he didn't let up. He continued to breathe against her, lick her, and pleasure her until she didn't even know where they were anymore. She melted into his ministrations, lost track of time, and fell completely into pleasure.

He only stopped when the light returned and their boat left the cave. He lowered her skirts, a satisfied smile climbing his face. Smiles were so rare with him that she basked in it. She knew she needed to sit up and gather herself, or the patrons would soon see exactly what they had been doing in the dark.

Nightmare lifted her up and placed her back on the seat, kneeling in front of her. He placed a gentle kiss on her lip.

"Thank you." Her voice was low, but she knew he could hear it.

He nodded. "You may want to know a mirror bargain is snaking through the air." Nightmare sniffed. "It seems like an enchantment from the Mirror of Luck."

Jane's heart skipped. "What?" She wasn't sure what he said because she was still lost in his tongue on her clit. "Can you say that again?"

"A mirror bargain is taking advantage of the club."

Jane blinked and remembered she was at work, where she was supposed to be the Pit Boss. She absolutely couldn't have the casino being had while she was in charge. "Is there any way to stop it?"

He clutched her chin tightly. "Bargain."

She placed a hand on his chest. No heartbeat. He never had

one. "What could I possibly bargain with? You already own the most important parts of me."

"You could give me your firstborn child." A wicked sneer played on his cheeks.

She dug her fingers into his suit. "Wouldn't you already have my firstborn child? You're my husband and the only person I am remotely close to having sex with."

His smile widened. "Precisely."

"Fine." Jane swallowed. "Nightmare, I will trade my firstborn child to your keeping if you break the spell on the club and add protection to all of the Fantômes businesses from spells and mirror bargains."

"Nicely done." He ran his thumb over her bottom lip. "It shall be."

Because this night couldn't just go simply, it was then that another problem accosted Jane.

Harlowe Merriwether appeared on the bridge above them, not even noticing the man kneeling in front of Jane. When she did see, Harlowe gasped and said, "Oh, I didn't realize."

Jane bit her bottom lip, her hand hovering over Nightmare's chest. "It's fine."

He glared over his shoulder but used his shadow magic to pull the boat into the wall. Once again, he lifted Jane like she weighed nothing and placed her on the walkway above them. Then he simply disappeared into the smoke and reappeared behind Jane, his hand possessively touching her waist.

He couldn't keep his hands off her tonight. A flame stirred in her stomach. Jane both liked it and hated it. Hated that she wanted him so much when he was her tormentor.

Facing him, his hands sliding along her torso as she moved. A shiver skated through her bones. "Can you please go find François or Emrys or and tell them about Luck's Bargain?"

He grumbled but nodded in the affirmative.

"Oh, and maybe have a drink of whiskey with him. You could use a night with friends."

"I have no friends," he said through his teeth.

Jane smiled. "Of course not."

Nightmare tipped her chin up, and he placed a rough kiss on her lips before he whispered into her hair as he left. "Just so you know, you become invisible when you cum."

Jane's mouth dropped open as she turned to Harlowe to deal with whatever the other girl had in store for her. She immediately pulled Jane into a dark alcove, secrets oozing from every pore.

"You and the Silver Man?"

What was the question? Jane cocked her head. "What about him?"

"He's the Mirror of Nightmares, right?" Harlowe asked in hushed tones, her eyes darting around as if she were afraid they were being overheard.

"Yes."

"And he's your lover."

Jane coughed. *Yes, technically, but not at all.* Jane let out an indistinguishable sound. What did she say to that?

"You made a deal with him?"

"Yes."

"What was it?"

Jane signed and touched one of the icicles dangling from the roof. "Why?"

Harlowe wrung her hands, her eyes darting again, her voice higher than usual. She clearly wanted to tell Jane something but was afraid. Jane didn't trust Harlowe because she was a walking ball of fire, and she hated Jane and the role she played in the Fantômes. But perhaps Jane could give her a chance.

What harm could it do?

Nightmare already owned her in every way imaginable.

Jane's gaze hardened on Harlowe, and she reached out and squeezed both of her shoulders to interfere with her fidgeting. "I sold my body and soul to him and became his anchor."

A horrified sound dropped from her lips. "What?"

I see, so she didn't make as bad of a deal with the Mirror of

Beautiful Decay then. "What was your deal with Beautiful Decay?"

"Nightshade?" her voice tremored. "Not that bad. I don't think." Her gaze trailed down to her left arm, where a tattoo of a tear rested with a smattering of leaves.

"But you did make a deal with him?"

"I don't remember doing so." The vein in her neck jumped. "I owe him a favor for every leaf I have on this tree, and he can ask for anything."

"Oh." Jane bit her lip. "That's not ideal."

"Is your deal similar? Can Nightmare make you do anything he wants?"

Jane swallowed past the lump in her throat. "Yes."

"Anything, even kill?"

Yes. But he's never asked for that. Jane only dipped her chin.

"Is he the monster he seems to be?" Harlowe asked. "Does he make you kill people for him?"

A gust of cold wind snaked through the cave, causing both girls to shiver and goosebumps to crawl over their flesh. "Half my life is spent trying to keep Nightmare from murdering everyone. He has no moral code and no empathy. He'd rather kill and ask questions later."

Harlowe inhaled sharply, and a dark shadow fell over her eyes. "How do you handle it?"

How did Jane handle it? It had been so long that she barely even thought about it anymore. Nightmare was a villain in most stories, and half the time, he was also the villain in hers, but he also treated her better than anyone else had in her life.

This was sad because he was still awful most of the time, although not often to her anymore. It was all too confusing to focus on, which was why Jane never did.

"Gain his trust. Making him want you alive and healthy and whole more than he wants to hurt you. He needs you as his anchor, and he needs your favor. You are valuable to him."

"Anchor?"

If Harlowe didn't know about anchors, then how did Beautiful Decay come to the Gilded Alliance meeting? Jane had just assumed he'd forced Harlowe to be his anchor.

An interesting question, but one Jane couldn't focus on. "Can I ask you a question?"

"Of course, anything."

"You used to be Emrys's lover, right?"

"Yes."

"What does it feel like?"—Jane's voice dropped an octave—"when you have sex? Does it hurt?"

Harlowe stared at Jane like she was solving an intense puzzle. "Does sex hurt for you?"

Jane glanced around the room. "Yes, and be quiet about it."

"Does Nightmare abuse you? Does he not care if you're ready?"

"Oh, Nightmare and I haven't really—" Jane paused, not knowing how to put it. "We don't."

"You've never fucked Nightmare?"

"No," Jane glared at the other woman and held a finger to her lips.

"I'm just shocked." Harlowe's white eyebrows drew together. "With the way he looks at you, I imagined you two fucked like rabbits every night."

"We... I've never—"

"So you're saying he's not even touched you?"

Jane flushed. No. He very much had touched her.

"He's," Jane gulped, "He's um..." Jane motioned to her nether regions.

"Oh, he's gone down on you?"

"Yes. But when he touched my..." Jane paused again. Gods, this conversation was painful. "It hurts. It tenses up, and I get a sharp pain."

Harlowe ran a hand through her frozen white hair. "I have heard of that happening from some of the courtesans. Apparently, some women suffer from pain when the pelvic floor is touched."

"So it's not normal?"

"No."

"Do you know how to solve the problem?"

Harlowe shook her head. "No, but I know someone who might. Give me a day or two, and I will get you the answer."

"Thank you."

Harlowe's face rose in a sad smile. "Thank you, too. I guess it helps to know someone else is going through something similar to me."

Somehow, Jane felt the same. She pulled the other woman into a hug, which was met by a tense, motionless Harlowe. Did she hate touch? Or just that she was starved of it?

When Harlowe moved to accept the hug, her white hair slipped and grazed against Jane's face, and the pain was instantaneous and terrible. A burn so cold it was hot. Jane flinched and instinctively pulled away.

"Oh, fuck, I am so sorry." Wetness gathered at the corner of her eyes.

Jane waved it off. "It's okay, Nightmare can fix it."

Chapter Seventeen

AGE 27.

"Who did this to you?" Nightmare growled, appearing in front of her and pushing her up against the wall as soon as she entered his mirror. His large, veiny hand lifted to her face, and he caressed the burn.

"No one did it."

"I told you the one thing you never do is lie to me."

"It's not a lie." Jane gently grasped his wrist. "It was a mirror consequence when I hugged a friend."

"Mirror consequence?" he asked, fully unconvinced.

"Yes, Harlowe Merriweather's hair causes frostbite, and before you think of killing her, she's Beautiful Decay's anchor, and he won't look kindly on that."

Nightmare watched her as if she were a ghost, fragile and unable to catch. "Heal," he commanded, and like every other time he did, her face instantly fixed itself and became perfect and pristine—even better than before.

"Thank you."

The tension was uncomfortable because he hadn't moved to

let her go and hadn't moved to touch her further. It was like the moment was steeped in both insecurity and longing.

But, just as quickly, it was done. Nightmare disappeared.

There were times when Jane spent days in Nightmare's mansion without seeing him. She had no idea where he was or what he was doing, and during those times, she acquainted herself further with the house. The place was like an invisible, magical friend.

Although sometimes not so invisible.

Tonight, it called to her. The artificial wind snaked around her body as if holding her in a lover's embrace.

It coaxed her, sang to her, and asked her to come to the ballroom of briars.

But it wasn't just the house calling her to the room. It was her feelings as well.

Sometimes, Jane's feelings were ravenous, and she was beginning to realize it was because of the magic burrowed in her bloodstream. It slept—and it hungered. It needed her to find something.

Something beyond the Ballroom of Briars. Something in the forbidden wing of the house, The Shadow Wing. Beyond the briars rested only shadows. Jane would have liked to say she considered not going, but she didn't. She had no hesitation at all. Something she would look back on every day for the next two years.

Perhaps she should have cared. Perhaps she should never have violated Nightmare's privacy.

But at this moment, she was merely a curious cat being egged on by her magic.

A mixture of dread and determination devoured Jane's stomach. Her strapped heels clicked against the marble floor and traversed through a dance of gnarled thorns. They were like prickly garlands twisting through the room, trying to ensnare her.

Yet, at the same time, they didn't cling on. They allowed her to slowly and skillfully maneuver through until she reached the other side. Candlelight swayed as if on an ocean breeze, and a sweet harp melody played.

Leaning slightly too far to her left as she cut through, Jane's arm scratched against a thorn, and as her blood trickled onto it, flowers blossomed along every single branch in the room.

Jane let out a sound of amazement as she turned and took in the sea of colors. It was gorgeous.

As she reached the other side of the ballroom and was first met by pure darkness, and shadows cocooned her body. Her heart leapt into her throat. Had Nightmare's castle guided her into a trap?

As if in answer, warmth spread across her skin, and from the shadows came a glowing door handle. A flock of butterflies took flight in her stomach. The handle called to her, begging her to open it, and so she did.

In hindsight, one should not necessarily answer the call of a magic door.

But she did.

On the other side of the door was a riverbed. The sand, holding in brilliant blue water, seemed to be formed from purple starlight—granule after granule of glowing violet. Its beauty was almost indescribable, and Jane wanted to run her fingers through it, basking in its beauty and serenity.

The place was supposed to be a nightmare, but nothing about it could possibly be considered nightmarish.

The river glistened, and the moon rose in the sky, a stream of red-golden light falling from its trail. Sunset in what seemed to be a serene fairyland.

The air tasted of cherries, and it smelled even sweeter.

A dragonfly landed on her finger, and a bright smile lit up her face. She loved dragonflies—their strength, resilience, and beauty.

Where was she?

Why would her magic lead her here?

The question was answered moments later when she found a stone path with walls formed from granite and sapphire. At the end of the path was a grand gazebo, and in its center was the diary they'd searched for four years ago, along with a ruby-red memory stone. Jane had never seen a memory stone in real life, but she had heard of them. They were rare magical objects, created by mirrors to hold copies of one's memories.

Was this one Nightmare's?

Jane should have been more interested in the diary. She should have been, but instead, all of her attention was drawn to that stone.

And without thinking, she wrapped her fingers around it and was immediately thrown into a set of memories.

Nightmare's memories.

A band of horses kicked up dirt, trotting in a circle around a young man with dark black hair who looked to be barely twenty years old. He wore a crimson tunic with a surcoat and cloak, and although young, he was exceedingly handsome, with sharp cheekbones and lean muscle.

"Lord Rendragon, will you not join me for a ride through the forest?" a beautiful redheaded girl around ten years older than he called from her horse. Her bright, enchanting, and intoxicating smile made everyone in her presence stand in awe. It was as if the girl were weaving spells through the air, causing all who looked upon her to fall in love immediately.

She wore a silk, embroidered bliaut—a style of dress from thousands of years ago. She was rich, but more than that, from the number of guards accompanying her and her general demeanor, this girl seemed to be of noble birth, perhaps even royalty.

The hair on Jane's arms rose. She was, in fact, using magic. Jane sensed it.

"I am not Lord Rendragon. That would be my cousin," the young man called back.

"Then pray, tell me what your name is."

"Count Draculei, Nephew of the king."

The redhead smiled, stopped her horse, and motioned for all of her guards to ride on without her. They complied, which was strange enough in itself. "Well, hello, King's nephew. And from the smell,"—she sniffed the air—*"a Hawthorne witch. A rather powerful one, from the feel of you."*

"How did you know that?" the boy asked.

"I am an Ash Witch." She wiggled her nose, and he let out an impressed sound. "I am Helene Ashwood, Princess of the Northern Realm."

Nightmare's face lit up. "I have always wanted to meet an Ash Witch."

"And now you have. Come into the forest with me."

"Why?"

"Because I like to collect powerful things, and I think I shall collect you."

Jane coughed. The smell of the enchantments soaking the air was thick and all-consuming. But why did the girl need them? She could have easily convinced the boy to go with her without all the dramatics and spells.

Nightmare mounted Helene's horse behind her, and they rode into the thick trees together. They finally stopped at a clearing, where they dismounted and continued to talk.

"It must be so boring living in the human realms. Do you even know how to do any magic?"

"Some."

"Ah, that's cute." She flicked his nose. "There is no way you know anything of significance."

He seemed to be offended by this, but he kept quiet.

Without any warning, Helene said, "Take me on this tree. I want to feel you inside of me." She pointed at a random tree.

"That does not seem wise, my lady."

A spell coaxed through the air, and Jane nearly vomited from its cloying taste.

"No," Jane whispered and turned away. She did not need to see a young Nightmare fucking the redhead in the forest, and from the sounds of it, that was precisely what was happening—especially since it was hard to tell if he wanted to or was simply being compelled.

Grunting and passion-filled cries painted the woods, and Jane smashed her hands over her ears.

When they were finally done, Helene said, "Be the Ambassador of Men to the Witchly Realms. Come stay with me as my lover, and learn to truly harness your magic."

He was young, naive, and spellbound. Of course he said yes. And there had to be a piece of him who wanted to leave the human realm and learn his magic while fucking one of the most beautiful women who ever existed. It was a young man's dream.

It was unclear how much convincing it took because the memory faded, switching to Nightmare in a different land working as the human Ambassador to witches while nightly fucking Helene. The memories flashed quickly, moving from one to the next.

Years passed, and Nightmare, a twenty-year-old, became a far too attractive, far too muscular thirty-year-old man. When he reached the age of thirty-five, Helene said, "You are aging like a mortal, and it disgusts me."

Apparently, Ash Witches didn't age. They were forever young and immortal.

"I cannot fuck an old man." She crossed her arms. "In five more years, you will be too old for me. And I do not want to lose you."

Nightmare had nothing to say to this. He was neither the bright, young, and joyful boy of his youth nor the emotionless man Jane knew. He was somewhere in between.

"Do you love me, Gavriil?"

"Of course I do."

"Would you do anything for me?"

He hesitated for a moment. "Yes."

A wicked and bright smile twisted on Helene's lips. "Perfect. I found a spell to make you immortal forever. Like me. Will you do this for me?"

"Yes."

"Take me as I cast the spell."

"Is that necessary?" he asked.

"No, but your dick makes my power surge within me."

Jane honestly did not want to know if that was true. Moments later, she had to avert her gaze again. The sounds of slapping flesh and ancient spells drifted through the space between them, and Jane groaned. It felt a little like torture watching the man she cared about sleep with someone else over and over again, watching this rotten woman toying with him over and over again. Helene wove the spell while she rode him.

Although Jane couldn't see it, she heard all of it. From the pounding flesh to the frantic moans.

It was disgusting, but Nightmare seemed to be enjoying himself, and he no longer seemed coerced—if he ever had been to begin with.

Helene's voice died out, and all that could be heard was wet gurgling. Jane finally looked back at them. At some point they must have changed positions because now, Nightmare was on top, crimson spilling from him.

Jane gasped, holding her hands to her mouth.

Helene had slit open his throat, and blood poured onto her naked breasts. She let out a moan as if she were enjoying Nightmare dying on top of her.

An evil smile painted her face.

When the light left his eyes, she pushed him off of her, and she stood up, her naked body covered in crimson.

Jane wanted to run over to him and help him, do something. But this was only a memory. She couldn't do anything. He couldn't be dead, though. He still had to become Nightmare.

Nightmare jolted awake and sat up. The first thing he did was sink his newly formed fangs into Helene's neck.

Unlike when Nightmare had fed on Jane, Helene did not get aroused. She got angry. When she managed to push him off, she cursed at him, called him an abomination, and banished him from her side and her court.

The memory shifted, and Nightmare was back in his realm at Castle Wryte. But vampirism looked good on him. He smiled more, laughed more, and his general demeanor was that of contentment and peace. And he looked healthy. His black hair shone with life. His muscles rippled beneath his black tunics and suits. He was thriving, and the people in his town were thriving as well. He was a lord the people loved, and if it were a little strange that he drank some of their blood from time to time, none of them seemed to care because he was good to them.

A lord with honor, integrity, and joy.

Nothing like the man Jane knew today. Although, to be fair, he was still mostly honorable and indecently honest.

He lived for hundreds of years as the lord people loved, until she arrived once more at his doorstep. Helene was an envoy to the human lands, and she had heard about the powerful and merciful wizard at Castle Wryte. Upon learning it was Gavriil she marched into his castle and ripped out his heart with her bare hands.

"I curse you from henceforth to be a man with no heart," Helene hissed. "You will not know empathy, passion, or love for as long as you have no heart."

"Why?" he sank to his knees. "What have I done to you to deserve this?"

"It's not what you have done, but what you've become."

The memory shifted again, and it was another hundred years later. The memories flickered rapidly from one to the next., and Jane gathered that with revenge in his heart and mind, Nightmare had enacted a plan to hurt Helene where it mattered to her most. Nightmare was going to steal her lover from her and turn him into a vampire like himself. He kidnapped Draven Darcy Hawthorne and his twin sister, distant cousins of his, and turned both of them into vampires, starting the first vampire and witch wars. Over the wars, many vampires were created, and their power and strength became something that could rival that of the witches, causing the wars to last until all the witches were eventually destroyed. But during those wars, Nightmare was captured, and fifteen of the most powerful witches in all of the realms, including Helene, used their magic to bind him within a mirror—at the cost of their magic.

Draven and his twin had managed to escape being captured and turned into mirrors, and they continued the war as the leaders of the vampires.

The memories came to rest on Nightmare inside his mirror, looking out at a world that was not New Swansea. It was something different. Something new. A land called Transylvania. Nightmare lured a beautiful blonde woman to his mirror and made her his bride. Together, they established Castle Dracula in Transylvania, creating vampires, making love, and living a life of grandeur.

Jealousy cut through Jane, and she rubbed her chest. Nightmare wasn't capable of love, but with the blonde woman, he was at least content. Over time, they brought in two more brides, a brunette and a redhead—although Nightmare seemed to have very little interest in ever touching the redhead.

It hurt Jane to see how unimportant she was. She was just like all of his other brides. Used to allow him to leave his gilded prison. Pain ricocheted through her, and she sucked in a strained breath.

The memory shifted, and Nightmare was lying on a couch with his blonde lover, watching a revelry. Suddenly, it all came to a crashing halt. Three tall male figures entered the room: a pair of black-haired twins and a man with golden-brown hair who looked to be related to them.

"Gentlemen, how may I help you today?" Nightmare asked, tone dripping with sickly sweetness.

One of the twins stepped forward. "You were recently visited by Jonathan Harker, an associate of ours."

"Why yes, we remember him." A vicious smile crept across Nightmare's face. "And who are you?"

"We are the Lords Ashbrook. Sent to retrieve the English Ladies."

"Ah, but they have no interest in being retrieved.

"Because you have ensorcelled them."

"Have I?" Nightmare disappeared and reappeared behind the second twin, but as he reached out to grab him, his hands slipped right through the man as he had become a ghost. Translucent and uncatchable.

"As you can see, we are monsters much like you," Lord Ashbrooke said. "Now, release the girls to us or begin a war."

A war did ensue, and all three of Nightmare's brides were brutally murdered.

Nightmare held his limp blonde bride in his hands, a stake plunged into her heart.

It didn't make sense to Jane because all vampires in New Swansea had Blood Paintings, which protected vampires from dying this way. Was that not the case in this other world?

Nightmare growled and met one of the dark-haired twins' gazes. He held up an amulet almost as if taunting Nightmare, who growled louder. And as he was distracted, the other twin appeared behind him and plunged a dagger into his back where his heart should have been.

Nightmare looked over his shoulder as if not bothered one bit by being stabbed. "I don't have a heart."

As the words left his mouth, his form began to disappear, his body being forced back into his mirror. Without an anchor Nightmare was forced to abandon his castle and return to New Swansea and the Looking Glass.

The memory shifted once more to show Helene entering Nightmare's mirror.

"Being a dark Lady does not look good on you," Nightmare said, leaning against the wall with his arms crossed. "It's very brave of you to enter into my mirror where you hold no power."

Helene looked terrible. Her eyes were sunken, her skin pulled far too tight, and shadows rippled under her skin, protruding from her veins. She had been so infuriated about losing most of her magic that she turned to dark and tainted forces to restore her magic. It corrupted her.

"I always hold power."

"To what do I owe this pleasure, Helene?" His words were poison.

"I want you to make me the most powerful within all of the lands, far more powerful than the Ashelles."

Nightmare narrowed his eyes. "And what is it that you would give me?"

"My soul."

A flash of disgust flashed over his features. "I do not want that tainted thing."

"I can tell you a vision of your future." She wiggled her nose. "I know you'd love to know."

"That would not be worth the prize."

"Fine, then give me the ability to read minds, and I will tell you the prophecy I saw when I first fucked you."

Nightmare paused for a long moment in thought. "I will grant you this magic, but no more. And you will never return to my realm."

"A deal is a deal." Helene held out her hand Begrudgingly, Nightmare took her hand, and indeed, they did shake on it. Then Helene said, "Thousands of years from now, a redheaded Ashelle witch will replace the heart I stole—and she will destroy you."

The memory was wrenched away as real-life Jane was suddenly thrown off balance and pinned against the wall. In the process, she dropped the memory stone to the ground. Blinking up at a furious Nightmare, his hand around her throat.

"How dare you?" The vein in his forehead bulged, as did the ones in his jaw and neck. Fury dripped from him like spilled ink.

"Nightmare, I—"

"Somehow, I forgot that you were designed to destroy me." His hand tightened around her throat. But the pressure was forward, not up. He wasn't strangling her—at least not yet. "I shall not forget again."

"Nightmare," she breathed, a tear stroking down her face. "Plea—"

"Never call me that," he snapped. "What you have done is unforgivable. You have infected my sacred halls, and stolen memories which were not yours to have."

"Alexei, I am so sorr—"

"Sorry will never be enough, little witch. Get out of my sight," he seethed. "I am done with you. Leave my rooms and find another. You are no longer my bride. Only my prisoner."

"What?" The word was raw and full of pain. She felt like she had been stabbed in the heart with a venomous blade.

A strand of her hair fell in front of her face, and as it did, all of the colors leached from it, turning it into the color of liquid silver. One singular strand of silver in her red hair. But it wasn't out of fear. It was out of belonging.

The mirror was claiming her, just as Nightmare denied her.

PART FOUR
TO HEAL
SOMETIMES
WE HAVE
TO GO
BACKWARDS

CHAPTER EIGHTEEN

Nightmare didn't talk to Jane for two years. No words, no notes, no messages—nothing. He didn't come to dinner or sleep in her bed.

Yet he still kept tabs on her through his magic.

She felt his eyes on the back of her skin. Sometimes, the feeling was so strong she became itchy. But he didn't have the house watch her out of the kindness of his missing heart. He did it to protect his precious anchor.

Nightmare didn't care about her. He cared about his freedom. He cared about himself. Always, always self-centered.

And Jane didn't know if she deserved this punishment.

She had completely violated him in ways she could never take back.

So maybe she did.

CHAPTER NINETEEN

Age 29.

It felt like betrayal, as if her skin were coated in tar, burning and sticky.

"Red, you're really hampering all my fun here," Emrys said in his smooth and semi-obnoxious manner. "You look like I just pulled out one of your teeth."

Jane was once again intentionally rifling through the morgue, disrupting evidence and placing her sister in a terrible position, yet again. If they stole any files or accidentally touched anything they shouldn't, Quinnevere would be blamed for it. This was precisely what had happened after the last time Emrys and Harlowe came to the morgue together. Emrys had lit Quinnevere's case file on fire. It was to protect Harlowe from a murder charge, which Jane ultimately agreed with, but it was still horrible for Quinnevere's standing. Not to mention, Jane had to lie to her sister after it happened.

Jane sighed. She hated lying, but unfortunately, it had become second nature to her. The last thing she wanted to do was to put her sister in harm's way. Quinnevere could *not* be involved with the mafia, Blood Mirrors, or vampires. This life was just too dangerous.

She would have everything Jane originally wanted—the ballet, fame, and fortune.

Not obsessed gods, obsessed mafia bosses, and obsessed vampire kings.

Jane sighed again and glared at her new partner in crime. When Nightmare stopped talking to her, she had to turn to someone else for help in investigating her parents' deaths. Prince Emrys Avalon seemed the best choice because he had the most interest in the case.

Her parents' murders were tied to a Blood Mirror. It had been destroyed the same night the Ashelles were murdered. With considerable effort, Jane managed to extract the truth from Emrys. The Mirrors held the vampires' great weakness. When vampires were created, the blood that fell during their deaths became twisted portraits of them. That painting then held their life force, and if destroyed, they died. During the Vampire Accords seven hundred years ago, all the remaining vampires agreed to have their paintings held in three Blood Mirrors, which would be hidden from the eyes of history.

One of them had been found. The Ashelle's then agreed to guard it, but they were brutally murdered. But no one knows by whom.

But Jane would find the answers if it were the last thing she'd ever do.

So that was how she ended up betraying her sister and breaking into the morgue with her sister's archnemesis. Jane had been looking for the last two years, while Nightmare left her alone, without uncovering anything. Unfortunately, she needed help. And if help had to come in the form of her vampire boss, then so be it.

They had come to the morgue to steal the Ashelle murder case file.

The file room was filled with rows and rows of metal cabinets that held paper reports for each case. It was one room away from the lab where Quinnevere did the majority of her autopsies.

"Shouldn't you be able to find it with your witchy powers?" Emrys asked, shutting one of the drawers a little too harshly.

Jane rolled her eyes. That was the last time she'd tell anyone her secrets. "Shouldn't you be able to find it with your shadow powers?"

Emrys flashed her one of his signature smiles that melted most girls and some boys, too. "If only it were that easy. But you hold the powers of ancient witches. Some say they were once gods. So be a god, Janey, and find these files for us."

Jane shook her head and glowered at him. "You're so very annoying."

"You are not the first to say it."

"Right."

But he had a point. Jane pinched her eyes closed and listened. Everything in life let out a frequency—everything had a magical sound and shape to it. She just had to tap into the plane of magic. She was fairly certain there was a realm that existed on the other side of a veil where magic roamed, and when people wanted to use it, they pulled it from there.

But it's possible that was all in her mind. Magic was like wildflowers, growing in twisting patterns through fields, in gardens, and along the edges of roads. Untamable and showing up in places one didn't expect and sometimes didn't want. The objective was to find those flowers, pull them out, and use them.

Each flower was different, with its own tone and heartbeat.

She just had to find the right one.

There it was. Jane opened her eyes and saw what looked like a glowing source of light surrounding a bundle of reports. Jane pushed Emrys out of the way, and it must have been hard because he stumbled back into a shelf with a glass vase on it. It rocked from side to side before finally falling, shattering on the floor.

A little yelp sounded from the other room.

Fuck. Quinnevere had heard.

"You couldn't have caught that?" Jane whispered through her teeth.

Emrys shrugged like he had very much meant to let the vase shatter. Oh, Jane was going to kill him.

Turning back to the cabinet, Jane pulled out the case file, trying to get it before her sister entered the room. But when she closed the drawer, the light didn't go away. The magic wanted her to grab something else.

She opened the drawer again, and three more files lit up like a floating lantern. Once again, she grabbed them and closed the file cabinet, but as she did, three more cabinets lit up. Jane was unable to get to them because the door slowly opened as Emrys said, "Don't worry. I'll distract her."

He wrapped Jane in shadows, but she waved them off and disappeared into the air instead.

"Impressive." He smiled and faced the door.

Quinnevere gasped at the sound of his voice, opened the door all the way, and walked in, clicking it behind her, leaving them in the room alone, or at least that's what she thought. "What's impressive?"

"I am... obviously." Emrys waved at his body.

Quinnevere's face fell. "Oh, you. Have you not done enough damage here already?"

"There will never be a time when I have done enough damage." He slowly strolled toward her as if to block her gaze from seeing Jane, but he also did it like a cat on the prowl. It was a sign for Jane to continue her goal.

Jane's gaze moved back to the magic lights. Slowly, methodically, she moved to the first cabinet and inched it open. Of course, it made a sound, which Emrys tried to cover up with his "flirting."

Quinnevere's gaze shifted behind him, but he stepped in closer to her and leaned into her, placing his elbow on the door above her head. With his pointer finger, he moved her chin to look up at him. "Eyes on me, Ginger. I don't like to be ignored."

"Is there someone back there?" She tried to lean over and look behind him.

Jane held her breath.

"Don't be ridiculous." He moved so Quinnevere could see behind him. "It's probably just a rat."

"The morgue doesn't have rats."

"Really? You'd think they would be drawn to dead bodies."

"Maybe I could make another dead body," Quinnevere said under her breath, and Jane had to clamp a hand over her mouth to keep from laughing.

Emrys did laugh, and stepped back into Quinnevere, blocking her view once more. "Don't threaten me with a fun time."

Jane gagged.

"Hilarious."

"I can be. Would you like to find out?"

Quinnevere crossed her arms protectively across her chest. "What would that consist of?"

He tipped her chin up and whispered something into her ear that Jane could not hear and, frankly, was glad she didn't. Sexual tension dripped between them, like a flame in slow motion etching toward the fuse of dynamite.

And that was the last thing Jane needed or wanted to see.

So, she fully threw her attention back into her task, and within a minute, she had all the files within her grasp.

"I'm done," she whispered, low enough that only one with near-perfect hearing could hear it as she turned back to her sister and the prince, holding all the files.

Emrys stepped back and clapped his hands together. "Well, it's time for me to get going."

"Wait, why were you in here?" Quinnevere asked, blocking their exit.

"Quickly, I can't hold my invisibility much longer," Jane whispered once more to the vampire.

Emrys shrugged. "I was just poking around. I like to do that."

"You better not have stolen anything."

"Do you want to pat me down?"

Quinnevere's mouth dropped open, but her gaze traced his body, undressing him with her eyes. "No, of course not."

"Your eyes would beg to differ."

"My eyes were checking to ensure you didn't steal a file."

A dark laugh rumbled in his chest. "Sure. Now, if you could get out of my way, I'll be going."

Quinnevere glowered at him one more time, but then she grabbed the door handle and walked out, waiting for Emrys to follow. He held open the door so that Jane could slip out before him.

"See you next time, Ginger," Emrys said, sauntering to the exit like he knew Quinnevere was watching.

Quinnevere pinched her eyes shut. "Please, never come again."

"Now, where would the fun be in that?"

Five minutes later, Jane and Emrys were full out of the morgue and walking to University Square's flying gondola. She rounded on him. "Leave my sister alone."

"Ah, so she is your sister."

Well, fuck.

"You didn't hear that."

He made a zipper motion over his lips. "Hear what?"

"Stay away from her."

"Why?" He shifted his weight onto one leg. "I have so much fun teasing her."

"Which is precisely why you need to stay away," Jane said. "You are going to hurt her."

He shifted his weight again and let out a lazy, exaggerated shrug. "Maybe."

"Touch her, and I will kill you."

"I can't die."

Jane shook her head. "Oh, but you can. I can find your Blood Painting and light it on fire."

Emrys held up his hands in surrender. "Gods, Jane, I was just joking. No need to threaten me so seriously."

"Then stay away."

"Fine, fine." His eyebrows crinkled. "You know you can be quite terrifying."

"I am Nightmare's wife. What else would you expect?"

CHAPTER TWENTY

Age 29.

It had been three hundred and ninety-five days since Jane had seen Nightmare. He was a ghost haunting his own mansion. Sometimes, she felt him on the wind and moving in the shadows. Lingering. Always lingering.

But anytime Jane got too close, the presence disappeared.

She wanted to ask for his help so badly. Jane needed him for many reasons. He was a heartless monster, but his presence was strangely calming, and now, in the absence of it, she felt empty. They were never ones for much talking, but they didn't need to talk to communicate. They spoke in desperate glances, coiled muscles, and rare smiles.

Nightmare was her companion—an evil one, but hers. And for someone so wicked, he seldom hurt her—never intentionally. Jane didn't believe he took dance from her to harm her—it was the result—he was trying to help her and trying to keep her from getting injured.

And she had lied to him.

The one thing he asked her not to do, without the compulsion.

But then, Jane hadn't meant to hurt him either. The difference between them was the drama. Although that wasn't fair either, she hadn't spoken to him for a year after he'd hurt her.

Perhaps they were both wrong. Both were ridiculously stubborn—both self-sabotaging.

Jane sighed and flipped through the autopsy reports for the hundredth time. There was something in here. She knew it. Otherwise, why else would her magic tell her to take them? Random murders of teens, vagrants, and ladies of the night. They didn't have anything in common. Not even the manner of death.

Some were drained of blood. Other victims had their throats ripped out like a dog had mauled them, and others still were stabbed or maimed in some other way. So what was the connection?

Could it be vampires?

Emrys had confirmed that none of his vampires had been attacking anyone. According to the Blood Accords, vampires were forbidden from making new vampires, at the pain of death. However, Emrys did believe that the person who killed Jane's family was ignoring those laws.

And if Jane could find the vampires responsible for the attacks, then she might find the man responsible for killing her parents.

Jane knew it was a man because she repeatedly heard his voice in her night terrors.

But to find them, she needed to find the connection between these victims. Jane closed her eyes and tried to call upon her magic, but it was in a mood tonight. Like a crusty, infected wound: red, raw skin oozing green pus. When her magic felt like this, it never complied, but she tried anyway.

Jane curled her fingernails into her palms, forcing them to bite into the skin. A small sense of discomfort helped her appeal to her magic. She closed her eyes and asked, *Show me the way. Help me see with your eyes, your strength, and your smarts.*

Seducing her magic and complimenting it always did

wonders. It was not a person or a being, but sometimes it acted like it and loved praise.

Her intestines tightened, her pulse quickened, and her skin prickled. Something was happening—some kind of *knowing*. Jane opened her eyes and scanned all the documents again, her magic thrumming. When she finally saw it, she felt so foolish.

The location.

They weren't all found in the same place. That would have been obvious. But all had some sort of foliage on their body or nearby. Eucalyptus leaves or flowers. Notable, because they were in only one place in the city. The Nature District, located on the west side by the Lake of Mirrors.

Eucalyptus trees weren't native to New Swansea. They came from a country far across the Kardic Ocean. So, the only place these victims could have died was the Nature District.

Jane jumped up, grabbed her tweed coat and gun, and promptly left Nightmare's mirror. Her magic vibrated in her bones—pleased she was going on a dangerous adventure. Possibly even directing it.

Sometimes, Jane was just a little too impulsive. Running out of the mirror and taking the first cable car to the Nature District was not the smartest choice. Only one cable car station was located in the Nature District, and it transported people to the trail that led to the Lake of Mirrors.

It was still a twenty-seven-minute hike to the mirrors, and unfortunately for Jane, most of the Eucalyptus trees surrounded the mirrors.

Church bells struck midnight. The ringing was heard all the way from the Spirit District. Jane jolted at the sound. She *should* just turn around and go home, but as soon as she had the thought, her magic tensed, causing a sharp sensation through her body.

So, her magic *was* driving this mission.

It didn't make Jane feel better. The last thing she needed was an inanimate force deciding her actions.

But here she was, so on she went, taking the trail to the mirrors. A sliver of moonlight cut through the forest canopy, formed of mostly cypress and pine trees, and illuminated the path.

Moving slowly and purposefully, she tried to get as far along the trail as possible while avoiding cracking sticks and crunching foliage beneath her feet—she did not need to attract the monsters hiding in the Nature District.

The Nature District was a hunting ground.

Jane swallowed past the lump in her throat. The area devoted to parks and wildlife was no place for a reasonable person to be after dusk. Black market dealings and gangs canvased the Verona Forest. The good news was that she, too, was a gangster—an armed one.

Yet, danger still lingered on the wind.

Insects buzzed, and low grumbling howls and owl hoots echoed through the trees, their branches scratching the heavens. The trees, shadows, and midnight hid all that should not be seen. All that should not be done.

Her stomach grumbled loudly at the sight of twinberries, her mouth watering. Her limbs weakened, and a daze hit like a boulder as she realized she'd not eaten in hours. Unfortunately, twinberries were toxic, and would kill her most unpleasantly. So she trekked on, searching for any sign of vampires.

What she would do if she found one, she had no idea. Because, like a fool, Jane hadn't thought this through.

Which was so unlike her.

Jane was meticulous and reasonable. She wasn't impulsive or reckless.

But her magic was.

It was hungry for something. It was directing her actions, and senselessly, she was listening.

When an owl cry came from next to her ear, Jane's heart

stumbled. The forest was not a safe place for a woman at night. Jane really should have brought Emrys or, if not Emrys, then at the very least, François and some of the Fantômes' guards.

Jane reached a clearing and was met with the face of a tortured statue. Hundreds of such statues surrounded a vast and glamorous mirror. She was here.

Sweat dripped from Jane's temple, and her left calf spasmed. The hairs on the back of her neck rose as she sucked in a labored breath.

The Lake of Mirrors was a lake formed from seven separate mirrors. The most well-known of which was the Mirror of Chaos.

When mirrors were sleeping or inactive, they were simply mirrors—solid silver glass. Hence, they got their names as mirrors—not doors, which Jane honestly thought would have been a better name for them. When mirrors were active, they swirled with magic and pulsed like living, breathing things, taking on the personalities of the gods that rested inside them.

Nightmare had a massive, commanding personality, and so too did his mirror.

Enthralling.

The Lake of Mirrors were all dormant. But they sparkled with a heavy darkness. It was an attraction that people often came to look at, because while it was dormant, it was still beautiful and sinister.

It was truly an experience to behold them.

The Lake of Mirrors glimmered. A sea of pink peonies, white roses, and ice-blue forget-me-nots laced the silver and was lined with diamonds—all frozen under an expanse of ice. It was the cursed crown jewel of New Swansea. An intricately crafted tiara, jewel after jewel, rose after rose, banded together into a magnificent creation.

But in its beauty lurked a dangerous power.

Jane tried not to get distracted by the mirrors because she needed to search the Eucalyptus trees for evidence. Luckily, they were now in sight. It only took her five minutes to find a clue—a cave set into the rock at the western edge of the district. Voices dripped from inside it.

Curiosity climbed up her throat, and she took a step closer—but sometimes, it felt like Jane must be forged from bad luck, because she immediately stepped on a twig.

In a blink, Jane was surrounded by ten people—vampires. Seven men and three women. All looking starved.

Fuck.

Well, magic, you got us into this mess. You better get us out of it.

The ringleader—presumably—stepped toward her and sniffed the air. "You smell... Strange."

"What a compliment." Jane smiled. "A woman always loves to hear that she smells strange. I know it's not because I am on my cycle." Jane took a step back from him but ran into one of his minions behind her.

Her heart stormed, pounding like a thunderclap. The worst part was that they could hear it, too, with their vampiric hearing.

"Just out of curiosity, do vampires like it when a woman is on their cycle? I have always meant to ask Emrys, but I always manage to forget."

The ringleader cocked his head. "Ah, so you know what we are. Curious, since humans are not supposed to know of our existence."

Jane held up her arm, its blood-painted tattoo visible. "I am a Council Member." Though, Jane had only gone to three council meetings, and they were boring and filled with useless information Emrys and Nightmare had already shared with her.

"The Blood Council," he seethed, clutching her chin tightly. It was not pleasurable, like when Nightmare did it.

Jane smiled through the fear ticking in her chest. "I would not recommend it. The meetings are very tedious."

He squeezed her face harder, his claws piercing into her skin and causing a trickle of blood to fall down her face. The iron hit her nostrils a moment before the blood touched her lips.

The vampire licked it away, his tongue running over her lips and cheek. Every muscle in Jane's body grew taut, and disgust licked her core.

His eyes became heavy lidded. "Oh, you're divine. I am going to enjoy sucking you dry. Or perhaps I'll keep you, and you'll do the sucking."

"I wouldn't do either if you prefer to live," Jane said. "You do not want to make an enemy of my husband."

A low, dark laugh rumbled in his chest. "I am not afraid of humans, girl."

It was Jane's turn to laugh.

He glared at her but said, "Time to take you to our little meal."

In an instant, he grasped her by the waist and dragged her into the cave, placing her down in a makeshift living room.

Jane's stomach rolled, and she leaned over, catching herself with her hands on her knees. Bile climbed her throat. Oh, that speed was worse than the travel void and teleportation.

The place hummed with enchantment, making what would usually be a cold, bleak, and dark cave into something livable, even nice—a mirror enchantment.

Jane clutched her knees tightly for a moment and inhaled sharply, trying to get her bearings. She needed to pull herself together and fight back. She had practiced with Nightmare long enough to be somewhat decent at manipulating wind. Even when Nightmare was no longer speaking or looking at her, she still religiously practiced.

Jane could do this—the only problem was that ten vampires turned into nearly twenty. Probably too many to control for long. But she'd try.

You better fucking work. She reprimanded her wind a moment before calling for Nightmare in her mind. She wasn't sure if he could hear, nor did she know if he would come, but it was worth a try. Jane stood up quickly and twisted her hands, feeling the wind and calling it to her bidding. The song it sang back to her was beautiful because it became an extension of her.

With a snap of her fingers, Jane pulled the air from every single vampire's lungs. They all toppled and clawed at their throats.

Even vampires needed to breathe.

"Oh, I should have mentioned I am a Wind Witch." A vicious smile painted her face. "And the bride of Nightmare. I am not one to be trifled with." She took a taunting step toward the ringleader. "So where were we?"

He clutched his throat and glowered at her, trying to take a step toward her to presumably snap her neck or something equally as vile.

Jane clicked her tongue. "Ah, no, no. You won't be moving." Jane twisted her hand and squeezed the wind around his body, holding him tight. "Isn't this fun?"

His lips were tight, and his nostrils flared.

"It looks like you have something to say." She released the hold on his air supply, allowing needed oxygen to enter his lungs once more.

"You are psychotic."

"Oh, thank you for the compliment. I definitely get it from my husband." Jane paused in thought and tapped her chin with one finger. "And probably my bosses. They can be quite insane, too."

"Let them go."

"Why should I? Weren't you about to make me your dinner?"

"They weren't."

Interesting. He cared about them. It was very possible that these vampires were victims, too. If someone held their weakness, then they would be able to compel them. This meant that Emrys might be right about the person who killed her parents being responsible for them. What other option was there because, with the Accords, only freed vampires could create new ones?

"I know you are not the boss." Jane squeezed her hand tighter, making the wind, in turn, squeeze harder. Extremely painfully. "So, who do you answer to? Who holds your weakness?"

"I am not telling you anything about us."

"Because you can't or because you don't want to?"

The vein in his neck pulsed, and he gritted his teeth tightly. It seemed to be the former. Interesting. Were these vampires controlled by her parents' murderer? Could she be closing in on the truth?

But as soon as Jane had the thought, her body quivered. Her magic was fading. She was doing too much. She swallowed and tried not to show her weakness. But her limbs went weak, and she barely kept herself up.

She stepped forward and had to reach out for the couch to steady herself, but she didn't quite make it, and her knees hit the rock floor hard.

"Ah, your magic has limits." He smiled. "So, all I have to do is wait you out."

Jane glared at him. Her mind felt like wet sand; slow, dense, and sticky. Holding on to her magic like this was tiring—it was hard. Pain reverberated from where her knees had hit the rock so hard.

Jane placed her palms solidly on the floor and lifted herself to her feet like a newborn fawn. Step by step, she tried to leave the cave. But the process was slow, and she was losing her grip on the vampires.

But she kept walking, putting as much distance as possible between them and her.

"This isn't over, girl," the ringleader called from behind her. "I will find you and kill you."

"I look forward to it," she said with a shaky voice.

Halfway to the opening, Jane slumped completely to the ground. She rested her hand on the rock, begging her magic not to break. She had no idea how she was going to get out of this, and it seemed like Nightmare had forsaken her.

Jane pinched her eyes closed, and her hold on the vampires slipped. She braced for an attack that didn't come.

Instead, she heard haunting screams from inside the cave.

With all the strength she could muster, she made her way back inside to find Nightmare ripping apart the vampires, limb by limb.

"I told you, you didn't want to piss off my husband."

It wouldn't kill them, but it would definitely slow them down. The process of rebuilding the body was a long and arduous one.

It only took Nightmare a minute to take them all out.

"Thank you." Jane stared at the massacre. Not all of the vampires were torn apart. Some of them had just had their necks snapped.

Did he just come to rescue her because she was his precious anchor, or did he actually care?

Nightmare stood with his back to her, surveying his mess, blood trickling down his arms and coating his clothing. The strong muscles of his back coiled under his white, disheveled dress shirt. His head cocked slightly back as if he were listening for her —but he still didn't look at her. Not directly.

"Night—" Jane swallowed the name and sucked in a deep breath, staring desperately at him. "Gavriil, please look at me. Speak to me."

He didn't. The muscles in his back tensed.

"Please." Her voice was shaky and raw. "I miss you." *I care for you, and I shouldn't.*

Without warning, he was in front of her, cupping her face so tightly she thought he might snap her neck, too. "Give me a reason..."

A reason? Jane's eyebrows crinkled. *A reason to miss him? Love him? A reason for him to kill her?* A trickle of fear pierced into her chest like the talons of a deadly predator—the fear taking on a physical form.

Then, perhaps the worst thing slipped from her mouth. "I am not Helene."

His hands slid into her hair and curled. He tilted her head like he was going to feast on her carotid artery. Jane placed a steady hand on his chest. If he were going to kill her, she would make him feel her... *love?*

It couldn't be love. Could it?

Either way, she would feel his empty, heartless chest. Except...

Jane gasped. Nightmare jerked and froze. With her free hand, she touched her own chest. Then his.

Beat. Beat.

Beat. Beat.

His. Hers.

Beat. Beat.

His. Hers.

"Oh," Jane whispered.

Nightmare's grip loosened, and she was able to dip her chin enough to meet his gaze. His liquid mirror eyes sparked with an emotion she could decipher. "Take your hand off my chest." His tone was flat.

The words pierced her heart, but she did as he asked. Jane's eyes stung, and wetness pooled behind them.

Nightmare's brow furrowed, and he cocked his head like a snake, staring into her soul. Then he dropped one of his hands from her hair and grasped her wrist, placing her hand back on his heart. Once again, Jane felt the pounding, like a drum vibrating under her hand.

Nightmare growled and removed her hand again. After a moment, he placed it back over his heart again.

Jane's nose scrunched. What was he doing that for? Her skin prickled, and she was so close to understanding but so, so far away at the same time.

"It only beats for you." His voice was husky with liquid darkness. "Hollow without your touch."

A redheaded Ashelle Witch will become your heart. Was *she* his heart? Impossible. Jane slid her hand up from his chest, along his neck, and up to his face.

"If I destroy you, it won't be because I wanted to." She stood on her tiptoes—on pointe, and with her hand, she leaned his chin down so she could touch his lips to hers. She kissed him softly before pulling back. "I will be your heart for as long as you let me."

His nostrils flared. "I don't know how to forgive you."

"I don't know how to forgive you either."

He lifted an eyebrow as if to ask, *What for?*

But she didn't want to get into how he stole dance from her— the only thing that allowed her to process her rotten emotions— not right now. So, instead, she said, "I can't take back what happened, and I am not sure that I want to." She paused, and her lips twitched, and a well of feeling stirred in her. "Because I want to know you; as much of you as you'll give and honestly as much as I can steal. But I know you don't want anyone to know you, ever. So, I am torn between accepting that and challenging it."

His throat bobbed.

"You own my body and my soul." A couple of tears rolled down her face. "All I'm asking for is a little piece of you. Anything, Gavriil."

He swallowed again, the muscle in his jaw bulging.

"Anything," she breathed.

Her eyes searched his, but as usual, he was an unbreakable vault. A groan sounded from the ground behind one of the couches, and someone stirred to their left. The vampires were waking up. It was past time to leave. Nightmare must have thought so, too, because his arms circled her waist, and they disappeared into the travel void.

He was taking them home.

Chapter Twenty-One

From the travel void, Nightmare stepped out and into the grand entry hall of his gothic castle. His fingers slowly drifted off her waist, leaving an echo of his touch.

A rumble moved through his chest. He sniffed the air, and his knuckles hovered for a moment over her hair as if he wanted to touch her again, but he didn't. He whirled around and walked deeper into his castle.

"Gavriil," she hedged, unsure how to ask him for help. She never truly had before. He'd given her help without her realizing it, but she'd never really asked anything of him—save the time he stole her dancing away.

"Yes," he said. Only one word, but at least he continued to speak to her. She was afraid he'd stop again. Swiveling on his heel, she saw a mixture of unreadable masks climbing onto his face. He was hiding from her again.

"I need your help."

He stepped toward her quickly, eager to help, but seemed to rethink his eagerness because he froze midstep. "That much is clear." He waved a hand. "Out with it, bride."

Jane gulped, and moisture played at the edge of her eyes. Had he just called her bride again while being quite rude at the same time? "*Bride*?"

He closed the distance between them and ran one of his large hands through her hair, grabbing the thick strands at the back of her head into his fist possessively, forcing her face up to meet his. "You will always be my bride, even when I hate you."

"Do you hate me?"

"Sometimes." He sighed dramatically. "Now, what do you need?"

"Will you come with me?"

He released her hair as an answer, and she walked out of his hold, guiding him to her new rooms. The autopsy reports were strewn everywhere: on the bed, across the richly woven rug, and even one hanging off a hook.

"You wanted to show me that you are an abhorrent mess without my presence?" He let out a low chuckle. "I already knew that."

"No, not that." Jane placed her hands on her hips. "And I am not that messy."

He raised an eyebrow, as if to say, "Have you met yourself?"

It was good that he was teasing her. He wasn't really a teaser, so perhaps he was trying.

"Fine," she sighed. "The autopsy reports. They are from my parents' deaths and a slew of vampire attacks over the past nineteen years. They are connected to the destruction of the first Blood Mirror. I think whoever killed my parents stole the vampire's Blood Paintings from the mirror and has been controlling them and creating more."

He cocked his head, but the gleam in his eye said he agreed with her.

"So, I need you to help me remember my parents' deaths." Jane bit her bottom lip, glancing at the reports. "I witnessed it, but I don't remember. I think I locked it away, and I know you can help me access the memories."

He ran a thumb along his bottom lip. "I'll help you, but not in here." He turned toward the door, waiting for her to follow. "We're going to my sanctuary."

"Your forbidden wing?"

"It's not forbidden anymore. Just ask, if you want to know something, and then respect me if I don't want to tell you."

It was fair. "Alright." She nodded. "Thank you."

He grumbled a response, leading her through the brambles and into his picturesque riverscape. It was night inside, and the sky sparkled like the ocean at sunset. Fireflies danced through a gentle breeze, and a sweet waterfall crashed in the distance against red-orange rocks. Rock sculptures littered the landscape, arches, and water-carved designs. The place was like a god's intricate finger painting—and now that she thought about it, it was.

It was Nightmare's.

He was a god, but also a vampire. Did that mean *he* had a Blood Painting? She asked as much out loud.

"Why, do you want to kill me?"

"No, of course not."

"I don't have one."

"Did you ever?"

"No." The answer was short and marked the end of the conversation.

He led her to the riverbed, had her take off her shoes, and made her sit in the sand. "I want you to feel the sand. I want you to be present. Close your eyes and listen. Feel the granules between your fingers."

She did as he asked. Nightmare sat opposite her, his knees touching hers. He was the first thing she felt. His demanding and commandeering presence—he ruled every room he entered and always stole her breath away. He might have stolen attention because on nearly half of the occasions he entered a room, he murdered someone in it.

It was impossible not to notice him.

"Breathe, and hear the birds singing to you and the water dancing in the grooves of nature."

Jane sucked in a deep breath and fell into the sounds and feelings. She scooped the sand and felt it fall through her fingers; with each movement, her soul settled. Peace stroked along her body like a physical force, warm like strings formed from contained sunlight, like a blanket or a hug.

But it was too real...

Opening her eyes, she saw his magic light stroking along her body, wrapping around her arms, legs, and waist. He was holding her, comforting her; but also giving her space. She smiled and closed her eyes again.

"Now, keep your eyes closed and bring yourself back to that night." The light strings warmed on her skin.

She did as he said again, and the first thing she saw was her wicked dreams. She shivered, and the ropes tightened on her skin, letting her know he was there.

The walls bled, but she couldn't quite distinguish what the walls looked like or where she was. The blood just piled up, thick and clotted, down the sides like a waterfall of old, clumpy paint. The smell stuck in her nostrils. A horrible, indescribable scent.

Once again, Jane held a hand over her baby sister's mouth and squeezed her to keep her from screaming—he couldn't hear them, he couldn't find them—and with her other hand, she pressed her fingertips into the marble floor to ground herself and keep herself from screaming.

Glass flew through the air, and Jane screamed in her mind, or maybe she screamed out loud.

It was hard to tell anymore.

Then she heard his voice... The man who killed her parents was asking, "Did you get them?"

"Yes," her mother's stern voice. "Now leave. Get out of my house."

But the memory ended and was filled with swirling smoke and haunting calls. "Come find us, Jane. Find us."

The words repeated endlessly.

It was a mixture of magic and a present request.

And suddenly, she understood what she needed to do to regain her memories.

Jane jumped up, quickly threw her shoes on, and ran out of the room to exit the mirror because her magic was guiding her. Her mind wasn't going to give her all the answers like this. She needed a Blood Mirror, so she let her magic pull her. She let the mirror call to her. Mirrors always had, especially the one in the Royalle Ballet, and all Jane needed was to clear her mind and listen.

And listen she did.

She ran, her dress covered with sand and disheveled, her shoes barely holding on. Onlookers probably thought she was unhinged, especially when they saw a tall, dark figure following her, strolling unconcerned behind her.

Nightmare had no anxiety or even emotion coloring his footfalls. It was quite the contrast.

But Jane didn't care. She followed her magic, her senses. Much like Nightmare's warm strings of light, her magic lit a path to the Ruins.

The Ruins.

Jane halted at the entrance. A sea of creepy mirrors and wicked gates formed the place. The viciously beautiful mermaid statues on the gate whispered to life, their tails flicking and hair bouncing in the wind—the sapphire gates.

"Enter at your peril, little witch," the mermaids said in sinister unison.

The hair on Jane's arms rose.

"Ah, and the man formed of Nightmares," they said again in unison as Nightmare stepped up next to Jane.

Two things happened at once: the sea of mirrors behind the gates let out a wave of shrieks, the sound piercing the night sky, and an invisible barrier tried to attack their bodies, but Nightmare broke the enchantment with a wave of his arm. When they stepped through the gates, the plane was blanketed in shadows and misty, unnatural smoke.

Jane's nostrils flared as she tried to ignore the screams and caged souls. But the mirrors were relentless, chanting evil things mixed with horrific lies.

They said things like, *We want to devour you, Jane*, and *You're going to die soon.* They continued, whispering cruel and damaging words into the blackened night.

"Ignore them," Nightmare said, linking his arm into hers. "They are just echoes of the souls inside other mirrors. They can't do anything to you."

Echoes? Jane wanted to ask what he meant by that, but she didn't have time or energy for that. So, instead, to the best of her ability, she ignored them, swallowing and following her magic past the mirrors.

When they finally reached the clearing beyond, it was like breathing for the first time. And, as she sucked in a deep breath, she turned her gaze upon the towering vampire ruins—a place that had once been their beautiful palace. Before the Blood Rebellion, when King Emrys won the war and slaughtered all the remaining vampires, at least until the survivors turned him into the same monster he hated so much.

Stone crumbled from the seams of turrets and looked like the jagged edges of a shattered stained-glass window. The once majestic castle festered and rotted like the bowels of a river-soaked corpse. Darkness's wings surrounded the place and covered it in death. Vines snaked up the shattered stone, and mold grew along the walls like parasites feasting on flesh. Moss and mildew covered the ground, and everything about the place screamed, *Get out*! Including Jane's gut.

Monsters worse than death haunted the grounds. Decay had breathed life into this place, and nothing was free from its chokehold.

Above the entrance were dripping words written in blood. *If you wish to enter the ruins safely, a blood sacrifice must be freely given.*

Without hesitation, Jane picked up and ran her palm against the jagged rocks hard enough to cause a bloom of blood to escape. Then she walked through the barrier. The effect was immediate. Wisps of shadow and glowing blue light leaked out of her body. The same thing happened to Nightmare when he repeated the process.

Jane clutched her chest and reached a hand out to catch herself on the rocks. A piece of herself had been stripped away.

It had stolen her magic.

"Don't worry," Nightmare said, wrapping a hand around her waist and helping her up. "It will return when we're done here."

The inside of the castle stared up at the cursed night sky. Stars leered down with wicked intent, the rays burning with cruelty. The room shone with crimson light that illuminated the shriveling castle. At its center stood a scarlet mirror—a ruby the size of a boulder.

The crown jewel in a sea of rot.

A Blood Mirror.

Even without her magic, the mirror sang to her, and it was in the same key as the song from the towering invisible mirror in the Royalle Ballet. Maybe even the same song. Because they were both Blood Mirrors.

Fuck.

Jane had found both of the remaining two.

"What do you want to tell me?"

A force hit Jane in the chest, and she fell to her knees. The memories flooded into her.

A scream pierced the night, coming from down the hall. Little Quinnevere ran out of her room toward it, and before Jane could yell to warn her, the girl had turned the corner. So, dressed only in her shift and no shoes, a ten-year-old Jane sprinted after her sister and caught her just in time. Jane wrapped a hand around her mouth and threw them both underneath the side table. The girl had run to the ballroom, where the massive mirror rested.

Only Jane and Quinnevere could see the thing, and her parents had told them they were not allowed to tell anyone about it.

And Jane hadn't, right?

Except Uncle Gideon—he wasn't her uncle, only her father's best friend—had asked about it last week. So, of course, she had told him. But he was family, right? Well, she hadn't technically known Gideon. She'd only seen him in pictures, but she first met him last week. But her daddy loved him; they were often seen together in many photos. Her daddy had said he died tragically, but then here he was, alive and standing before her, asking about her dad and the mirror.

Mommy had told her not to tell anyone except family.

Had she done something wrong?

Another scream rang out, and the floor grew red. A pool of redness was coming toward them. Quinnevere tried to scream, but Jane held her tightly.

So much red.

"Gideon, you're supposed to be dead," Daddy said in a low, shaky voice. "We killed you."

"Well, it didn't seem to stick, did it?" Gideon's voice was wicked, cold, and cruel, taunting her father. "Don't worry, next time, maybe it will. Unfortunately, you won't be alive to see it."

Just as Jane peeked her head out from the tablecloth, she saw the tall man with redwood hair and hazel eyes stab her father in the heart. Gideon, her father's once-best friend, killed him. Jane couldn't contain her scream.

Gideon's harsh gaze landed on her. "Ah, the little snitch." A sinister smile lifted on his lips. "Come out, little dove."

Jane shook her head and held her sister's mouth tighter.

"Now, girl."

Jane gulped. She knew if she didn't move, he'd come over and find her sister, too, and that could not happen. So she turned back to

Quinnevere and whispered, *"Do not make a sound. If you do, you will die. Do you understand me?"*

Quinnevere nodded and slammed her tiny little four-year-old fingers to her mouth, tears leaking from her eyes.

Jane placed her hands on the floor and slowly lifted herself up and out from under the table. As she did, her eyes scanned the room. Five bodies littered the floor, blood gushing everywhere, but as her gaze tracked through them, she realized her mother wasn't there. "Where's Mommy?"

Gideon pointed to the mirror with his thumb. "In there, getting me some paintings."

"Why do you need paintings?"

"Hush, child, I am trying to think." He took a menacing step toward her. "I want to kill you, but they say the little Ashelle girls are special. They say old magic rests in your veins, girl."

"Magic?"

"And that could one day be useful. So call me your savior, girl, because today is your lucky day." He pinched her face between both hands. "Forget me, forget this." A tingling sensation clawed at her brain, and she fell to her knees and collapsed into a dark slumber, blood sticking to her dress and hair.

It was the last thing she saw. Jane never knew if her mother made it out of the mirror alive. But she learned from the reports and aftermath that she never came back, and that mirror was destroyed and killed, too. So, if she never made it out, she would have died inside it.

Jane screamed, coming out of the memory, and found Nightmare holding her. Jane turned her head into his chest. "It's my fault," Jane sobbed. "I am the reason my parents died. I told him about the mirror. I even told him where it was."

"Who?" Nightmare asked darkly.

"Gideon."

"Gideon," Nightmare parroted, his voice laced with shadows. So he knew the name.

Jane squeezed his thigh and looked up at him. "Have you bargained with him?"

"Yes," Nightmare seethed. "I made him a monster, gave him too much power, including the ability to change and morph his appearance. But I thought your father and his vampire friend killed him about thirty years ago. So I didn't worry about it anymore."

"He can change his appearance."

"Yes."

"So, he could be anyone?"

"Theoretically, yes."

Well, that was fucking terrible news. Now, she had to find a man with a changing face and far too much power for his—or anyone else's—good.

PART FIVE
DOES FALLING IN
LOVE FEEL LIKE DYING?

Chapter Twenty-Two

AGE 29.

It was a ship of dreams, and he was a man formed from nightmares. Four days after discovering the Ruins Blood Mirror and realizing that the other one was at the Royalle Ballet, Nightmare told her they were taking the Titan across the Kardic Ocean. To find a magical object somewhere in Grand York.

Honestly, Jane wasn't entirely sure what Nightmare wanted. It was just another one of his many machinations. But she was realizing that he wasn't just doing things at random. He was preparing.

Preparing for *her* return. Helene. His nemesis.

His hand rested on the small of her back as they walked up the gangway and onto the most opulent steamship in the world. The morning smelled of paint, ocean air, and smoke. It was the ship's maiden voyage, sailing from New Swansea to Grand York.

The ship was gorgeous. Opulent white paint coated the walls, and gilded crown moldings and massive chandeliers adorned the entire ship. The finery and company were like nothing Jane had ever experienced. Yes, once her parents and even her former husband had both had money, but she was too young when her parents died to be invited to any parties, and her husband was never respected enough to be invited into the upper echelons of society. The only true wealth Jane knew involved the Royalle Ballet and its parties and engagements, and possibly her involvement with Emrys and the Fantômes. But the majority of her role with them was clandestine and coated in a life of shadows.

This was different.

This was out in the open, with the most handsome and dangerous man Jane had ever known.

It made her both uncomfortable and excited.

After settling into their first-class stateroom, Jane wanted to explore the decks. She wanted to experience this moment, to feel the joy of living and take it all in. Deep down, she felt the end nearing. Whether it was her magic or simple dread, Jane felt Death nipping at her heels. And, instead of being terrified of that feeling, she simply wanted to live. It was a once-in-a-lifetime experience to travel on the maiden voyage of the largest ship in creation. And she would enjoy it.

The ship was a marvel of engineering, and Jane wanted to see it all.

Especially as the ship set sail.

The smoke stakes towered into the air, scraping against the light blue sky, and as the ship began to move, black clouds poured from them like a pool of ink spilling out, dancing with the sky.

Jane smiled as she walked, nearly skipping to the front of the deck, getting much closer to the bow of the ship. She almost shivered with joy as she leaned over a railing to see a dolphin jump next to the ship. It was the first one she had ever seen, and it was so... so utterly beautiful.

She glanced back at Nightmare to share her excitement with him. He stared at her, his expression empty of all emotion, his hands in his pockets.

"Come see, Alexei." She smiled, not letting his typical apathy affect her.

Without argument, he strolled over beside her and glanced down at the water, the side of his lips twitching as he slid an arm around her waist.

"Aren't they beautiful?" She turned her face up to meet his gaze, her red locks fluttering with the ocean breeze.

He nodded and held her a little tighter. He'd never admit to enjoying anything, but deep down, Jane knew he had sparks of feeling, and she knew, despite his complete lack of outward expression, he too liked the dolphins.

"Have you ever seen one in person before?"

"Yes." His tone was monotone, but his eyes sparked.

Jane turned her attention back to the ocean as the boat carved through the waters. The midday sun sparkled on the water like a sea of diamonds. Jane tried to count the refracting rays of light, but there were far too many of them.

After a while of simply watching the calming sea, she moved on to exploring the Writing and Reading Room before wandering around the promenade deck. It was all so... glamorous and new. The ship was like a floating palace, and Jane wanted to see everything.

But time slipped away from her, and before she knew it, it was time to change into her evening attire and make her way to the dining salon. She looked forward to dinner because the first-class passengers were mingling and had to sit at a table with multiple parties. It was a time when people could meet new people and socialize.

And this was something Jane had never gotten to do freely in her previous life. Her last husband had had far too many enemies for her to make friends, and although Nightmare was a grumpy man at best, he also allowed her to have a life outside of him. He let her have friendships and teach dance class, and he wanted her to work for and be a key member of the Fantômes. She even thought her rise in the mafia's ranks made him proud.

In almost every way, Nightmare was the antithesis of her horrible, dead husband.

As she entered the sparkling dining room, she grinned brightly. It was all just new and fascinating. Even the food was captivating. They served a variety of meals, from a luscious steak to fresh salmon, and peach ice cream for dessert.

After a time of mingling with guests, talking about all things from the weather to the magnificence of the ship, and things about the first-class passengers' homes and families, they were finally seated at their tables.

Their table was set for eight, but two of the party hadn't arrived yet. Those who had were content with keeping to themselves. Unfortunately, their quiet dinner was quickly interrupted by their table partners—a rail-thin, overloud woman and her husband, who looked to be thirty years older than her. But when Jane saw his face, she stiffened and tried to disappear into her chair. All the excitement from the day vanished in an instant.

Nightmare's fingers glided over her thigh in response as he stared at the late newcomers.

The man had a dusting of grey in his dark hair, and wrinkles spread across his face, but it was his cruel eyes Jane remembered the most. A gloved hand drifted to her neck as she sucked in a breath and begged him not to recognize her. The silk fabric scraped against her delicate skin as she remembered his fingers circling it.

He liked to cause pain. It was the only way he came.

For the life of her, she couldn't remember his name. She tried not to remember their names. It was hard enough to forget their tiny cocks.

Jane sank further into her chair, wishing she could turn invisible, but using her magic in such a fashion would be highly inappropriate. So she just begged any god in existence to spare her from what came next.

But it didn't work. When the older man's eyes landed on her, the recognition was immediate. Time froze as he opened his mouth to say something awful, and Jane pinched her eyes closed, waiting for the onslaught of embarrassment and trauma, but it never came because Nightmare cut in before he could say anything. "Have you met my wife, Jane Whitfield-Wryte?"

"Ah, you remarried?" The older man's eyes latched onto Jane.

"Yes." She smiled tightly.

"This one seems even richer than your first one. Good on you."

Jane smiled through her teeth. "Thank you."

Nightmare tactfully steered the conversation away and onto lighter topics, but during a moment of quiet, he leaned into her and asked, "What did he do to you?"

"Nothing." Jane swallowed. "He's done nothing to me."

"Liar," he whispered into her hair, his tone dark and fingers still curling into her thigh.

"Gavriil,"—she jerked her gaze to him—"you know what he did. Don't make me say it."

Nightmare growled and turned his eyes to his food, but his attention was soon brought back to the conversation. He laced a facade of cordiality onto his face, but he vibrated with fury.

While he expertly maneuvered the conversation, Jane watched the man's wife—she still couldn't figure out his name, but then he didn't deserve to have one. His wife couldn't have been much older than Quinnevere, and as Jane studied further, she realized that the exuberance and loudness of her conversation were a finely crafted mask. The girl also barely touched her food, and when she did, her husband reprimanded her under his breath. He used it as a form of control, just like Jane's dead husband had. It was also probably the reason the girl looked like a gust of wind might topple her over.

An anchor sank inside Jane, dropping to the deepest depths of the ocean. The girl was a mirror. The reflection of all the abuse she'd suffered.

Wetness gathered at the corners of Jane's eyes, and her stomach churned.

She bit her lip and turned to the beautiful god sitting beside her, his hand still clutching her thigh protectively. Maybe her monster was right. Maybe she should take her revenge. Maybe it was time to stop denying the past and embrace it.

Jane's gaze tracked over Nightmare's sharp features and silver hair, taking him in fully. His beauty. His anger. His magnificence.

Leaning in, she whispered in his ear, "Will you help me kill him?"

Like a dangerous bird of prey, he cocked his head sharply, meeting her gaze. "Yes."

And on their first night aboard the Titan, they killed a man who deserved no name.

Chapter Twenty-Three

Age 29.

There must have been something deeply wrong with Jane because as Nightmare and Jane walked side by side to her former abuser's room, a thrilling sensation bubbled inside her.

Jane was hoping her humanity had been rubbing off on Nightmare, but his wickedness might have been corrupting her instead. But she didn't know if she cared.

No matter. Sometimes, evil men deserved to be purged from the world. Nightmare had taught her that much.

Without knocking, the two of them swung open the door to the man's estate room to find him fully naked, his miniscule pecker on full display as he hovered over the bed. His wife sat up, tangled in the sheets, her fingers clutching them as if they were going to save her from whatever came next.

The man let out a protest as his hands covered his penis protectively. "What are you doing in here? Get out."

Their first-class room was much smaller than Jane's and Nightmare's. So it was much more crowded. The bed was placed next to a small vanity with a chair slid into it, and when neither

Jane nor Nightmare moved to leave, the man took a protective step behind the vanity.

But nothing would save him.

"Get out," he yelled again. "I will—"

But Jane didn't get to hear the following words because Nightmare didn't let him finish. In an instant, he was on him, and a second later, he had ripped off both of his arms before slamming him into the wall by his throat. Nightmare truly had a taste for the gruesome.

The act splattered blood all over the room, coating everything in the dripping red liquid, including the left side of Jane's face.

"Would you like to do the honors?" Nightmare's voice was liquid fire as he turned to her.

"Yes," Jane breathed, and stepped up next to them.

She pulled out the chair of the vanity and placed her leg up on the seat. Slowly, oh so slowly, she slid her dress up until she reached the knife holstered at her thigh. Being a top member of a gang meant she always had a weapon stashed somewhere.

She slid the knife out of its sheath, slowly, the metal sounding against the leather. She flipped it in her fingers, playing with it, toying with him for a moment. Just one moment.

A wicked smile climbed her face as she swiftly thrust the blade into her ex-tormentor's heart.

"You could have played with your food a little more." Nightmare's blood-soaked fingers gently stroked her waist as if he couldn't keep his hands off of her.

"I am not you."

"No, you're not." Nightmare released his grip on the man, and the body slid to the floor, its lifeless eyes staring straight at the ceiling. Jane cocked her head, taking in the destruction.

The vein in Jane's jaw ticked, but she didn't feel bad. It felt right. Killing her tormentor *felt right.*

Nightmare ran a thumb along her jaw. "No, you're you."

He leaned in and licked the blood off Jane's face, moving

from her jaw up to her cheek and along her temple. As he fed, his fangs dropped, and at the sight, the girl screamed.

"Vampire!"

Nightmare jerked and twisted, the weight of his full attention now on the girl who screamed louder. Jane didn't have time to stop him. He disappeared from her side, and when he reappeared, he had the girl by the throat, dangling, her feet barely touching the floor. He flashed his fangs, and Jane knew she only had mere moments before Nightmare killed again.

"No," Jane said sternly, before stepping beside her avenging angel. "Please, don't kill her."

Nightmare growled.

"Can't you see? She's his victim, too." The word victim came out with a waver in Jane's voice. She never liked to see herself as a victim. "Please, she's been through enough."

"She saw," he said through his teeth, still holding the girl up by the throat, one of her toes scraping against the floor, keeping from choking her completely.

"I know." Jane's voice was soft, like she were trying to tame a lion—and in all reality, Nightmare was her lion. "Let her go for me. Do it because you *care for me*."

Blackness seeped into his eyes, and he flashed a look that said, *Why would you think that would matter?* His eyebrows scrunched.

"I can never—" The muscles in his arms bunched as he bit the words off, glaring at her. But it wasn't a cruel expression on his face; it was resigned. All the while, he still never let go of his prey.

"You don't care about me?" It was both a question and a plea.

His lips flattened into a stern line. "I don't have a heart, Jane. Whatever it is you want from me, you will never get it."

Jane swallowed past the lump in her throat. "I know." She nodded. "I know that I am only your anchor, and you will only ever care about me in that capacity. I will only ever be a useful tool to you." She stretched her hand out and placed it on his chest. "But I can care about you." His heart thumped beneath her hand.

"Maybe I can care enough for both of us." It thumped harder. "Maybe, I refuse to give up on you."

His nostrils flared, but he reached his free, blood-soaked hand up to cup hers.

"Let go of the girl, Gavriil."

Beat. Beat. Beat. Beat. His heart stormed in his chest, and his gaze raked over her.

"Please."

He tilted his chin and, without taking his eyes off Jane, he not-so-gently threw the girl down onto the bed.

Before the girl could scream or do anything else, Jane said, "Remain silent and don't run, or I will let him kill you."

The girl nodded, tears streaking down her face.

Jane's attention drew back to her monster. She drew up on her tiptoes and placed a chaste kiss on his lips. "Thank you."

Chapter Twenty-Four

Age 29.

"What's your name?" Jane asked the girl softly.

"Genevieve." It was more of a squeak than a word, and her eyes darted to Nightmare, fear etched into her every pore.

Jane slid her fingers into the girl's and squeezed, trying to give her some comfort. "If you promise not to say anything about what you saw here, we will let you live. We'll clean up this mess, and if anyone asks where he is, tell them he went to the smoking room and never came back."

The girl bit her lip. "Yes, I promise."

"Bargain it." Nightmare crossed his arms, his muscles rippling with the movement. "Bargain with me that you will keep the secret, and you can have your life, and we will cover up the murder, and you will not receive any flak for this."

Genevieve's eyes went wide. "Bargain?"

"Yes, bargain. I am the Mirror of Nightmares. I am sure you have heard of me."

She gasped. "The Looking Glass?"

197

It was Jane who answered. "Yes."

The girl sucked in a breath. "Alright then. I accept your bargain.

As Genevieve accepted, all the blood and the body evaporated from the room, leaving the place as pristine as when they had entered.

But as the magic worked, a sharp pain carved through Jane's torso, like a warning.

Jane clutched her chest. Something was off. She felt a knowing. A future whispering to her, and in that moment, she knew whatever the consequences of that bargain were, it was going to be far more than any of them anticipated.

The next two days passed without incident. They ate omelets in the morning before going to the ship's gymnasium on the boat deck, taking afternoon tea, and mingling with the other patrons in the evening at dinner.

On the third night, Nightmare surprised her with a fairly deep conversation.

"You said you wanted to know me," he asked at dinner. Tonight, they had a private table. "So, ask me a question."

Jane pinched her lips shut. Of course, she wanted to know everything about him, but where did she start? Why not the beginning? "You seemed to be a sweet teenager..." Jane trailed off, not knowing where she was going.

"Where is the question?" he smiled.

Jane swallowed. "I am honestly not sure. It's a lot of pressure to ask you a question."

"You can't do it wrong."

Jane raised an eyebrow disbelievingly.

"Fine. Others could. Not you. I just won't answer it if I don't want to."

"You were a happy, sweet teenager; you didn't have this darkness." She waved a hand over him. "Do you wish you could have some of that joy back?"

He sat perfectly still, his jaw tightening the longer he stayed silent. Jane restlessly shifted in her seat, wondering if she had done something wrong. But eventually, he said, "I don't know. Do you want me to be like him again? Because I don't think I ever can."

"No," she breathed. "I don't want the boy, or even his youthful joy. I want you to be fully who you are. Not pieces of yourself. I just want you to be able to have a piece of him back if you want it."

"I am not whole, Jane." He ran a hand through his hair. "I have no heart without your touch. I am a grotesque vampire."

"I would like to meet the person who called you grotesque. Have they seen you?" Jane waved a hand over his incredible physique. "Not to inflate your ego, but you're perhaps the most attractive man I have ever seen." She paused for a long moment, deciding if she wanted to bring up the woman he clearly hated so deeply that he talked around her presence. "That's why Helene targeted you to begin with." He flinched at the name, but Jane continued anyway, "She liked to collect pretty things. You and Darcy are two of the prettiest men who have probably ever lived. If she were alive today, I am sure she'd probably want to collect Prince Emrys too."

"She is alive." He clenched his fists tightly, all of his muscles taut like a bowstring. "She's entombed inside the Lake of Mirrors, and it's mere years, if not days, until she figures out how to escape."

"How could she? You've never managed it."

"I am here with you, am I not?" His chin motioned at the Titan.

Jane played with her teaspoon. "That's different."

"Is it?"

"Well, yes. You need me in order to be out here. She'd need an anchor, at the very least, not to mention enough magic to break the spell on her mirror, and she wouldn't ever have enough."

"No, she wouldn't." He stroked his chin in thought. "But she's ancient. Her parents were once lesser gods. She knows things we could never. She'll find a way. She found a way to get all of her power back after she accidentally drained it all, imprisoning me in my mirror. She will find a way. Evil always does."

Nightmare's eyes darkened, and his gaze focused on Jane, a hint of hatred lingering in them when he looked at her.

"Do I remind you of her?"

"Absolutely not." There was no hesitation in his answer. "Your—" His throat bobbed. "There aren't words to describe you, but you are her opposite in every single way. Every. Single. Way."

Nightmare's eyes shifted to the dancers, and he stood. He wanted this conversation to end, so he held out his hand to dance and asked, "Will you dance with me?"

"I can't."

"But you love dancing."

I did. How did he remember that but not that he stole dancing from her?

He raised a manicured silver eyebrow when she didn't move to stand.

"I love dancing, but I can't." Confusion painted across his face, and she gulped. "You must command me to do it because I can't."

"Is that what you want?"

"Yes."

He gave a downward glance before raising his chin again. "Dance with me tonight."

Jane bit her lip. It didn't break his original command completely, and his original command had barred her from speaking about it. So even if she wanted to bring it up now, could she? Jane didn't want to linger on that.

So she just wanted to experience this moment... With him.

She took his hand and let him walk her to the dance floor. It was a waltz. He grasped her waist tightly and slid his hand into hers, turning into her, and then he led her into the three-four rhythm of the dance. It was simple and sweet. Just the simple movement caused joy to stir in her blood and fill her with tranquility that she hadn't felt in years—a peace she missed.

It was beautiful and simple.

Jane closed her eyes and sucked in his scent, sharing this moment with him. He smelled of musk, black tea, and a hint of vanilla.

The night was perfect, but it was followed by a morning of horrors. Around five in the morning, Jane and Nightmare were woken by what felt like an earthquake. It was either the ship hitting an iceberg or a mine, but the effect was immediate chaos.

The ship went down in forty minutes, and all forty of those minutes were tumultuous.

Nightmare and Jane grabbed their jackets and life jackets and stormed out to the lifeboats, along with everyone else on the ship. They found one that allowed them to board, but as Nightmare was lifting Jane onto the boat, the sailor responsible for lowering the lifeboat into the water let go of his rigging, and it swung, hitting Jane at the edge of her temple.

A strike of pain surged through her head, then she fell sideways, nothing beneath her legs, and she tumbled into the ocean six decks below. As she hit the water, darkness poured into her vision, pain jolted her bones, and water filled her lungs.

She was unconscious and drowning, and that was the last thing she was able to recall before she heard him—her nightmares.

"You don't die. You never die," he seethed, his voice riddled with a darkness that rattled her bones.

She felt a hard pressure on her chest before her eyes flung open, and she was coughing up water onto the wooden deck. Her throat and lungs were burning from the effort.

When she was finally able to look at him, he said again. "You never die. Do you understand me?"

Jane's mouth ran dry, despite having just been filled with water. Because what could she say? And more importantly, what was she feeling? It was a buzzing in her chest like she'd never felt before. It was warmth, home, and rightness. But it was all wrong. All lies because Nightmare, Gavriil, was not her home. He never could be.

He was the greatest villain she'd ever known... Yet he was also more than that.

And that was dangerous.

"Is that a command?" she finally asked, her voice raw.

"Yes," Gavrail snarled, his eyes still wild.

Jane sucked in a slow, painful breath and felt her fingers on the deck, the wood grain coarse like her following words. "I don't think even you could command Death like that."

"I can't." His voice was raw and honest. "I can't command you back to life, Jane. So don't you dare die on me." He pulled her into a desperate hug.

"I won't," she lied, because she knew she was destined to die young and painfully.

"And stop getting yourself into so much trouble. I am rather sick of saving your life."

"No, you're not." Jane laughed and rubbed her head, a bump forming where the rigging had hit her. "You killed the boy, didn't you?"

She didn't have to look at him or hear his words to know the truth. Gavriil was one thing above all else: consistently wicked. It wouldn't even have been a question in his mind. The boy had hurt what belonged to him, and therefore, he would be eliminated. Simple. Swift.

"Yes." As Jane suspected, no remorse or guilt was evident in the words. It was hard and cold. It was what nightmares were formed from. "Now, bargain with me to make you a lifeboat."

"What should I bargain for?"

"A kiss."

"Alright," she said. "Alexei, I will kiss you if you give me a lifeboat."

"I accept your deal." He leaned in and touched his lips to hers.

It took two more days on a smaller ship, during which they had to sleep in the cold to get to Grand York City, the greatest city across the ocean. The travel would have been miserable if Nightmare hadn't been there to keep her warm and company. They sat silently for most of it, but also engaged in small talk, learning a little more about each other, such as their favorite colors and foods.

Nightmare's was red, and he said, "Like your hair." Jane's favorite was black, which he argued was not, in fact, a color but the absence of it.

When they arrived in the city, they didn't waste their time. For such a traumatic journey, they were only on the other side of the ocean for fifty-seven minutes, half of which was the cab ride to the Grand History Museum. Once they got to the Museum, Nightmare quickly found the exhibit with the magical item he was looking for—a cloak.

Jane didn't even want to know what it did or why he wanted it.

Nightmare punched the glass and didn't even bother to make a bigger hole; he just placed his hand through and pulled out the cloak, the glass ripping a tear in his skin and causing blood to trickle on the floor.

But he didn't care. He simply walked over to Jane, wrapped his hand around her waist, and hauled her into the travel void, pulling her back into his mirror.

When her feet hit the marble of his castle floor, she asked, "If you could do that all along, why did we have to take the ship?"

"I can return to my mirror from anywhere. I cannot always go anywhere from inside of it."

CHAPTER TWENTY-FIVE

AGE 29.

Jane's life was one of service. Serving and servicing powerful men, pleasuring her first husband and his debtors, being Nightmare's minion, working for the Mirror Mafia... Everything was for someone else.

Jane was done. She wanted her own life. She wanted freedom.

But at that moment, she wanted him.

All of him. Finally.

His back muscles shifted as he walked toward his forbidden wing to drop the cloak off.

"Nightmare, stop. I—"

He rounded on her and snarled. "Do not call me tha—"

"No," she cut him off. "I am going to call you Nightmare because you are my nightmare. *Mine.*"

She pushed him up against the wall with the force of her wind, and at first, he fought, standing his ground, but then he relented and let her. His back hit with a thud, and a rush of air came out of him.

She held him to the wall with a hand on his chest. He could overpower her at any moment, but he didn't.

"You are my Nightmare, the creature that haunts the night, slaying my enemies and keeping me safe. My entire life since I remember it has been a nightmare, and then I met you. and you were worse until you were better." Moisture curled at the edges of her eyes. "So, I get to call you my Nightmare because you made it better. Because even at your worst, you have always protected me, even if for selfish reasons."

Jane stood on pointe and fiercely pulled his mouth to hers, using his shirt as leverage.

The kiss was a conquering, a claiming. Jane was telling him that, while he might own her body and soul, she owned him, too.

He was hers.

The good, the evil, and the monstrous. It was all hers.

She pulled away for a moment and glared up at him. "And you are gonna fuck me now." Her chest beat to a frantic and needy rhythm. "Eight years is far too long to wait, far too long to want you and not have you."

His only response was a grunt before he flipped them around, causing her back to hit the wall, and engulfed her mouth again. It was all lips, teeth, and untamed passion—like two starving hyenas devouring a meal after months of starvation. In their case, years of it.

Her legs came up and wrapped around his waist, and she felt the thick bulge of his arousal against her core. She ground against him and let out a moan. And she suddenly realized they were wearing too much clothing.

She ripped at his white-collared shirt, splitting open the buttons, which fell to the marble floor.

He suddenly wrenched his mouth away and pushed her back further into the wall, his hand coming up around her throat. "Slow down."

"No," she whimpered.

He sighed and leaned his head against hers as if he were practicing great patience. "You're not ready for this yet."

"Nightmare, no, please don't pull away again," Jane begged,

her breasts rising with her frantic words and breaths. "I can't wait any longer. I can't."

He removed his head from her forehead and pinched his fingertips deeper into her neck, stealing some of her breath. "You misunderstand me. I am going to fuck you tonight, but I'm going to have to show some restraint, and that's not going to be very easy if you attack me like this."

"I don't want restraint." She managed to get the words out despite his hand on her throat.

"Yet, it's what you need." He released some pressure and slowly pressed his lips to hers again. "Let me show you something different. I promise later you will get my beast."

Nightmare scooped her up, threw her over his shoulder, and walked her to their room before throwing her onto the bed.

"Now, we do this my way."

"We do everything your way," she said, sitting back on her elbows and looking at his towering frame.

He lifted his eyebrow but didn't say anything.

Nightmare snapped his fingers, and her dress, petticoats, corset, and shift disappeared off her body, leaving her fully naked before him.

"You could always do that?"

"With you, yes." He prowled toward her, his hands first landing on her ankles.

His fingers danced up her calves, and when he got to her knees, he spread her open and placed a kiss on her inner thigh before moving up to her core and proving just how talented his tongue could be.

It took an embarrassing amount of time for her to fall apart. One of his touches was enough. While she orgasmed, he continued his ministrations, wrenching every spasm from her he could get.

"Oh, gods," she moaned as he slid a finger inside, but just as he did, she tensed and she let out a yelp, her head falling to the pillow.

Jane pinched her eyes shut, hating that he was right. She was defective. She couldn't just be fucked normally. The first time he touched her, she flinched and freaked out, and then the pain started. She wasn't normal, and if he had just pounded into her, like she had wanted, it would have been painful like all the other times.

But she hated that he was right, and he knew her so damn well, and she was such an open book when he was a book in a forgotten language.

"Jane," he growled, and with his free hand, he clutched her chin. "Look at me."

Her eyes flashed open.

"Trust me, Jane. Let go." He moved, curled his finger again inside her, and her walls tensed again. It was so frustrating because she'd been working on this, touching herself so she wouldn't have this problem anymore, and she knew that it had disappeared. "Breathe," he said, placing a kiss on her chin below her ear. "Breathe, and look at me." He moved so that his face hovered before hers. "Breathe, my doe. Breathe and trust me."

So she did; she sucked in a slow, steady breath and slowly let it out; all the while, his gaze held hers.

It didn't make sense. How was this man—this monster—so gentle with her? How did he know what she needed when he didn't even have a heart?

It didn't make sense.

But it was him.

"Good, now keep breathing." He curled his finger again, and this time, her pelvic floor didn't spasm and shoot an intense pain through her body.

This time it—oh, shit. She tilted her head back and grabbed at the sheets because he was caressing a spot that was oh, so.... Oh gods.

She let out a scream, and her body began convulsing in pleasure.

Nightmare stifled the scream with his mouth, plunging his tongue inside; all the while, his talented hands kept going.

But despite his fingers filling her, she felt empty. She needed more. "I need all of you."

Her hands raked down his chest and curled into his belt. "Please."

He pulled his large fingers out of her pussy, and they were dripping with her arousal. He sucked one of them into his mouth, tasting her.

It was the most erotic thing she'd ever seen.

Then, his hands moved to his pants, and he unbuckled them and pulled them off, finally releasing his beautiful, obscenely large cock.

Jane just stared at it, wondering how it would fit.

His hands skated up the insides of her thighs, and he pushed them open. He hovered above her, as if in slow motion, and positioned his cock at her entrance.

He thrust, and she watched the tip slowly enter her. Disappearing inside her. She inhaled sharply and held her breath, waiting for the pain, but it didn't come.

"Breathe, Jane."

She released the breath she was holding and swallowed, waiting for him to move, to go further. But he simply stared at her and caressed her face with the back of a knuckle. "Are you okay?"

She nodded.

"Any pain?"

She shook her head, unable to speak.

"Any words?"

"I uh—no."

"My golden cock has driven you speechless." She nodded again. "Wonderful, let's see how much I make you scream."

Nightmare smiled, and it was beautiful and bright. It wasn't a smile she had ever seen from him in person, but it was much like she had imagined the young Gavriil would give before he met Helene.

Then he moved, thrusting in fully, his knowing eyes locked on her face, watching.

Oh, so slowly, he increased his pace, his velvet thickness sliding and caressing her in ways she didn't know were possible, and she didn't think she needed. All the while, he watched her.

Her fingers dug into the sheets, and her head rolled back, a moan falling from her lips, followed by a scream when his talented hand flicked her clitoris.

Then, they did see how much she could scream. Over and over and over again. Nightmare was both attentive and monstrous, even in his passion and even in his restraint, and Jane was entranced—spellbound, and she didn't want it to end.

She wanted to be in his embrace forever.

She lost count of how many times she came—it had to be a record—and how many times he did too, because almost as soon as they'd finished, he started again as if he, too, wanted it to last forever.

But eventually, she was just too spent, and she passed out, only to wake to him taking care of her and cleaning her up.

Nightmare scooped her up into his arms and carried her to the white clawfoot bathtub, gently placing her in it. Her eyes went half-lidded, and she rested her head on the tub's lip while he cleaned her. His hands traveled over her body once more, but this time, he massaged her. When his hands got to her hair, she moaned.

"You like to be touched here?" he asked in a low, whiskey voice.

Too much. She let out a sound of agreement but didn't open her eyes. Sometime during his aftercare, Jane drifted off to sleep, but she couldn't tell anyone when it happened.

Chapter Twenty-Six

Age 29.

Jane yawned and blinked. His warmth surrounded her, and the world was a haze. Jane ran her hand up something hard, rock-solid yet somehow soft at the same time. Her head was on that same hard surface, and it wasn't until a hand stroked up her back that she realized exactly where she was—and who she was with.

Jane stilled.

Nightmare didn't. He ran a hand into her hair, massaging her scalp. Jane let out a soft sigh, pinching her eyes tight. The way he touched was better than magic. Jane was purring like a cat as he simply continued to run his fingers through her hair. There was nothing better than someone touching her head. It was maybe her favorite place to be touched.

Sex was great, for the first time in her life. It was, but this simple touch afterward was almost too much. Intimate in a way she'd never had before. Her body had been used by many men. Over and over and over again, but none of them had cared to just stroke her, to take care of her after.

"You really do love your hair being touched."

Jane's only answer was another moan.

"If you don't want to be thoroughly fucked, then you are going to need to stop that." For the first time in eight years, his tone was amused, tinged with a smile.

"And what if I do?"

The answer was immediate. He flipped her over onto her back and hovered over her. His gaze watched hers, and Jane's chest rose with her quick, anticipatory breaths. Nightmare leaned all of his weight onto one elbow, and his other large, warm hand ran over her naked breast, down her stomach, and to her folds.

"You're so wet. Already." A smirk lifted on his lips. Jane was fairly certain she hadn't stopped being so since the night before. "Are you ready for me?"

His hard cock pressed against her opening.

"Please."

He thrust inside her. Hard and unforgiving, Jane whimpered at the sensation.

"You're so tight." He moved again and again and again, and it was so good. "You're mine." He pounded harder. No softness.

This time he fucked her hard with no restraint. Halfway through, he flipped her over and took her from behind so that he could wrap her hair into his hand, pulling it taut and controlling her completely, letting her know that he owned her. She was fully his. The intensity was almost too much.

The sex was unforgiving and rough, but it wasn't like the other men. Then, she was as dry as a desert, and the sex was so painful. So rotten. But this? It was as if he were correcting all the other times. Showing her it could be rough and still pleasurable.

Showing her this time, it was different.

When Nightmare flicked a finger over her clitoris, Jane fell apart, having such an intense orgasm that she didn't know what to do with herself. But she didn't need to know. He did. He led and controlled.

He was in charge, and in this, she wanted him to be. The sound of flesh slapping again and again and again was all Jane could focus on other than the pleasure because it was all too much. Jane went over the edge again, and her pussy tensed around his cock even harder. He continued to move through her orgasm until he fell with her, coming inside of her and filling her up with his warmth.

Jane never liked it when a man came inside of her before. She thought it was disgusting, but not with him. She wanted all of him.

Always.

He stilled and pulled out, his weight leaving the bed. Jane leaned down on her elbows before rolling over onto her back and looking up at the ornate wood carvings on the ceiling's trim. When he came back, once more, he pulled her into his arms like she was a weightless doll—and given that he was a vampire, she bet she did feel like lifting a doll to him.

Once again, he walked her to the tub and put her in it, cleaning her up again. This time, she didn't fall asleep. Instead, she watched him show a hint of humanity. A speck of having a soul. And it was fascinating.

"Why do you clean me?"

"You are my bride," he said simply and then cocked his head like he was lost in thought. "If you wish me to stop, all you need to do is ask."

But she wouldn't ask. He knew it. She knew it. Anyone with half a brain would have known it. Nightmare was the villain of the night. But he was also her safety. Jane didn't know when that changed, but it had. He was still utterly awful. The reason she no longer danced. Yet he protected her.

He owned her. Body, soul, and even parts of her heart. But she liked to believe that she owned a couple of pieces of him, too —the only pieces he'd let anyone have.

Nightmare wasn't capable of love, and he never would be. And Jane wasn't quite sure if she was capable of love, either. Nightmare wasn't just a pleasure. She wasn't able to label what he was. He was a selfish creature, but Jane fulfilled one of his needs, and until she held no more value for him, he would keep her safe.

But was that it?

Jane didn't want to think so.

"Nightmare," Jane said slowly, not fully knowing where she was going with it. She brought her knees up to her chest, splashing the water around her body. "Would you let me go? Would you break our bargain and free me?"

His face paled, and his mouth fell into a flat line, and fear laced the edges of his eyes. "I don't want to." There was more he wanted to say, Jane could tell, but he didn't say it. He pinched his mouth shut and almost stared at her pleadingly.

"But would you?" she asked and stopped breathing for a second too long. But she was met with silence, and a dark sadness swirled in his eyes.

He grunted. "You want to leave me?"

"No," she said quickly. "No, I don't."

His silver eyebrows crinkled together. "I don't understand." The words seemed to be hard for him to say.

Jane didn't know what to say. She had gotten her answer. He wasn't willing to let her go. She would forever belong to someone else. So there wasn't much left to say. "I should probably get out and get going. It's my sister's Mirror Rite tonight, and I have Royalle Ballet auditions this morning. I may not be home until very late."

He sat back on his heels, examining her. "Have her bargain with me."

"No, fucking way." She sat up more, moving the water, her fingers curling around the porcelain.

He winced. "You don't trust me?"

Jane swallowed past the lump in her throat. It wasn't that she didn't trust him. She did to a degree. She understood that he would never let her be physically harmed. But he didn't have a heart. He didn't understand emotions, and Jane feared he might accidentally hurt Quinnevere and not mean to, because he so rarely did anything for selfless reasons.

In fact, she'd never seen him do anything for a selfless reason.

The silence dangled between them like a spiderweb. Unsettling yet beautiful in its way.

"You don't." He nodded, and a hint of something flashed across his unreadable features. "I would never do anything to hurt you."

Jane pinched her lips and ripped her gaze from his, instead looking at her bare legs and callousless feet. Feet that no longer belonged to a ballerina. "You already have." Her voice broke. She thought she was over it. She'd thought it no longer affected her. But she was wrong. It felt like her ribcage was being pried open with rusty clamps.

He leaned into the bathtub and tipped up her chin with his thumb. "You said that once before, after your husband's death, but I didn't care to know what it meant." He rubbed his thumb along her jaw. "I wish to know now. I think I would like to know you, too."

He echoed her sentiment from the vampire lair when she had said she wanted to know him.

"I—" he paused and tapped his empty chest. "I remember what it is to care about someone else." He sighed, frustrated. "While I no longer truly have that ability. I would like to try." *For you*. The words lingered in the air between them, unsaid.

Jane's throat bobbed, and she placed her hand on the surface of the water, feeling it and pondering if she should let him have this—if she should let him see her pain. Because this pain was the unbearable kind. She could endure torture and assaults, but showing him how much he'd taken from her felt so much harder.

"You have to command me to tell you," Jane said.

"Why?" His eyes narrowed.

"Just do it."

"I command you to tell me how I have hurt you."

Jane pinched her eyes tight for a moment. "You stole ballet from me." The words were a breath.

"Ballet hurt you. It caused your bruises," he said so earnestly.

Jane scoffed. "You can't truly believe that."

"I believe the words you tell me are true."

Jane shook her head. "Then you're naïve."

"And you lied." His voice was rough, and she thought it was possibly a little hurt.

"The night you killed my husband was not the first night he hit me." She absentmindedly rubbed the phantom marks of her dead husband's fingerprints on her neck. "He would hit me daily if he could. It was a sport to him."

Nightmare snarled. "If I could kill him again, I would do it slower."

Jane pinched her eyes shut for a moment, her held-back emotions bursting at the seams, stinging and painful. "You took away the one thing that brought me happiness in a sea of brokenness."

Then she let him see everything. Six years of pain. No, nineteen years of holding in pain—everything from the moment her parents died. She gave him all of it and, strangely, he held it. Quietly and calmly, he gave her room for all of it.

In a moment of lull, after twenty minutes of just being there with her, he said, "I'm sorry." Only two words. He let her see him, and she believed that, possibly, he might have meant his words. He might actually feel bad about what he had done. "I wish for you to dance. I wish for you to do whatever you would like to do with your body." A command. A magical one. It was the most freedom he'd ever given her... possibly breaking all the commands that came before.

Jane whimpered. Her chest ached with pain and a hint of happiness. She'd longed so long for this—to get her dance back. To be whole again.

"What else do you want... no, what do you need from me, Jane? he asked.

"Let me go," she breathed. "Let me be free."

He dipped his head, nearly hanging it. "I can't."

"Why not?"

"Why do you want this?"

Jane frowned, sinking into the water, allowing it to cup her skin. She ran a finger along the porcelain. "I want space. I want to choose what happens to me for the first time in my life. I want to be free to do whatever it is *I want*."

He lifted his head and leaned over the tub to see her fully. "I left you alone for two years."

"Because you were angry. You withdrew your presence because you were hurt. That wasn't for me, and it hurt me too, Alexei." Her lips fell below the water, and only her nipples peeked out. The chain of the necklace holding her wedding ring floated for a moment between her breasts and then fell between the mounds. She submerged herself fully, closing her eyes and sinking into the heat. When she came back up, she said, "You were still present. I felt your anger like a ghost haunting me, and even in those two years, you still commanded me. I always do what you want. I live at your whims."

Nightmare grazed the water with his fingertips, next to one of her breasts. "You want to be free," he parroted her earlier words.

"Yes." Her body twisted into the water, and she faced him more fully.

"I'll give you five days."

What? Jane sat up, bringing her head out of the water. Was he serious?

Nightmare's silver eyes swirled and sparked. He was serious.

Jane wiggled her nose and bit her bottom lip, narrowing her eyes on him. "Twenty days. Free me from our bargain for twenty days."

"Six."

"Fifteen."

"Eleven."

"Deal." She smiled, water trickling down her forehead, and he glared. "I will come back to you. I promise. But I want you to prove that you can think of what someone else wants besides yourself."

He growled. "I care about what you want."

"I believe that... sometimes."

"Eleven days, but our deal will automatically shift into place again, no matter what happens."

"No matter what," she agreed. "But I want to be fully free, Gavriil. I am going to leave my ring here. I will not be your anchor, and you will not spy on me. You will actually let me have a week outside of your influence and eyes."

"I didn't always spy on you." It seemed important to him that she know that.

"I know, it only started after you killed my first husband."

He grunted. "I will leave you fully alone. It will be like you don't exist to me, as long as you are safe. Drop your investigation and stay out of trouble."

Jane laced her fingers through his. "I promise I will not investigate my parents' murders without you. I just want a week outside of here. A week to think and figure out who I am."

He sucked in an audible breath. "Alright." Then he leaned in and sealed their deal—like their very first one—with a kiss.

The effect was immediate, a cold splintering inside her chest. It felt like someone had pierced their claws through her skin, muscles, and tissues and pulled out a chamber of her heart.

It was awful and empty.

Nightmare gritted his teeth and stood up, removing his hand from hers and turning his back to her, and walking out of the room, his back muscles bunching as he moved.

Jane was hit with the feeling that she had just made a terrible mistake, and an even worse feeling like she should have told him she cared for him, that she loved him—in a way.

She wasn't in love with him, she didn't think, but it was the closest she'd ever come. to a romantic love and now, stupidly, she'd made him think that she didn't want to be with him.

She'd begged him to let her go, and he had essentially begged her to stay. But she believed this was what they needed.

Right?

Jane lifted herself out of the bathtub and placed her dripping feet on the rug covering the tile. Grabbing a towel off a rack, she dried herself off and walked back into their suite.

Nightmare stood with his back to her, fully dressed and tying his cravat.

Jane inhaled sharply and walked to her wardrobe, and as quickly as she could, she dressed for Royalle Ballet practice, which thankfully didn't require a corset. When she was all finished, she unclamped her necklace, curled it into her palm, and walked over to Nightmare, who still had his back to her.

She ran a hand along his lower back before twirling around him with ballerina-like grace. When she reached his front, she cupped his hand with hers and furled the necklace into his palm, closing his fingers around it.

"Gavriil, I—" *love you*. Then, on pointe, she grazed her lips across his, for a soft moment. "I'll be back."

She didn't know then just how wrong she'd been. Jane would never be back... At least not like this.

Not alive.

CHAPTER TWENTY-SEVEN

AGE 29.

Jane didn't know who was more nervous for Quinnevere's Mirror Rite, her or Quinn.

Jane was an utter mess. She had been all day. Earlier at Quinnevere's Royalle Ballet auditions, not only had Jane let it slip that Blood Mirrors existed, but she'd also asked Quinnevere about her necklace.

The last thing Jane needed was for her sister to get wrapped up in the dark underworld of New Swansea City.

And now they were standing in front of the Mirror of Midnight, waiting for Quinnevere to get enough confidence to enter it.

The only problem was that Jane didn't think her sister should make a deal with The Mirror of Midnight—aka Periwinkle.

No one else thought she was dangerous. They all thought Periwinkle to be a harmless, quirky, sad mirror, but Jane knew better. She was the most clever of all the mirrors, and she always had a nefarious scheme up her sleeve. If there were a true puppet master of New Swansea City, it would be the Mirror of Midnight.

So, Jane couldn't let her sister bargain with her.

Quinnevere gulped and clutched her necklace for comfort, taking another step toward the Mirror of Midnight.

She visibly shook and reached out a hand for comfort. Jane instinctively curled her fingers around her sister's, trying to be comforting.

Quinnevere took another step toward the swirling galaxy surface of the Mirror of Midnight. She reached out and touched the liquid nebula, flinching back from the mirror's icy cold

Jane's heart surged. She couldn't let her sister do this. "I think this is a mistake." So, without warning or forethought, Jane wrenched her into the *wrong* mirror.

Into one of the wickedest mirrors in all of New Swansea.

Beautiful Decay.

At least he was a friend. After a tumultuous beginning, Harlowe and he first became lovers and then partners in all ways. Except they weren't married. A true happiness for now.

And because Jane and Harlowe had gotten over their differences and actually become friends in the last two years, Jane had gotten fairly close with Draven Darcy Hawthorne, aka Nightshade, aka Beautiful Decay, and technically Nightmare's first cousin once removed.

Jane's life was rather strange.

Quinnevere sucked in an audible breath and rounded on Jane. "You shouldn't be here. It's my Mirror Rite."

"That's not a real rule," Jane said, grasping Quinn's wrist. "You're going to be fine."

"Fine?" Quinnevere whispered through gritted teeth. "This is Beautiful Decay."

Quinnevere's face blanched as an icy wind ruffled the petals of the flowers surrounding them.

Beautiful Decay's realm was a sunken garden with lily ponds and magic cottages. It was like a fairy wonderland.

"What the fuck was that? Why did you do it?" Quinnevere rubbed her temples.

Jane held up her hands. "I'm sorry, but I couldn't let you

bargain with Midnight. Her bargains cause permanent consequences."

"Are you out of your mind? Beautiful Decay is—" Quinnevere's eyes darted around, realizing the mirror god might
hear her.

Jane wrung her hands. "I know how it seems. Nightshade is
known for cruel bargains, but he's my friend."

"A friend?" Quinnevere's voice pulsed with what sounded like
intrigue and shock.

"Do you trust me?" Jane's tone was a plea.

Quinnevere hesitated, and hope sank like an anchor in Jane's
heart.

"Trust me, he won't hurt or take advantage of you. He only
punishes the bad—the people willing to trade anything for selfish
gains."

"Coming from the person who made a deal with Nightmares,
that's *the* Looking Glass, Jane."

"He's not *as* bad as he seems, either. I wouldn't bring you in
here if I thought you'd be harmed. This is going to be okay, I
promise." Jane paused and bit her lip. "I would never do anything
to hurt you."

Quinnevere gulped. "No, it won't be okay." Frantically, Quinnevere turned on her heel and tried to leave the mirror through
the magical portal door that they had entered through, but just as
she ran toward it, a figure appeared on the path in front of her,
halting her steps.

"Leaving already?" A sinister smirk rose on Darcy's face, and
Jane's eyes lifted to the heavens. He was far too pleased with
himself. "We haven't even started yet. You don't want to ruin all
the fun."

Darcy crossed his arms, his muscles bulging under his white
dress shirt. Jane was surprised he was even wearing a shirt. Inside
his mirror, he often walked shirtless, especially when Harlowe was
around. But tonight, he wore black slacks and a white button-up
shirt with the top three buttons hanging askew, exposing the top

of his chest. He raised a cocky eyebrow, his swirling silver eyes alight with mirth.

"Hello, Quinnevere Ashelle, friend of Jane Whitfield-Wryte and the Daughter of Blood. I've been waiting for you."

"I—" Quinnevere started, but was distracted by her necklace. As were Jane and Darcy, too.

It began to buzz. Inside the iron cage, the shard of glass became a flaring crimson metal that swirled to a smooth rhythm. Jane's jaw dropped. She knew it. She now knew the necklace was a shard of the Blood Mirror that was destroyed the night their parents died. She hadn't realized her sister had stolen a piece but when Jane saw it now, she instantly knew.

It called to her. It sang songs of sorrow and pulled her to it. This Blood Mirror wanted her attention in the same way the second had—in the same way the one had always called to her at the Queen's Royalle Ballet. Now, Jane had found all three Blood Mirrors, but she would never tell another soul.

Their secret was safe with her. Not even death would rip it from her. Jane was excited to meet this one. The final one.

But then, as soon as it started to morph into something else, it froze, reversed, and solidified into a ruby, almost as if something had blocked its magic.

Jane screamed with frustration inside her head. It was going to be her chance to ask the necklace what happened to her mother after she entered the mirror. She'd never been seen again, and Jane needed to know the truth.

"I do not allow other magic in my domain," Dracy said, his tone dark and threatening. Jane narrowed her eyes. It wasn't that he was a soft man. He wasn't, but this seemed like an act. Draven Dracy Hawthorne was a villain, oftentimes worse than Nightmare, but he was also fair, unlike Nightmare.

"Nightshade, stop scaring her." Jane folded her arms.

"Is that your name?" Quinnevere asked.

The side of his lips turned up. "It's one of them." He turned back to Jane. "You will remain silent for the rest of our adventure."

It was a command but not a binding one. Jane smirked. "As you wish, oh terrifying one."

Nightshade glowered, clearly not amused. Jane simply smiled back. Two could play this game.

"Now, you." He angled his head, his gaze devouring Quinn like prey. "You've come here to avoid getting bad luck, so what do you want?"

"How do you know that?"

"I am a god, little ballerina. The things I know would rattle your bones and rip apart your heart."

"I think I should leave now."

A muscle in his jaw feathered. "If you leave now, you will incur the seven years of bad luck, and you and I both know that you wouldn't make it into the ballet if that happened."

"Okay, then." Quinnevere paused, her hands trembling, but she tried to cover it up with determination. "What do you offer?"

"What do you want?"

"Aren't you going to offer to make my dreams come true? To give me unending beauty or eyes that make everyone fall in love with me, or a life filled with no pain, or wealth that won't dry up or magic or something?"

A wicked sneer climbed up his face. "I could give you all those things, but why would I offer you any of that when I know you wouldn't accept it?" He cracked his neck almost as if irritated with how much of his time she was wasting. "You've come here, so what do *you* want?"

Quinnevere sucked in a visible breath. "Is Jane truly your friend?"

"Yes."

"She pulled me in here so I wouldn't face horrible consequences."

Jane opened her mouth to respond, but Darcy narrowed his eyes at her, and she closed her mouth.

"Interesting. That would depend on how well you can bargain." Darcy's tone was like a dark, smooth whiskey. "What is it you want?"

After a long, long pause, where thoughts flashed across Quinnevere's face like a silent picture show, she finally said, "I want to have an emotional expression in my dancing, but I am not willing to pay the cost and the consequences for that."

She crossed her arms protectively over her chest.

Darcy rubbed his chin. "Here is the only deal I will offer you. I will give you the ability to express emotion in dance. I will give you such incredible artistry that no one can look away—if, and only if, you passionately kiss the prince you despise so much."

"Nightshade, what are you doing?" Jane cut in, her eyebrows crinkling. He was fucking ridiculous. Was he punishing Jane for bringing her sister in here? Darcy knew she wanted the prince as far away from her sister as possible.

"Quiet, Red," the god growled.

Jane threw her hands up in mock surrender but said under her breath, "I thought you two had settled your issues."

"Anyway, Quinnevere," Darcy's voice was rough, "kiss the prince with passion, and I will give you everything you want."

"I can't kiss Emrys," Quinnevere gasped out.

"And yet, it is the only deal I will make with you." His grin sharpened like the edge of a dagger. "Take the deal or receive seven years of bad luck."

"Why would you ask this of me?" Quinnevere shivered. "What do you get out of it?"

"Torture." A sneer twinkled in Darcy's eyes. "I know you hate him above all others for making you look like a fool to your medical superiors. I want torture for you and possibly a fun show for me. I think you may enjoy it, though, my sweet, innocent Quinnevere Ashelle."

"And if I fail your task?" Quinnevere stuttered, her voice quivering. "What happens then?"

"If you fail, you don't reap the rewards of our deal."

"And the consequences?"

"Kiss him passionately, and I won't give you any—"

"Nope," Jane interrupted, "this is where I step in. He can't promise you that because it is not the Mirror Gods who determine mirror consequences." Jane learned long ago that it was the magic's choice. And magic often acted like an unruly teenager, doing whatever the fuck it wanted.

Jane's magic was very rarely helpful without begging or bargaining. But in this particular case, it was Harlowe who had confirmed Jane's suspicions that the Mirror Gods weren't fully in control of their deals.

Darcy rounded on Jane. "For the love of all the gods. Stop giving our secrets away. The Looking Glass should know better than that."

Jane scoffed. "While he has told me that, it was your lover who told me that first. If you want your secrets kept, speak with Lowe about them."

"Who determines the consequences?"

"The magic," Jane said, "whatever force exists beyond us, that is greater than the mirrors. The cost is upfront. It is determined during the deal by the god." She pointed with her thumb at Darcy. "The consequences are unknown. It is possible to get none or horrible ones."

"So, how do I avoid having horrible consequences, or even just visible ones like Harlowe Merriwether?"

At the mention of Harlowe's name, Darcy's eyes darkened, but it was Jane who cut in, "A lot of her consequences were actually costs that she knew about before making her deal, and she trades for powerful magic. That always carries harsher consequences." Jane touched the god's arm, calming him. "What Nightshade is offering won't carry that kind of consequence."

"Will you stop helping her now?" Darcy pulled out of Jane's grip.

"She's family to me," Jane said. "You know better than anyone else. We *always* help family."

"Fine." Darcy gritted his teeth. "Back to your deal. Do you have any questions before you accept it, which we all know will happen?"

"I could leave and not make any deal at all."

"Then you would get the bad luck," he said. "I know stubbornness is a trait of redheaded ballerinas, but if we could just get this done, I have places to be."

"Stuck inside a mirror?"

"You've seen my realm." He motioned to everything around them. "Maybe I want to frolic through the fields."

Quinnevere glared at him and crossed her arms. "What if I can't kiss the prince with passion?"

"Then I assume it will be very disappointing kiss."

Jane snorted, and both the god and Quinnevere flashed her a glare. Emrys would never allow that to happen, which was the problem with this deal. He would get his claws into Quinnevere, and she'd never be able to get them out. The last thing Jane needed was Emrys breaking his sister's heart, but in the scheme of deals, this one was fairly innocuous.

Quinnevere thought on the terms for a very long time before she inhaled sharply and seemed to decide. She nodded and said, "I accept your deal."

"Wonderful." He clapped his hands. "Oh, and remember, dearest Quinnevere, if you don't at least *try* to kiss Emrys, you will receive seven years of bad luck. And trust me, your life is about to fall apart, and you probably won't survive it even with good luck."

CHAPTER TWENTY-EIGHT

Jane sat quietly in the corner of the cable car, her fingernails digging into the wood, her eyes gazing off to the distance of the city. They were riding from the Spirit Sector to the Pleasure District to get to the Viridian so Quinnevere could finish her bargain, and Jane had another Gilded Alliance meeting.

The first one without Nightmare. It would be interesting, to say the least.

While Jane's mind wandered, her sister and friends were discussing vampires and various ways to die. But Jane's mind was focused on Quinnevere's Blood Mirror shard.

She was the only person alive who knew the location of all three Blood Mirrors—the location of every vampire in New Swansea City's greatest weakness and the only way to kill them. People would kill for that information, including some of her closest friends like Emrys. But more than any of that, Jane wanted to speak to the third Blood Mirror. It might be the only creature alive that knew what happened to her mother.

But how to manage that?

Quinnevere never took off her necklace. Jane knew because

she'd been drawn to it since the moment she saw it, and there was not a day that her sister didn't have it around her neck. So, how would she get to it?

The truth was not an option.

Could she drug her sister?

That sounded awful.

Fuck.

Jane was wrenched out of her rumination when Constance said, "Quinnevere, your necklace is... glowing."

A glowing red light reflected in Quinnevere's green eyes. Jane sucked her lip into her mouth, entranced. Inside its iron casing, the shard of mirror liquified into a flaring crimson metal that swirled to a slow melody.

At that exact moment, a high-pitched scream sounded from beside them—trapped Souls Row. They were Mirror Echoes as Nightmare called them, but also one of the barriers between everyone and finding the Third Blood Mirror.

The Mirrors were talking to each other.

Jane felt it on the air like a conversation. No longer focusing on her actions, Jane reached out and wrapped her hand around Quinnevere's necklace. Instinctively, she knew it wanted to talk to her too.

And it did.

Time froze. Her friends were statues, and the lights bent like an abstract painting, blurring and swirling together in a beautiful dance. Sound stilled, and an icy chill skated over her arms. The sound returned first, and it was a haunting soprano she'd never forget and had heard in countless night terrors.

"Darling Janey, you must stop." The necklace spoke with her mother's voice.

Shock rattled through Jane's bones. "Mom?" Jane whispered, a tear leaking down her face.

"Yes, my Jane," her mother said softly. "You need to drop your investigation. You are getting too close to things that are too dangerous to unearth."

"Mom?" Jane's nose flared.

The glass in her hand heated as what might be Jane's mother spoke another unsettling warning. "You are going to die. You must leave all of this now..."

Jane opened her mouth to respond and ask a million questions, but she never got the opportunity because time snapped back into place, and the glass flamed, searing her skin. This was a final warning.

She jumped backward and nearly fell off the cable car, but Constance caught her, keeping her from falling out of the moving vehicle.

"It burnt me," Jane breathed, and staring at a coin-sized burn in the center of her palm. "So it's true." Was it truly her mother? It was definitely a Blood Mirror, and it was the last place she was seen. Jane knew better than anyone that humans could live inside the glass.

Was her mother trapped? Jane needed to find out. There was no way she would drop anything now. She would simply have to find a way to incapacitate her sister or distract her enough to get her hands on that shard again.

"What's true?" Quinnevere asked, protectively pulling away from Jane.

Jane blinked, and her hand fell into her lap. "What?" she asked as if coming out of a daze.

"You said 'it's true' while staring at my necklace." Quinnevere gripped the jewelry in between her fingers, the lattice cage digging into her flesh.

Jane bit her lip, and instead of answering the question, she said, "Did you get the mirror shard when your parents died?"

Quinn's fingers tightened further around the necklace as she contemplated the question. "I—" she started. She blew out a breath. "Yes."

Jane didn't quite listen to the conversation after that. It was all the information she needed to know. One of the city's greatest secrets was also her mother's prison, and Jane would figure out how to get her hands on it again.

～

The Viridian's grand ballroom pulsed with dread. It was all around her—in the air, sizzling like flame. Jane couldn't put her finger on it, but ever since she'd discovered the vampire lair, she'd felt a sick feeling tingling at the back of her spine.

Ever since gaining witch magic, Jane sensed things. Periwinkle had even called her a seer, despite the fact that Jane never saw anything. But sometimes, she just *felt* things—knowings. These "feelings" were part of the reason Jane had intervened in Quinnevere's Mirror-Rite earlier. She simply felt that she had to, so she did.

And right now, something felt off.

The problem was that she had no idea what it could be. Quinnevere's Mirror Rite? Les Fantômes business? The Gilded Alliance meeting?

Emrys had called the meeting because he had somehow discovered some information that he needed to address immediately. The man had ears in the walls, he found out everything.

The meeting was to take place after the cabaret's opening number, so Jane still had time to find her sister and give her a birthday present. But she had to hurry.

Glancing through the horde of people, she looked for the glint of fiery hair, and when she finally spotted it, her stomach twisted.

Jane glared through the crowd, her gaze latched on fucking Emrys Avalon, who was once more flirting with her sister. Jane was going to castrate him. And he didn't even have the decency to be alone while doing it. He had that vampire bitch Teagan Atwater dangling off one arm, and Nia Cross—Jane's replacement as the prima ballerina of the Queen's Royalle Ballet—on the other arm.

The cad.

As a business partner and friend, Jane rather enjoyed Emrys, but as a suitor for her sister, she was less enthusiastic.

This was bad.

Worse, Darcy was forcing them to kiss. What in all the hells? Jane trusted Darcy, mostly because she trusted Harlowe, but this was ridiculous. If Quinnevere followed through with the deal and passionately kissed Emrys, he would fuck her—because he couldn't help himself—and then he would toss her away like all his other girls, and it would destroy Quinnevere.

It was a disaster waiting to happen.

"Oh, Jane, there you are," Giselle said, grasping onto her arm and pulling her through the crowd. "I found us a spot to watch."

"What about Quinnevere?" Jane asked, pointing in her sister's direction.

Giselle glanced for a second at Quinnevere and Emrys before tossing her hair and continuing on her path. "Isn't the point for her to kiss him?"

Well fuck. Jane let Giselle lead her to a ledge overlooking the crowd and the stage. It even gave a better view of Quinnevere and the soon-to-be-murdered Vampire King.

But Quinnevere didn't pull Emrys aside to seduce him. Instead, she scurried away like a rat on a sinking ship before quickly finding their ledge just in time for the show to start.

The lights grew dim, and the dance floor cleared of patrons. With a loud pop and an explosion of blue fire, the show began, and dancers glided in, feathers grazing the floor. They ran in with quick steps and high kicks, exposing as much of their petticoats as possible.

It wasn't surprising because the club was made as a vessel of seduction—everything about the place catered to dark desires.

And the dancers embodied it. They became seduction itself. It could be a good teaching moment for Quinnevere, who was still incapable of showing anyone her emotions.

"Do you see their emotional expression?" Jane leaned into Quinnevere and pointed at the dancers.

Quinnevere rubbed her palms together nervously. "Yes."

Jane squeezed Quinnevere's hand empathetically, knowing the depths of the struggle. Quinnevere was too young when their parents died to remember the horrors of it—she didn't even remember having a sister—but Jane was fairly certain Quinnevere's inability to feel anything outwardly stemmed directly from witnessing the bloodbath. Jane had her own scars from that night. Different, but just as dark.

"As dancers, we are also actors. And to act, we need to have access to emotion—either true or imagined."

Quinnevere let out a breath. "But that's the problem. I can't do that."

Jane smiled kindly. "Yes, you can. In the four years I've mentored you, I've seen you connect with your emotions on numerous occasions. You can do it. You just don't *want* to."

Quinnevere bit her bottom lip as a storm of thoughts played in her eyes. Jane wanted to pull her into her arms and tell her everything would be okay—tell her everything and help her process through her past, but she just couldn't get herself to do it.

What if, when Quinnevere discovered the truth, she didn't want anything to do with Jane?

Jane could withstand anything in her life except losing her sister—again. Once was enough. So, she lied to, and withheld from, the one person she loved more than anything else.

"If it helps, pretend to be a different person with a different past," Jane said. "Sometimes, letting go can be the very thing you need."

Quinnevere sighed and fiddled with her fingernails, watching the dancing.

I love you so much. Emotion pooled behind Jane's cheeks, and she did everything she could to hold it in. *I think you're perfect, baby Quinnevere.*

Jane pulled a small box from her pocket behind the bustle of her dress. "I got you a present." It was a bracelet with a single charm on it. A gold ballet pointe shoe with a heart inside. But not a cute heart that a schoolgirl would dot an "i" with; a human heart, the organ, cradled in a pointe shoe.

Quinnevere told the world she didn't want to be a medical examiner, but Jane sometimes stalked her sister, made so much easier with being a Wind Witch, and she saw the way her sister lit up when she had her hands deep in a corpse.

Ten years ago, Jane would have found it creepy and revolting. But that was before she'd watched Nightmare slaughter hundreds of people and helped the Fantômes with their more nefarious adventures.

Now, blood, guts, and dead bodies were just a Tuesday to her.

Jane rubbed a wrinkle in her skirt. "I know ballet is your dream, but I also know, deep down, you love carving up dead bodies. You love being smarter than everyone else, and there is a world in which you can have both of your passions."

"They aren't both my passions."

"Sure, sure." Jane suppressed a smile. "One day—" A flash of something in the crowd caught Jane's eye. Her brow furrowed.

Was that one of the vampires Nightmare had beheaded a few weeks ago? Of course, Jane knew they couldn't die without destroying their Blood Paintings, but they'd all gone missing since she found their lair.

Were they looking for her?

That could be a massive problem because, foolishly, she'd forced Nightmare into a deal to leave her alone and taken off his ring. She wanted him to prove he had self-control—prove that, for once, he could put her needs above his. But the deal left her vulnerable. If they were here for her, she needed backup. Thankfully, François was in the club for the Gilded Alliance meeting. She'd just stick close to his side.

"I have to... go. There's a meeting..." Jane jumped down from her perch and misjudged the distance, stumbling and falling.

Before anyone could help her, she sprang back up and disappeared into the crowd.

Ever since Jane got her dancing ability back, she'd been far more agile—like a ballerina again. It only took her two minutes to get through the crowd and find the alcove where the meeting was to take place, but François hadn't arrived yet. Only Nightshade—Darcy—greeted her.

"Hello again, Red." A wicked smile climbed his sculpted face. "You think your sister has tried to kiss her prince yet?"

Jane shook her head and crossed her arms. "Why in all the hells would you make that deal?"

"Besides the entertainment?"

Jane rolled her eyes.

"I want to see Emrys suffer. Whether that's from you cutting off his balls for daring to touch your sister, or him trying and failing not to touch her."

"So you set her up to fail?"

His smirk widened. "Oh, no. Emrys won't be able to resist her. She is his poison, and that's what makes it beautiful"

"I thought you were over your grudge."

"He murdered me." His eyes darkened. "I may be forced to work with him and not kill him because of Harlowe, but I will always hate him."

"The feeling is mutual," Emrys said, pulling back the curtain and strolling through.

Chapter Twenty-Nine

Age 29.

"Where is your Nightmare?" Emrys asked, gesturing at Jane, who was clearly sitting alone.

"Off doing Nightmare things." She shrugged.

Emrys groaned. "Please don't tell me he is off killing people and I am going to have to clean up his mess... Again."

Jane didn't know. She'd asked him to prove that he could let her make her own choices without interference until after the Winter's Eve Ball. She asked for her freedom to do whatever she wanted for eleven days: no deals, no spying, no anchors.

"Most likely not. He's 'stuck' in his mirror."

"Well, that's a blessing." Emrys smiled with brightness and mirth.

It wasn't. But Jane didn't say anything else.

The next one to enter the room was Periwinkle, her bubblegum-pink hair bouncing with her footfalls.

Goosebumps rose on Jane's flesh. The Mirror of Midnight always freaked her out. She talked in riddles and code and was far too clever for her own good. Jane was glad she had forced her sister to bargain with Beautiful Decay instead.

He was at the very least stable, or stable enough, and more so since Harlow had entered his life.

Speaking of the now white-haired woman, she was the next to enter the alcove with François on her heels. When her eyes fell on Periwinkle, she winced but tried to hide it under a smile.

Harlowe and Jane agreed that the pink-haired Mirror God was not to be trifled with.

"Aww, sister," Periwinkle's voice was coated with cherry-sweet candy—"it's so good to see you again. My irritating baby brother here likes to keep you from me."

"We like to keep everyone from you," Darcy said under his breath.

Periwinkle heard the comment, wiggled her nose, and winked at him. "Ah, yes, very prudent of you twinny."

Draven Darcy Hawthorne and Periwinkle—no one, save her brother, knew her real name—Hawthorne were ancient fraternal twins. Born over two thousand years ago.

"Shall we get started then?" Emrys said.

"By all means." Darcy glared at him.

Jane cleared her throat to break the tension, and Harlowe slipped her fingers around her lover's arm, calming him.

"If Nightmare were here, he'd want you to know that the tremors from the Nature district are getting stronge—"

"As important as that topic is," Emrys cut in very much, meaning the opposite of his words. "I'd rather discuss the rumor that you found the second Blood Mirror."

"How did you hear that?" Jane asked.

"So you aren't denying it." He shook his head as if disappointed, and a bit betrayed.

"How do you know?" Jane asked again, worry digging its claws into her back. No one save Nightmare should know, so the fact that he did was very bad. And more so, very dangerous:

"Oh, I might have let it slip," Periwinkle said brightly.

Jane's brow furrowed. "And how do you know..." She trailed off. "Oh, never mind, you're... you." Periwinkle was the keeper of knowledge. Of course, she would know almost everything.

"Creepy," Harlowe said under her breath. Then she cursed and said, "Oh, for fuck's sa—" and blinked out of existence, the last part of her sentence eaten by the wind. Every hour, for seven minutes at a time, Harlowe would randomly disappear. No one could see her or hear her. It was one of her very infamous mirror consequences. And while that consequence was a curse, it was often a blessing in disguise because, for those seven minutes, she could do anything without being noticed. Including breaking into things without setting off alarms. A valuable skill set in the Mirror Mafia.

"Ah, brilliant idea. I, too, shall disappear." Periwinkle clapped her hands together excitedly. "The walls have ears, so it's best to avoid their eyes, too." Then, with what had to be wind magic, she popped out of sight.

She must have guessed Jane's thoughts because, at her right, the other girl whispered into her ear. "Yes, I am a Wind Witch too. Technically, I am a Wood Witch, too, but I expect you to be all five types one day. When one goes through death and fire, one can be reformed. You know?"

Jane shivered. No, she definitely did not know. Jane didn't get time to think about what that could mean because Emrys broke through, stepping toward her and growling like Nightmare often liked to do.

He boxed her in, his demeanor dark. If he were a color, he would be empty black.

"You have to tell me where it is," Emrys Avalon said fiercely to Jane, nearly shaking her. "We need to know; it's life and death."

"I can't tell you." Jane folded her arms and stood her ground.

A glow from the wall sconce flickered in Darcy's silver-ringed eyes. "But you do know where it is?"

Jane's gaze jolted to his, and she said, "Shouldn't you already know exactly where it is?"

"It doesn't work that way," Darcy said, cocking his head. "Peri might be able to find it, but she's more talented with knowledge than I am."

"Then ask Periwinkle, not me." Jane pointed to the space around her. *She's right there. Probably.*

"This isn't a game, Jane," Emrys snarled. "I need to know where it is."

"No one should ever know where it is," Jane crossed her arms, "it's too dangerous—and so are you."

Just as Jane said it, a floorboard at the alcove's entrance squeaked, and everyone's gaze shifted in that direction.

Quinnevere.

The walls have ears. Periwinkle knew she was listening. God, the mirror was creepy.

Quinnevere stood at the entrance, all color leeching from her face. She shifted and slowly stepped deep into the shadows, but it was too late; the room had already seen the girl, and when she realized it, she let out numerous curses. "Fucking, filthy, nasty mirrors. Well, fuck."

Jane chuckled to herself. Her sister was adorable when she cursed.

"Hello, Ginger." Emrys's smile was wicked but not disturbed. He clearly didn't care that she was listening. Instead, he walked toward her as if she were prey.

Jane did not like the way he looked at her, like he wanted to devour her whole.

"I am sorry..." Quinnevere sputtered. "I didn't hear anything."

"You are a terrible liar." Emrys's eyes sparkled with amusement and mischief, and his mouth curved further with sinister delight. "It's okay. We weren't talking about much of interest. You should just forget about it." His voice was laced with sugar.

Nope. It was too much. He would not compel Quinnevere. Not when Jane was around to see it. Or ever.

Jane rushed up, grabbed the prince, and harshly said, "No. Don't you dare!"

The prince's lips turned into a hard line. "As you wish." He waved his hand, and the enchantment he was spinning unraveled.

She needed to get her sister as far away from these fucking vampires and Mirror Gods as possible. Jane glanced back at Darcy. "Remember, Darcy, hurt her, and I'll hurt you."

"You're worse than my paramour, Harlowe." Darcy rolled his eyes. "Besides, what's done is done. It is her actions that will decide her fate."

"And yours, it would seem." Jane stepped forward, laced her arm through Quinnevere's, and guided her away from the scene and back into the Viridian grand ballroom.

One crisis semi-averted.

At least it was until Quinnevere said. "Wait." She pulled out of Jane's grip. "You are going to tell me what that was about later, but first, I have the Mirror Rite to complete." Before Jane could stop her, Quinnevere turned and strode back to the alcoves.

Jane rubbed her face and let out a long-suffering sigh.

"That rough of a night, huh?" François strolled beside her and slid his hands into his pockets as he leaned against the wall.

Jane pinched her nose. "It's been rather interesting."

"I've found that most nights are, with this gang of misfits—especially the godly ones."

Jane nodded, and the hairs at her nape stood up. A sickening and terrible feeling suddenly hit her. It was like when the mirrors called to her, but far more sinister. It was her intuition, a kind of magic, warning her of something, giving her foresight. And at that moment, she knew what she had to do. "François, will you do a favor for me?"

"I would say anything, but I have long since learned not to make that promise to anyone." He slid his glasses up his nose with his middle finger.

"If I die, will you deliver these letters for me?" Jane pulled out four folded and sealed letters from the pocket behind the bustle of her dress.

François leaned back into the wall, bending a knee and placing his perfectly shined shoe against the wallpaper as he examined his friend. "Are you planning to die?"

"Of course not..." *But I just have a feeling.* So much so that she had picked up the letters she had written after the sinking of the Titan steamship and placed them in her dress.

François reached out and took the letters, combing through the envelopes. "What, I don't get one?"

"Do you need one?"

He shrugged.

"If I wrote you a letter, it would say, "Be nicer, and smile more—and not like you want to rip someone's head off—but you don't need that reminder since I tell you that daily."

"Like this?" A mocking smile lifted on his cheeks. "But yes, you are the bane of my existence."

"Precisely... " Jane smiled warmly back at him. "Although if I had written you a letter, I probably also should have warned you that a girl from your past is plotting against you."

"Jane?" He raised a well-manicured eyebrow. "Is this something I should be concerned about?"

"If I thought she was dangerous, I'd let you know. And honestly, with this one, you kind of have coming."

"Jane..."

Jane clicked her tongue. "Perhaps you might even enjoy it."

"Jane?"

"Oh, and one more thing,"—she completely ignored him—"if I die, there are casefiles and autopsy reports in the Mirror of Terror. I would like you to return them to the morgue."

The Mirror of Terror was where the Mirror Mafia kept all of their secrets. Jane had moved the reports there in the morning because, although she agreed not to investigate during the eleven days, she still wanted access to them without going back to the Looking Glass—and Nightmare's realm.

His eyebrows went from slightly amused to terribly concerned. "Is there something you're not telling me?"

"No, I just have a bad feeling." She rubbed her chest, a trickle of fear climbing her ribcage like a spider weaving its web. Her magic's inklings were never wrong. "Anyway, you should go enjoy the night. You don't have to be patrolling a casino floor or overseeing a light maiming."

"Hilarious," he said, starting to walk away. "Are you not joining?"

"I will, but first I need to eavesdrop on the prince and my sister."

The side of François's mouth twitched. "Now, that is dangerous."

Jane sighed. "Yes, it is."

François's expensive shoes clicked as he strolled away from the alcove.

"Oh, one more thing," she called after him. "Stay away from fiery brunettes tonight. Just trust me."

He laughed. "Will do."

Jane scrunched her nose as she turned back toward the alcoves. The last thing she wanted to do was watch or listen to her sister kissing the Playboy Prince, but Jane needed to make sure her sister's bargain was successful.

But gods, she did not want to overhear any of it, and it wasn't like there was much she could do.

"Are we snooping?" Periwinkle said in a fairy-sweet tone, popping out of thin air. Jane jolted and nearly came out of her skin. "I do love snooping."

"We are not snooping."

"It certainly looks like we are." Periwinkle tapped her nose. "Is it a redhead thing to lie about eavesdropping? Or an Ashelle thing? Maybe it's an Ashelle fated ballerina thing. Hmmm, one may never know."

"Fated?"

"One shall die while the other blossoms, but time shall tell if they are possums." Periwinkle paused and scratched her head. "No. That's not right. Not possums. Hmm, well, I don't remember the rest of the prophecy. It's something, something, save the world. Shatter ceilings... no, not ceilings. Red, rose, murder, fun. Life, death, and as bright as the sun? Well, it's along those lines. Do you understand?"

No, none of Periwinkle's word salad made sense.

"Ah, I see you do not. Alas, one day you shall." Periwinkle flicked Jane's nose and skipped off into the club, a wave of pink curls bouncing as she went.

Jane touched a hand to her heart and let out a little gasp she'd been holding in. The god was sometimes a little too much for Jane to handle, and what she had just said, at the very least, was confusing and, at the most, quite terrifying.

And Jane didn't want to think about any of it.

She just wanted one night of fun. One night for herself. For once.

So she allowed herself to be swept up in the jubilance of the night, celebrating her sister's birthday. All of her closest friends were there: Constance, Jevon, Giselle, and Quinn, as well as the infuriatingly charming Prince with eyes for her sister, and her boss, François. They all handed her a drink at one point during the night. Causing her to be far too lubricated with spirits.

Darcy and Harlowe had left. Something about a mission across the sea: apparently, they were leaving on a steamship in the morning to be gone for seventeen days.

But they weren't very fun anyway. Darcy could be, but Harlowe's personality was formed from razor blades and sour candies. The festivities would probably be better without them.

Regrettably, Jane might have been allowing herself to imbibe just a bit too much, as all her friends were handing her drinks and contributing to her poor decisions.

She found herself lured to and trapped in a quiet section of the club by a man she'd thought was a friend.

Her feet were too unsteady and her vision just a bit too hazy. But she could see the danger.

And fortune was not on her side, for Death was on the prowl, and nameless monsters lingered in the dark.

Chapter Thirty

"Gideon, I presume?" Jane said, eyes darting around the small room as ten vampires penned her in. Her legs felt like jelly, and her mind was hazy and unfocused, but she tried as hard as she could to stay standing and strong.

But she'd been drugged.

She had to have been.

She wanted to call on Nightmare, but she couldn't. She'd severed their bond and broken it at maybe the worst possible moment.

One of the vampires had a malicious and hungry smile on his face—the ringleader from the vampire lair. He wanted to devour her like a snake eyeing its prey, getting ready to pounce.

Jane had been betrayed by one of her closest friends, but with her mind in an utter state of fog, she couldn't grasp and hold onto their name. The drugs were taking bits of her. But she knew the man who stood before her was her friend. And the worst bit was that she never imagined Gideon would end up being close to her —would end up being someone she'd trusted so deeply.

It was unclear why her mind couldn't grasp any names, save the one who murdered her parents. Maybe it was a sick trick of the drugs.

But here, her parents' killer stood with his hands in his pockets, a sickening smile twisted on his face.

As he chuckled, his face morphed from what she knew to something else—into the man from her nightmares with dusty red hair, freckles, and hazel eyes—confirming her thoughts. This was indeed the true Gideon. He was still attractive with his true face, maybe even more so, but no kindness remained.

"You flew too close to the sun, my dear, and now you have discovered too much," Gideon said, his once beautiful face twisting into horrors—and not the kind she cherished. "And you know the location of an object I very much want to possess."

Jane took a hesitant step back, but the ringleader vampire was there just as she did, and she knocked into his sturdy, muscular chest. "Not so fast, little mouse," he whispered, his voice vibrating against her ginger hair. "My food isn't getting away from me this time."

Jane's knees wobbled, and she pulled at her magic as if she were ripping out her hair. But it, too, was unsteady. It, too, was drugged.

Fuck.

"Compel her to tell me where the second Blood Mirror is," Gideon told her captor.

"What?" she spat. "You can't do it yourself?"

"You know why I can't, Jane." He raised a manicured brow.

The ringleader vampire whirled her around and cupped her face between her hands. His gaze was evil, but his hold on her body wasn't nearly as harsh as she'd expected it to be.

Jane sucked in a breath, desperately trying to get ahold of her magic. But it was like training to lift an ancient statue in the Gilded Museum all by herself.

With his sharp, retractable claw, the vampire pricked her jaw, and blood bubbled out before he dipped his fingernail into it and placed the blood on her tongue.

"Where is the second Blood Mirror?" His jaw tightened after the words, and he clamped down so hard that she heard his teeth rock together.

Jane pinched her lips shut. She would not tell. She'd die before allowing that information to slip. She expected to feel the familiar tug of compulsion, the undeniable hold, but it didn't come.

Nothing—absolutely nothing—happened.

"Hmm, compulsion doesn't work on Nightmare's whore." Gideon's atrocious smile widened even further. "Good to know." Gideon took two steps forward and clutched her jaw tightly as the ringleader held her shoulders tightly. "Tell me where the mirrors are."

"No."

"Tell me, Jane." He squeezed her face harder.

"I will never tell you. You'll have to kill me."

"That can be arranged," Gideon snarled, holding his hand out to another vampire, who handed him a dagger by the hilt. "But first, I think I'll try to torture it out of you."

He slowly took the blade out of its sheath and held it in front of Jane. Showing all the angles of the blade. "Hold her tight."

She felt the vampire behind her nod in agreement just before Gideon slammed the knife into her stomach. At first, it felt like only a punch, a brutal force hitting her stomach, and it wasn't until Gideon twisted that pain spiked through her. Horrific pain.

Her knees buckled, and a whimper escaped her lips.

The ringleader held her up, steadying her body. Into her ear, he whispered, "Hold true." Jane didn't know what he meant by that, but he pulled her tighter into his chest. "You're okay. It's just pain."

His hand slid from her shoulder into her hair and cupped her nape, nearly massaging her head as he went.

The ringleader was trying to comfort her.

"Where are they?" Gideon asked again, sliding the knife out and plunging it back in again and again to different parts of her torso.

Jane let out a cry, and her knees could no longer hold her. Instead of trying to hold her up, the ringleader let her fall to the floor, but he went with her, holding her tight, almost as if cradling her.

"Why?" she whispered so only the vampires could hear her.

His lips touched her ear. "Most of us don't have a choice. He holds our Blood Paintings."

A vampire's only weakness. The objects the Blood Mirrors held. The reason Jane would never tell another soul where the mirrors were. If someone got their hands on a vampire's Blood Painting, they would control them as thoroughly as Nightmare had controlled her.

"You can fight this, Jane," he breathed into her neck. "Fight this, you're a fucking Wind Witch. An Ashelle prophesied to save the world. Fight him."

Jane pinched her eyes shut and tried to call upon her magic. It was hard, but it tried to fight, to budge the statue, and it worked — rocking just a little bit, as she called it.

But it wasn't enough.

Her head drooped, and she coughed, blood coming out of her mouth.

Gideon knelt and lifted her chin, softly saying, "This can all end if you tell me where those mirrors are."

Jane gritted her teeth, the taste of blood lingering in her mouth. "No."

"You are strong, but you won't always be." Gideon touched her forehead with the heel of his hand, and a rush of magic followed through her, mending all her wounds and healing her.

He was healing her.

In doing so, he also decreased the barrier between her and her magic. He was giving her the means to fight.

Jane closed her eyes and let the healing soak through her. All the while, she sang to her magic, seducing it and calling its name, humming the tune of its favorite colors.

When the healing peaked, Jane opened her eyes, looked directly into Gideon's azure eyes, and stole all the oxygen from the room—this time from all the vampires' lungs, too.

They collectively fell to their knees, like birds hit by buckshot and falling out of the sky. They clutched their throats, drowning in the lack of oxygen.

With his last breath, her ally vampire croaked. "Good, fig—" before slumping to the side behind her.

Gideon cackled and clapped his hands, the knife still in his hand. "Oh, spectacular job. Unfortunately, that trick won't work on me."

Without warning, he slammed the knife once more into her lower belly and pulled it upward, ripping her open nearly seven inches. A pain more horrific than anything she'd ever felt before tore through her. Agony dripped through her blood. He pulled the knife out, dropped it on the floor, then from his pocket, he pulled out a pill and shoved it into her mouth and forced her to swallow.

The pill was slightly sweet and nutty. "No," she whimpered. *Not Mirror-Poppy.*

Jane's hold on her magic slipped, and air filled the room once more.

"I'll ask once more. Where are they?"

"I will never give in to you."

He laughed. "You know, I believe that." He slid a hand slowly over her breast, giving it a tight squeeze as he traveled slowly, moving down to her stomach and hovering over the wound.

Healing once more spilled through her skin and muscles, but this time, it was far more isolated, only to the wound. Healing just her stab wound, but not the drugs he put into her system.

Jane reached out and tried to grab him, only managing to hit his pocket square and pull out a purple feather.

Gideon motioned with his chin at the vampire behind her as if saying, *Do your job*. The vampire complied and held her once more.

"Luckily for me," Gideon's words trilled off his tongue. "You have a sister with your same Witch abilities—albeit more dormant. And she's always been far more amenable to me, even when she doesn't want to be."

"No. Do not dare—"

"Maybe I'll seduce her and stick my cock inside her. She seemed so needy tonight. I'm sure she'll tell me where the mirrors are as she screams my name with pleasure."

"If you touch her—"

"What are you going to do, Sweetling? You'll be dead. Are you going to haunt me?"

"I won't need to haunt you. Nightmare will do that."

He laughed maniacally. "What fun I can have with my nightmares."

"You have no idea the horror you've just brought upon your-self with this." Jane's words began to slur as the drugs hit her system. She didn't have much time left with her rational mind. "He will come for you."

"No, he won't." Gideon's smile was a noose wrapping around her neck. "He can't. He made me, and I ensured he'd never be able to destroy me. It was a part of the deal, sweet Janey."

"There is more than one way to destroy a person. He might not be able to kill you, but he will destroy you nonetheless."

"He can try. But I am more powerful than a god. Especially one stuck inside a mirror—even more so now after I kill you."

Warmth spread through her blood, and glitter rained inside her mind. Bright and fun, like a summer dance. The drugs...

Fuck. Part of her brain tried to hold on to reality.

"Well, Janey, it's been truly fun knowing you, but I can see you're fading." He clutched her chin. "The last thing I want you to know before you die is I am going to make your baby sister cry... in so many ways."

Jane clenched her fists, and with all the energy she had left, she spat on him.

He wiped her saliva off his face with a slight chuckle and turned the vampire holding Jane. "Suck her dry. Make sure you get every last drop. I don't want any hint of drugs found in her system."

A deep snarl rumbled in the vampire's chest, and she felt it as much as she heard it. She also felt the fight in his muscles. He didn't want to do it. But, like anyone under compulsion, he had to.

"At least tell me the name of the man who is going to kill me," she said, her voice light and bright, happy and cheerful.

Fucking drugs.

"Aeris," his breath caressed her neck. "My little mouse, I'm sorry."

"I know."

As the words left her mouth, his fangs plunged into her neck, and he drank and drank and drank. With each gulp, her body grew weaker and weaker and weaker.

She leaned into him and allowed him to cradle her body as he killed her, seeking as much comfort as she could in death. And he gave it, pulling her close with one arm and stroking gentle circles on her back with the other.

Jane was born to die horrifically, just like her parents. So she wasn't surprised to be looking death in the face. What *did* surprise her was whose face it was—and how much it destroyed her, knowing she had been so cruelly betrayed.

But her surprises weren't over because a girl, another of her closest friends, appeared in her vision. At first, Jane thought she might be there to help, but then all she did was hold her hand, sniffle, and say, "I am so sorry, Jane."

"You too?" The words were merely mouthed with no sound escaping because her body was no longer capable of speaking.

The girl stifled a cry. "I am so, so sorry. He's just—"

But Jane would never know what her other traitor said

because it was at that moment when the drugs fully kicked in, and her mind was consumed with wicked pleasure and glittering hallucinations. In some way, Jane was thankful to be rid of the pain. Both mental and physical.

She heard one more command in her joyous haze—or at least she thought it was a command. One could never know, really.

In her dreamlike state, her mind shifted to her Nightmare, to the man formed from muscles and brooding. She closed her eyes and saw him as a sea of wisping colors. She was in a flowing, white dress, and he was in his signature black suit, but they looked more like abstract paintings than people.

But she touched his face and spoke to him one last time.

But what could one say to the person who had become their everything? What could be said? She didn't know.

So the ghost-like version of herself whispered to the ghost-like version of him, "*I will miss you, my Sweet Nightmare.*"

"When you're done, mutilate her face. Make it harder to recognize her. Then throw her body into the bay."

Gideon's dark voice cut through her fever dream just before true darkness slipped into her mind, and her eyes lost sight, but she didn't stop seeing. Jane looked down on herself—her lifeless body?— as if she were a ghost hovering above.

Aeris slammed her face into the marble hard, but he only smashed in one side, possibly out of protest. Then he and the lady traitor took her body to the Marina District and threw her body over a dock and into the water.

The female ran off and expected Aeris to follow, but he didn't. He looked down at the water for a long moment before checking behind him and diving in.

Aeris pulled her body to shore. He caressed her broken face and whispered into the wind. "I will try to keep her safe from a distance."

Jane wanted to hold on longer to see more—to hold on to life —but she was dead, and she had been since she'd lost conscious-ness. Now, she was just a ghost with a fraying tether to life.

And as much as she wanted to stay, she couldn't.
Her time was up, and her foresight was proved to be correct.
She was destined to die a horrific and early death.

Chapter Thirty-One

Nightmare

Eleven Days Later

Gavriil Wryte paced his mirror impatiently, waiting for his bargain with Jane to disappear. His eyes tracked to the hourglass, which represented the timeframe of their deal. It was about to run out.

He'd kept his end. He hadn't stalked her, checked on her, or even sensed her in the last eleven days. A considerable feat because the girl was his obsession.

He didn't love her. He barely even tolerated her. Gavriil possessed no ability to feel. It had been stripped from him ages ago. But she was his obsession, and one day she would be his end. She was destined to destroy him, and he should have killed her from the moment he met her.

He should have killed her every day since.

But he couldn't, and he didn't understand why.

She wasn't any prettier than any of the other women he'd bedded. She wasn't special, or unique, or all that tempting—not like the ancient witch courtesans of old, or even Helene. Jane was just a normal, mortal girl, albeit it with powerful potential lying beneath the surface. She was an Ash Witch, after all. However, she was still mortal and had barely received any training. She was nothing in the grand scheme of immortals. So, he shouldn't have been fixated on her, but to him, Jane was all those things and more.

When she was around, no one else existed. She was beautiful, unique, and the most tempting thing he'd ever seen.

And he couldn't reconcile it.

Because he also hated her and everything about her.

She was his curse.

So, he shouldn't be impatiently awaiting her return because she meant nothing to him. She would always mean nothing to him.

And the fact that their bond was broken, and he couldn't even feel her, even when he tried, angered him *because* she was nothing. Only a plaything that he would eventually discard because he didn't care.

But since she had been gone, something felt off—wrong.

He was more irritable and unstable, and his mind was beginning to fog, just as it had been for ages prior to meeting her. Jane Whittfield-Wryte was his anchor, but he was starting to realize that not only was she his anchor for travel outside the mirror, but she was also the anchor to his sanity.

But their bond was gone, and even more concerning was his heart. Gavriil placed his hand on his chest, feeling it beat beneath his fingertips. It had started beating again on its own, without her touching him, twenty-one hours after she had left his mirror. And then it never stopped.

For the last ten days, his heart beat on its own.

Without her, and he didn't understand why.

So when the last grain of sand fell through the hourglass, and the time limit ran out, Gavriil immediately searched for her. Using his magic and his mirror to see through the whole city, he could spy on anything in New Swansea.

When he found her locked inside a freezing chamber at the University Square morgue, her lifeless body cut open and dissected, he fell to his knees and roared. His fury caused the earth to shake violently, an earthquake splitting cracks into the roads and buildings of New Swansea.

She was dead. His Jane, his light, was gone, his anchor gone.

Everything was gone, and he vowed he would make them all pay, from the one who killed her to the one who cut open her body and dissected her. He would kill them all, slowly and torturously.

A roar shook all of New Swansea City again, and twelve words left his lips: "I will burn the world down to get you back, little witch!"

~

The End... for now

~

The story isn't over. To find out who actually murdered Jane read Gilded Wicked Mirrors and continue with Nightmare's revenge in Cruel Ghosts.

~

Next Books in the Series:
GILDED WICKED MIRRORS (out now)
CRUEL GHOSTS (coming 2026)

SNEAK PEEK
AT CRUEL GHOSTS

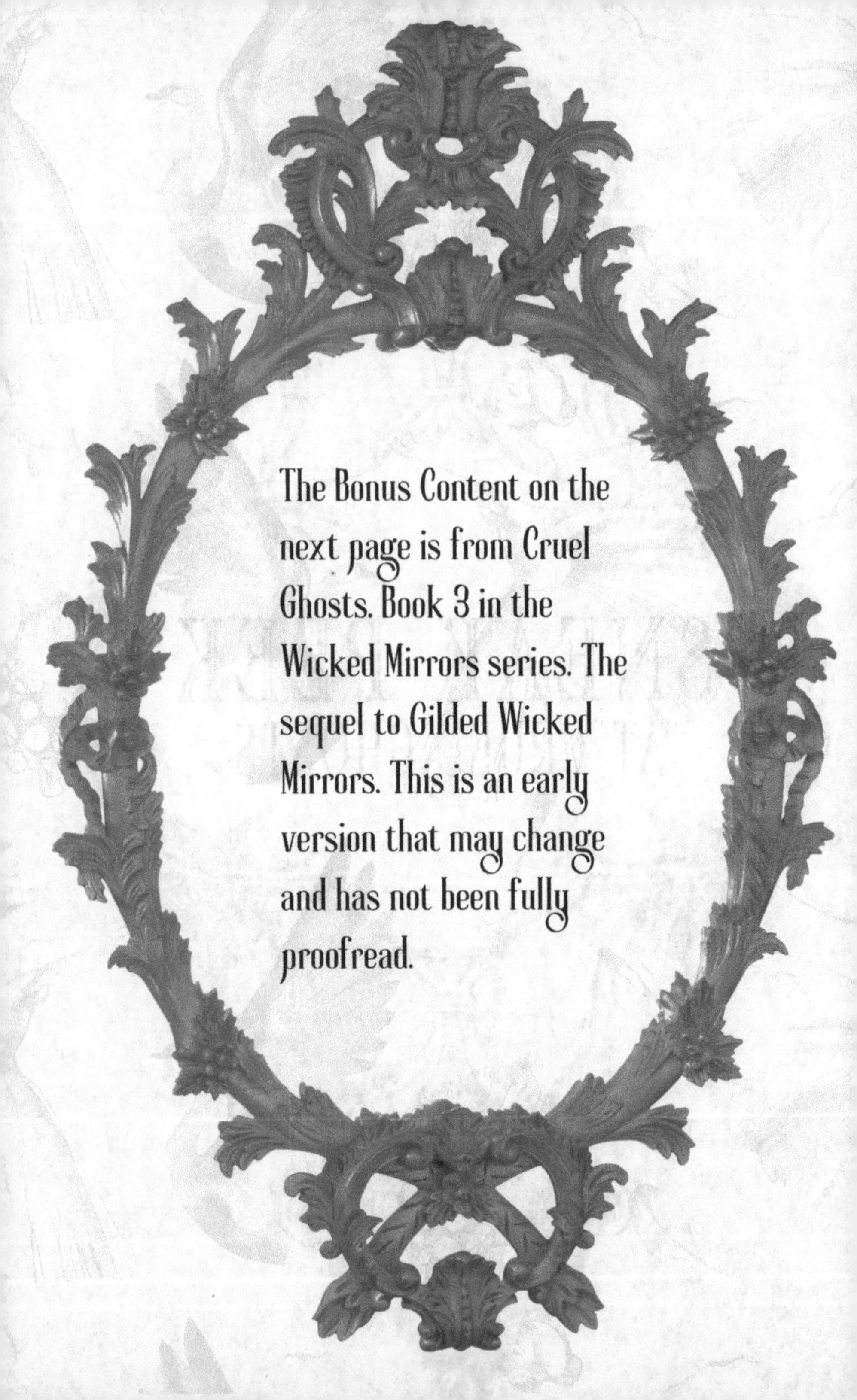

The Bonus Content on the next page is from Cruel Ghosts. Book 3 in the Wicked Mirrors series. The sequel to Gilded Wicked Mirrors. This is an early version that may change and has not been fully proofread.

Bonus Content

Periwinkle

92ND DAY OF AUTUMN, 700 AV

Why did she have a bucket of dirt again?

Periwinkle cocked her head to one side, her bubblegum pink hair bouncing with the movement as she examined the bucket more closely. No, it wasn't dirt, it was mud. Periwinkle loved mud. It was squishy and soft, and when she squeezed it, it felt so nice between her fingers. Yes, mud was nice. She loved mud.

Although her love of mud did not quite explain why she had it.

It was a fact of life that Periwinkle was always up to no good… or was it always up to too much good? Ugh, sigh. It was hard to tell, really. Either way, Periwinkle was up to something. And that something today happened to be…

She'd remember any moment now.

"Miss, you can't be in here," said a young man in his thirties, roughly, wearing a white lab coat — at least he looked that age. What did Periwinkle know? She barely understood these fragile mortals and their lifespans. In the blink of an eye, they were gone.

"And where is here?" Peri asked.

"The morgue, miss, and you can't be here."

"The morgue at University Square?"

"Yes, miss."

"Hmmm," Peri hummed and peeked down once more at her bucket. That was why she had the bucket. Good to know.

"Do I have to escort you out?" he asked.

Periwinkle bit the inside of her cheek as she glanced down at her wrist and the human hair that was braided together into a bracelet—the anchor she used to leave her mirror prison. Unlike her twin brother, she didn't use a human as an anchor. She used human body parts, and those faded far faster than humans. Humans died quickly, but they still lasted for years. From the look of her bracelet, Periwinkle only had about an hour left until the magic would force her back into her prison cell.

Peri didn't want to braid the bracelet too big because she wanted to save her anchors for other important things, and the more hair she had in the braid, the longer she could be outside the mirror.

"No, little human man, I am not leaving." Metal sprang out of her fingernails, and in a blink, she ran a very sharp claw along his collarbone, breaking flesh. She dipped her finger in the blood and plopped it into her mouth. Tasting the blood on her tongue.

Sweet iron.

Her claws retracted back into her skin, and her hands once more looked like a boring human.

She sucked on the blood again, savoring it. Periwinkle loved the taste of blood... but then didn't all vampires? Peri rubbed her chin and hummed again.

She didn't know. Or did she, but she had just forgotten?

She twisted her lips and hit herself in the temple with the base of her palm, trying to remember. Her stupid memory. It kept fading in and out.

"You're an abomination," the man whimpered, his face a storm of fear.

Periwinkle's brow furrowed. "I once thought so too." She paused, her brow furrowing further. "But that's not a very nice thing to say. I haven't even released my fangs yet. Now those are scary."

She smiled and then, to scare this rude little human, she made her fangs extend. He screamed, and she let out a wicked laugh. She wasn't against confirming their fears that she was indeed a villain.

And she was; how bad of one just depended on her mood.

The little stinky mortal peed his pants, and the tinkle of it against the floor echoed in the hallway. Was it loud or just her superhuman hearing?

"You're boring me," she sighed. Now that she had tasted his blood, she could compel him. "Tell me where the body of the redheaded ballerina is being kept."

Like a good little boy, the human pointed three doors down to a morgue lab.

"Thank you. Now, forget that you saw me and tell no one of this exchange."

"Yes, miss." He nodded, his eyes cloudy as he turned on his heel and walked away from her.

Periwinkle threw open the door to the lab as if she had no worries in the world, and then she skipped over to the cold chambers housing the dead bodies. She played a child's guessing game to choose which chamber she would open.

When she slid open the chamber, she whispered, "Drats." For being the world's greatest seer, which honestly wasn't saying much because all the other ones were dead, she should have been better at this. The problem was her memory.

Without her true anchor, she was adrift in the world. Perhaps she shouldn't have trapped him inside a prison far worse than hers. Because at least she could interact with the outer world. The Seven Wicked Witches didn't have that luxury. Nor could they interact with the other Mirror-Gods like she could.

They were trapped inside a black void prison inside the Lake of Mirrors. Although Gallagher, the Mirror of Chaos, had discovered a way to interact with people, and then she eventually made a deal with the Goddess of War in a different world, which helped her escape her prison cell completely.

Periwinkle let out a big huff of breath.

Craighton wasn't so lucky. He was her ex-lover, turned vampire hunter, who on at least five occasions had tried to murder her... truly rude behavior if you asked Periwinkle.

Oh, well.

She had come *here*—to the morgue—for a reason, right?

Periwinkle blinked and looked down at the death chamber that she held open. "I don't know you." She blinked again. "Why am I here?" Blinking once more, she noticed the bucket of mud in her hand. "Oh, mud, I love mud."

She closed the chamber and quickly opened the three others, making her way to the last one. She opened the drawer to find a very dead redheaded ballerina. "Oh, you. I have been looking everywhere for you." Periwinkle placed her bucket on the floor.

She scrunched her nose and playfully slapped the dead girl across the face. "You are very, very dead, Janey, and that just won't do with my plans..."—she cocked her head—"Or does it perfectly align with my plans?" She shrugged. "Who knows?" Periwinkle bit her lip. "He won't like you this"—she motioned to the woman's dissected body—"wounded."

Periwinkle dipped her finger into the mud and began to trace over every single wound on Jane Whittfield-Wryte's body. When she got the girl's face, she winced. Someone—no, not someone, Jevon the demon living inside Gideon's body—had bashed her face in, and Nightmare would not be pleased, so Periwinkle cupped a handful of mud and slapped it onto the dead girl's face, not so gently.

Wonderful. "I feel like I am missing something." She scratched her face, getting mud all over herself. She shrugged. Oh, well. She tapped her nose while she tried to figure out what she was missing.

Ah, yes, witch symbols.

Yes, she was a Mirror-God, but that magic only worked in deals. If she wanted to do magic outside of a deal, she would have to use either her witch magic or her vampire magic. Lucky for her, she was a very powerful witch and a semi-powerful vampire. After all, she was the third vampire ever to be created in the existence of the universe. It went Nightmare, then her twin brother, Draven—also known as Beautiful Decay—then her.

Dipping her finger once more in the mud, she drew witch symbols on the dead girl's palms, feet, and stomach.

There was once a time when witches were boundless, able to bend all energy and matter, like gods. But no longer. Now, witches were extinct... well, not all of them, she guessed. Periwinkle wasn't foolish enough to bind her magic into a mirror. How silly that would have been? However, witches were almost extinct, and over the generations, their magic weakened from boundless to mostly channeled through symbols.

But all that was boring, complicated stuff, and Periwinkle didn't care at all about it.

As soon as she finished her last symbol, the mud placed on the body began to glow, healing all the physical wounds of the corpse. But it was still a corpse—a vessel. Periwinkle was not in the business of resurrections.

If, say, a very angry Vampire-Mirror-God wanted to resurrect his 'not-love-of-his-life', then he would have to do it himself with much darker magic than Periwinkle wished to use. Dark magic had its consequences.

Periwinkle summoned water. She was a Wood Witch, a Wind Witch, a Water Witch, and a Seer. Like she said, she was unnaturally powerful. Although, to be fair, she had stolen her water magic from another witch, but that was another story—maybe one day she would tell it. But not now.

Shaping the water, she turned it into a magical ice, which would encase the body, preserving it until the oldest vampire in existence needed it. Periwinkle smiled and closed the chamber. Dipping her finger one last time in mud, Periwinkle drew a locking symbol onto the chamber, making it so it wouldn't unlock until the opportune moment.

Periwinkle might not be willing to resurrect the witch, but her resurrection would very much play into the wicked plans Periwinkle had laid.

All of her puppets were in place, and now she just needed to find where she had misplaced their strings.

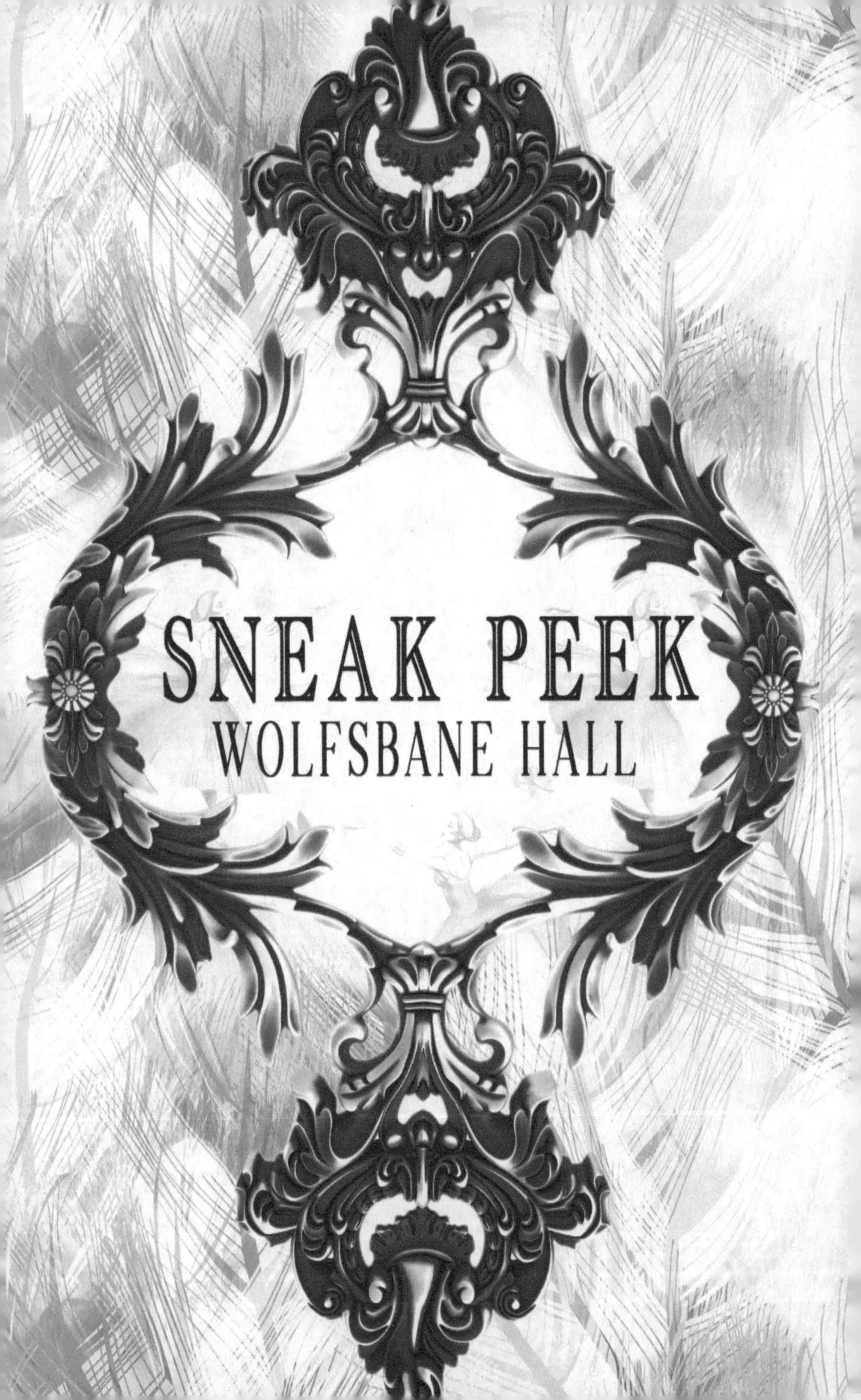

SNEAK PEEK
WOLFSBANE HALL

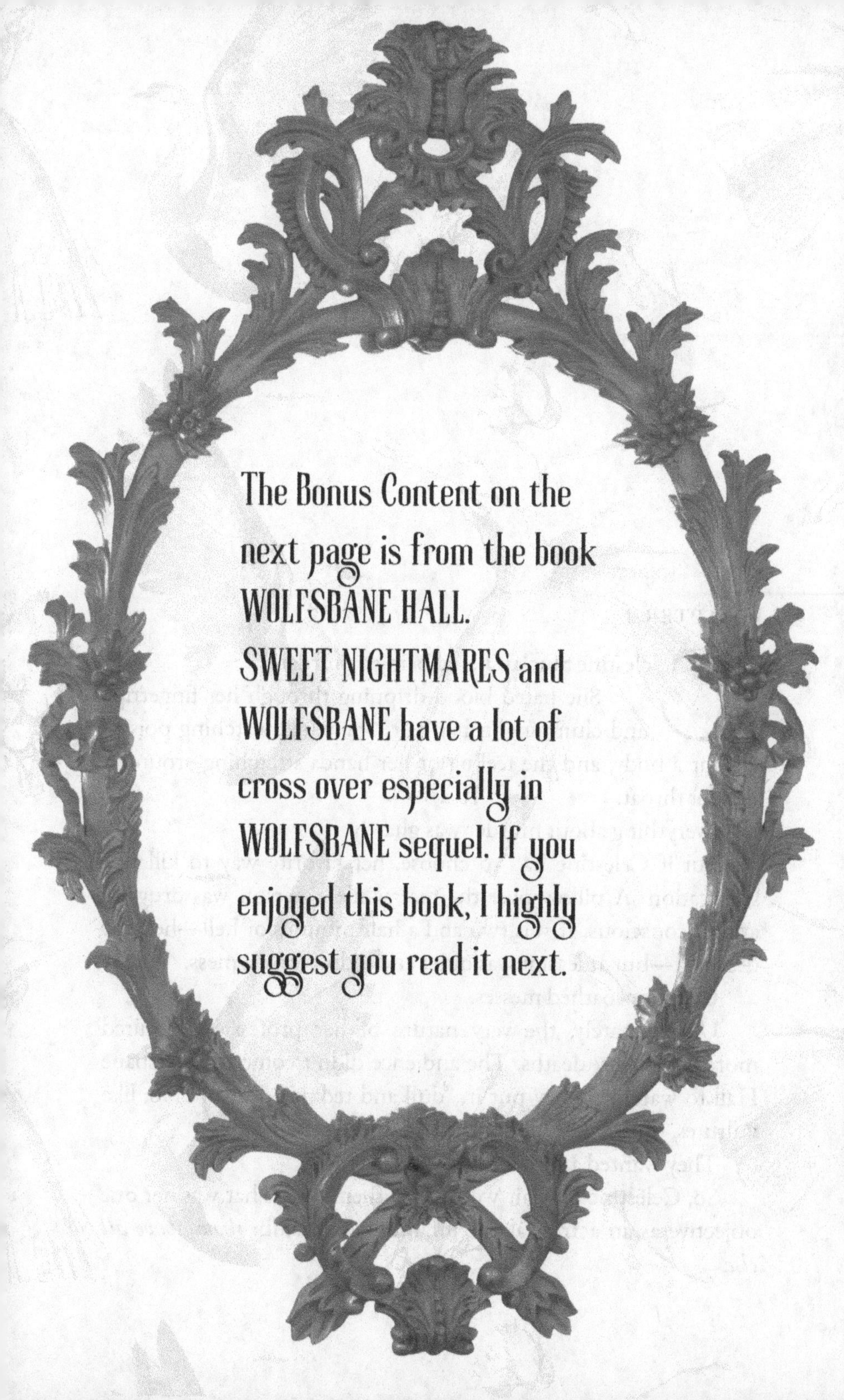

The Bonus Content on the next page is from the book WOLFSBANE HALL. SWEET NIGHTMARES and WOLFSBANE have a lot of cross over especially in WOLFSBANE sequel. If you enjoyed this book, I highly suggest you read it next.

Bonus Content

Chapter 1

Celestine Sinclair hated being a murderer.

She hated blood dripping through her fingertips and clumping in her hair. She hated watching poison devour a body, and the feeling of her hands stretching around a slender throat.

Everything about murder was ghastly.

But if Celestine had to choose, her favorite way to kill was suffocation. A pillow over the face while a person was drugged and unconscious. It was two and a half minutes of hell—hell she deserved—but at least it was quiet and didn't leave a mess.

Celestine loathed messes.

Unfortunately, the very nature of her profession required more...*theatrical* deaths. The audience didn't come to Wolfsbane Hall to watch, as they put it, "dull and tedious deaths." No, like vultures, the rich, pompous pricks wanted carnage.

They wanted a show.

So, Celestine Sinclair would give them one. That was her one objective as an actress at the infamous nightclub: *show above all else.*

Show above one's own sanity.

"You're wasting time," said a voice forged from darkness, twisting from the room's shadows. Smoky sweet, like honeyed whiskey. Sugary, yet potent.

The Specter—the magical and mysterious owner of Wolfsbane Hall, the glittering palace at the edge of San Francisco, filled with as much mystery as magnificence. It was a place where patrons became a part of a murder mystery show. Glitter, grandeur, and witchcraft were laced through every inch of the manor, interwoven into a tapestry of entertainment.

"You must prepare for your next murder," the Specter whispered in her ear, darkness twirling and cloaking her from the patrons meandering into the Grand Ballroom—the club's showroom.

"I know, Specter," Celestine breathed. She wanted to call him something else, but she didn't know his true identity—no one did. People saw glimpses of him in the shadows and smoke, or as an animated, talking painting. He appeared silhouetted like a ghost in the reflections of the house's grand mirrors. But no one ever saw his face. He was a beautiful voice, singing grand arias and speaking through the walls and the calls of mockingbirds.

The Specter was everywhere in the house, and yet nowhere to be found.

Impossible to truly know. Impossible to hold. Impossible to keep.

"Open your character card, sweet Cellie," he said, the darkness vibrating around her.

Celestine flinched at the words. Opening the card would only confirm her as the night's killer, and she absolutely didn't want to do that. There would never be a day or a lifetime or even an eternity in which Celestine would get used to killing someone. And she'd certainly never enjoy it like some of the sick patrons of Wolfsbane Hall.

People came here to play out their fantasies of either

murdering or dying, and to Celestine, both options were equally disturbing.

At least the Specter had given her a heads-up this time. She was tonight's murderer, and that fact made her both furious and sad. She wanted to curse his name or punch him...but then, she didn't know his name.

Besides, she wouldn't harm him anyway. She couldn't.

He'd saved her life, and she'd given him her soul in return. Not literally, but he would forever own her and could forever have his way with her. And oh, she often wished he would take physical form to do just that. Fuck her. Hold her. Whisper dirty things into her ear.

Nine years of unbroken tension were far too much.

Her core grew wet. That's all it took, the mere thought of touching him.

"You have thirty minutes to open your card and perform the deed." His voice snapped her out of the fantasy.

"I know," she repeated with a huff as she nervously ran her willowy fingers through platinum-blonde curls. Celestine detested this role, but she would do anything for the Specter. He was her family, her home, her everything, and all she ever wanted was to make him proud. So, even though Celestine despised it, she would kill for him.

Always.

"Timeliness is next to godliness." The Specter spoke through the mouth of a Victorian painting, using the fanciful duchess's lips to form the words.

Celestine bit her lip, slightly smudging her bloodred lipstick. "Right."

With her crimson fingernails, she lifted the corner of the envelope housing her character card and sucked in a deep breath as she prepared for the onslaught. Pinching her eyes tight, she tore open the envelope as if ripping off a bandage. The impact was immediate. Thoughts, feelings, a script, and a character background poured into Celestine's mind. She felt it like a physical blow, even needing to steady herself against the wall for a moment.

A character was transferred into her mind, teaching Celestine how to speak and behave during the game, while providing her with lines to say throughout the night. The role instructed her on whom to talk to, flirt with, and insult, as well as whom to avoid.

Every person at Wolfsbane Hall, from the patrons to the six cast members, received a card and played a part during the show, each becoming a new person. The only difference between the cast and a patron was that the cast helped the Specter progress the story along its desired path. Patrons tended to lose focus and meander, so they needed a push in the correct direction—sometimes physically.

There was only one rule at Wolfsbane Hall: *every murder must be solved.*

So, the cast became the Specter's hands during the show, ensuring it reached its conclusion. If a patron refused to be the murderer on any given night, the cast would step in for that, too —although typically, Everett or Babette preferred to take on that role.

Never Celestine.

She opened her eyes and officially became Dorothy Wolf, a movie star who had just signed a seven-year contract with a massive Hollywood studio.

A beautiful ingénue.

An object to be desired and a typical role for Celestine. She always played either the tempting seductress or the innocent ingénue. Beautiful, sweet, and all one's desires wrapped up in a tiny, busty package. It was a part designed for Celestine because she was the Specter's muse, and because she had considerable assets. Tits and ass, as the vulgar might put it.

"On with it," the Specter said as her shadow on the wall. "How do you plan to do it? And please, give me the short version. You can tell the longer story tonight in your rooms."

During the show, the Specter was often impatient and blunt,

demanding that she be succinct. He disliked long, repetitive stories. Celestine put up with it because late at night, after the games, the Specter was kinder and warmer—even a friend. But show Specter was driven, consumed by the story and his genius.

"So?" the Specter asked when she waited too long to respond.

Knives, the character, Dorothy, whispered in Celestine's mind. While the characters Celestine played sometimes felt real, they never were. It wasn't like being possessed. The magic gave her a script to follow and a history to portray. Still, because Celestine proscribed to Stanislavski's and Strasberg's method acting techniques, her characters often felt real. She became her role for one night only.

However, there wasn't much to imagine at Wolfsbane Hall.

Much of it was *far too real*.

"Stabbing," Celestine finally said. Short and straightforward, just how he liked it.

The character, Dorothy Wolf, planned to kill her lover and director because he wouldn't cast her in his newest film. A film worthy of Oscar consideration.

A slight that caused a murderous rage.

The script gave many options for completing the murder, but the character favored knives and intimacy.

"Wonderfully horrific," the painting said as the shadows followed up with, "Knives will be intriguing." The Specter loved using multiple communication mediums, like a hovering voice, darkness, and animating objects. All at once. It was often disorienting for Celestine. "Now go."

The darkness receded, and Celestine was left alone in the nightclub of dreams—or, more accurately, the nightclub of nightmares. However, some people reveled in nightmares. Celestine only reveled in the stage. At least she could do that well.

Every detail of the grand mansion was unique and dripping with money. Even the wall sconces were formed from electrum, because gold or silver alone wasn't special enough for the Specter. The ballroom was no exception. It sparkled as she stepped onto the floor, with ten crystal-carved felt tables and two ruby-sculpted bars on either side.

Friday nights were casino nights. Anyone wealthy enough to pay the extravagant admittance fee could gamble and take part in the murder mystery, which meant all the usual patrons were here —the usual suspects.

Trying to avoid them and focus on her work, Celestine made a beeline for the bar. Liquid courage never hurt anyone. She ordered a rum cocktail and swiveled to survey the room for her target. He was nowhere to be found, and she was getting antsy. The script forced Celestine to be excited to murder one of her lovers. The character was a real Bonnie Parker, this one. Ruthless, devious, and exceedingly foolish.

Because Celestine truly became her character, she, too, took on that excitement, but it merged with Celestine's own feelings of dread. The result caused heart palpitations and a bead of sweat to roll down her back.

She just wanted to get on with the show. But no one was around to act with.

"The ingénue again. How very typical." The words jerked Celestine out of her pondering, and she looked up seconds before a cocktail waitress threw a glass of red wine in her face and down her emerald silk dress. "Ah, now you're a soggy mess. At least it'll match your personality."

Celestine sputtered as her lipstick streaked down her chin.

How dare she? Someone fire this wretched girl! Lines of the script screeched inside her mind. The magic was adaptive. If another character altered the story, the Specter's magic would modify the script in real-time. It was like reading off cue cards, but the cards existed inside her head.

But Celestine didn't say her lines; she just swallowed and squared her shoulders, holding her head high like a regal queen as confusion struck her stomach. The person who had accosted her was Babette Fontaine, a fellow Wolfsbane Hall cast member who frequently played the French maid or mistress roles. But Babette and Celestine's roles were not supposed to overlap much tonight. They didn't even share the same storyline.

Celestine barely had any dialogue with her character, meaning Babette was going rogue.

It was unsurprising; the girl was like a rose in full bloom, with thorns dipped in vinegar and laced with poison. Babette was a tiny thing that seemed entirely harmless, but her bite was deadly.

"What was that?" Celestine whispered, her eyes darting to the crowd now forming around them. "That wasn't a part of the show."

"No, but it felt good," Babette said in a low voice as she placed the empty wine glass on the bar and leaned closer. "I am sick of you stealing my parts. I was the ingénue long before you, and I will be again long after you're gone."

Celestine shivered at the threat, but also because the liquid now varnishing her dress had mixed with the cold air, causing goosebumps on her flesh. "I'm not stealing anything." Nor did she even want this role. Babette could have it; she could bask in its cruelty.

Babette grunted, unconvinced, but she pulled away, and her face changed, the mask of her role sliding over her features. Thick, wavy chestnut locks bounced around her powdered porcelain face. "I am so, so, so sorry," she said with a thick French accent. An accent that was as fake as the beauty mark painted beneath her left eye. "I didn't mean to, mistress." Turning her head so only Celestine could hear, the brunette breathed, "I hope you choke on poison tonight."

All around them, patrons stretched their necks to listen and get a better view, for the show had officially commenced. Technically, the show started when a single patron entered the building. There was no big announcement; the mystery was a part of the spectacle.

But the audience's attention was a clear sign. Celestine needed to take on her role and become Dorothy fully.

"Oh no, my dress is destroyed," Celestine whined in an over-the-top, rich, spoiled lilt, keeping with the persona. The true Celestine wanted to say nothing. She'd rather grin and bear it, but the character would never do that. So Celestine gritted her teeth and fanned herself dramatically while speaking her lines. "Oh, my night is ruined—ruined, I say!"

Celestine patted her soaked dress with a napkin she'd grabbed from the bartop and sighed hyperbolically, the hysterics on full display.

Babette rolled her eyes and sauntered away smugly like the wildcat she was.

"Sometimes I want to throw my wine on you, too," James Ashbrook said as he approached, his eyes sparking with mischief.

Excited shivers danced in Celestine's stomach at the sound of his rich baritone, and she sucked in a breath, taking him in. His presence had a visceral effect. Some men were too handsome for their own good, like all the Ashbrooks. The three men, fellow cast members, were rich, too. James was the tallest and most refined. To Celestine's utter dismay, he was exceedingly charming and, oh, so good at tempting her into mistakes. It didn't help that he was blunt as a lead figurine, speaking in precise, concise, and sometimes cruel phrases. Unfortunately, she was drawn to bad boys who showed no emotion.

An added benefit was that they tended to have massive cocks and be great in the sack.

"No, you don't," Celestine finally responded.

He raised a midnight eyebrow as he chewed a piece of gum— the man loved chewing gum. It was like a tic. "Don't I?" When the sides of his lips drew up, she finally grasped his meaning. "It could be fun to lick off your smooth...folds."

Her center pulsed, wanting him to make good on that offer.

"James," she whispered and hit him with her fur scarf. "Don't be so vulgar."

He shrugged. "I can't help it."

"You very well could help it."

"Ah, but I don't want to." James stepped closer, and her back hit the bartop. "Nor would *you* want me to." With one more step, he pinned her, his arms snaking around her waist. "It seems like it's my lucky night. I get you all to myself, and my meddlesome cousins are nowhere in sight."

Celestine's eyes snaked through the room, not seeing the twins either, but they had to be somewhere. Despite being as rich as Croesus, they were in the cast, and the cast never missed a show.

James leaned in and placed a chaste kiss on Celestine's lips. The gesture wasn't new. Outside of the shows, they were sometimes lovers. Mostly when he was bored, or she was desperate for a human touch. James Ashbrook wasn't capable of true love or connection, and she would never ask it of him—or at least, that was the lie she always told herself. Because if she ever truly cared for him, he would break her.

James was a psychopath. He reveled in the murder—enjoyed both killing and dying. It was why he worked at the club. Only those who were truly desperate or fucked up worked here. James was no exception. He bathed in the carnage.

But he was good to her, and even more importantly, what they did together gave her a chance to numb herself. To fall entirely into pleasure and forget everything else.

A moment of respite.

Celestine pulled away from the kiss. "The show, James."

"Tonight, our little kisses fit into the show."

"Perhaps, but save some room for imagination."

He wasn't wrong. Dorothy had many lovers, and James's character was one of them. But the story required that piece of information to come out a bit later. Or, at the very least, be more obscured. So Celestine stopped him from making a spectacle by placing a hand on his well-manicured suit. Everything about James Ashbrook—including his clothing—was clear and measured. Studied like a scientist. And he always played characters like himself.

The Specter was far more accommodating to him than he ever was to her.

James's eyes examined her. "Fine," he sighed. "Perhaps not before the murder."

Celestine flinched at the reminder, and her eyes tracked to the clock. Seven twenty-five.

Shit. Celestine had only minutes to complete her task. So she leaned close to James and whispered into the shell of his ear, "Meet me in the Red Parlor in ten minutes, and then you can do whatever you want to me."

His lips curved further up. "I'll take you up on that." His eyes twinkled with domination and the promise of the depraved things he'd do to her later.

"Sorry, love, I must leave you," she said loud enough for the room to hear. "I need to change."

James leaned in and caught her hand before she could run off. "I have a beautiful dress in my room if you need it."

All three Ashbrooks had rooms in the East Wing. The Specter only allowed cast members to stay the night at Wolfsbane.

"Oh, thank you, but I have my own."

With that, she dashed out of the ballroom and stopped in her dressing room to prepare for her task. Rifling through her bag, she searched for the lipstick, the tool she needed. But as she grasped them, she braced her makeup table with her hand tightly, and she sucked in a pained breath. All the excitement and running had overexerted her, and she needed a minute to breathe.

Celestine's heart shuddered in her chest, beating asynchronously. No...not now.

Get yourself together. She didn't have time for her body to melt down. She needed to get changed and prepare. So she slid her fingers along the grooves in the wall, grounding herself and communing with Wolfsbane, sending it her intentions.

Wolfsbane, please fix my makeup and enchant my lips. Help me to complete this killing.

Every night, Celestine drank the Specter's elixir, a potion that allowed her to use his magic to further the show. It allowed her to interact with the house and ask it to do her bidding—create a musical ambiance, manipulate the audience's emotions, or even morph the setting and her clothing. The only way to use the magic was to physically connect with the house; the walls and floors were the most accessible connection points.

Sometimes, the house listened; sometimes, it didn't. Other times, it twisted the request so much, Celestine wished she'd never asked to begin with.

So tonight, Celestine asked for help with the murder...and to fix her makeup. She didn't bother asking to change her dress because it would get stained soon enough anyway; Babette didn't realize the gift she'd given with the wine-throwing stunt. It gave Celestine an excuse to announce she'd changed her clothing publicly.

An alibi.

The house complied. A rush of wind circled through the dressing room, and magic poured over her face, tingling. The enchantment the house placed there burned her lips.

Thank you. She patted the wall, but her face soured as she remembered what came next.

"You look like the wind's gone out of your sails and took all the sunshine with it, my sweet dame," came the Specter's voice from a shadow in the mirror. The Specter and his idioms. "Cheer up. It's going to be fun."

Celestine swallowed. "Death is never fun."

"Perhaps..." the Specter trailed off as a grandfather clock chimed.

Celestine cursed under her breath. She needed to get moving. She had a murder to complete. At least tonight's victim was a regular to this type of debauchery. He'd been murdered and done the murdering before. He wasn't new, which was a significant relief. Sometimes, the attendees didn't know what they were coming to. They were blissfully ignorant of Wolfsbane Hall's true nature.

A monster house.

The Specter loved to play with newcomers and render a horror show where everything felt real until the end.

Because everything *was real* until the end.

The killer physically murdered their victims, and every moment of the show was, in fact, not an illusion. But new guests assumed it was all fake, that Specter fashioned expansive fantasies to make the bodies feel and look deceased.

The Specter's true magic was in resurrection—although he could cast illusions and play with emotions, too.

The one rule of Wolfsbane Hall was: *every murder must be solved; then, and only then, would the body resurrect.*

Celestine stood in the Red Parlor, waiting for her prey. One minute until he was supposed to arrive, and James Ashbrook was always on time, even as his characters. He believed it was never appropriate to keep someone waiting.

As her character, Celestine raised her lips with feline delight and leaned against the side of a lounge like a seductress draped in silk and jewels, waiting for a midnight assignation.

James stormed into the room like a cowboy in a Western film about to rescue his damsel in distress. He walked with purpose, and, without hesitation, he cupped the back of Celestine's neck and kissed her fiercely.

The kiss was beastly and consumed by unfiltered vigor. Almost as if they didn't do this every week. But that was the nature of their relationship. They were a wildfire that burned until it would eventually flame out and die.

James was not for keeping.

No rich man was. A lesson she'd learned long ago. Poor girls don't end up with "the man," even if they desperately want to.

James was for fucking and, tonight, killing.

Celestine's back slammed against the wall as their mouths

devoured each other, his hands stroking up her legs and bunching the fabric of her dress up to her core with their movement.

"You taste of champagne," he whispered, his lips on her neck and his fingers digging into the curves of her thighs, their rhythm like magic. "And is that a hint of raspberry?"

The elixir. It tasted like champagne and raspberries tonight. But Celestine didn't mention it. She had a murder to complete, and too much conversation wouldn't do, so she pulled James's lips to hers again.

Kisses made such useful distractions, so she deepened their passion until he jerked, his hands stilling.

James pulled away, his eyes widening with betrayal.

"I'm sorry," Celestine breathed into his hair as his limbs went limp. "You're the Specter's victim tonight."

Celestine had poisoned her lips with a tranquilizer strong enough to sedate a horse. Only a thin layer of plastic and Specter's magic kept the lipstick from incapacitating her.

"How are you going to do it?" James croaked as his head lolled to the side.

"Stabbing." She caught him as his body slid to the floor.

"Ah...I've never been stabbed before." James smiled, lopsided and bright. A sick part of him enjoyed dying over and over again. He once said it made him feel alive every time he died in Wolfsbane Hall. He enjoyed it so much that he often volunteered as a victim, choosing to die every other week.

Although he enjoyed it, killing still made Celestine's stomach churn and her arms quiver.

"I'll see you after." And while he was still conscious, she gripped an ornamental knife from above her head, rolled her hand into the stabbing position, and thrust down.

"Thank you," he said, blood bubbling from his mouth as he stared gleefully down at his wound. She knew he thanked her for starting while he was still awake to experience it. He wanted to see and feel the knife as it slid in.

James had a terrible trauma in his past, which he refused to speak about. It caused him to enjoy pain and victimhood—to feast on it. But who was she to judge? She had her own crooked, scarred history.

Celestine pulled out the knife, then slammed it in again and again and again. It was a crime of passion, after all. Her character was overcome by rage and vengeful lust. But all of it made vomit snake up Celestine's esophagus. She continued her job regardless. Celestine Sinclair was loyal—the perfect employee for her Specter.

Loyal to a fault and to the detriment of her sanity.

ALSO BY HAZEL ST. LEWIS

BOOKS IN THE MIRROR UNIVERSE

WOLFSBANE HALL

COURTING WAR

WICKED MIRRORS SERIES

Book 1: GILDED WICKED MIRRORS

Book 2: SWEET NIGHTMARES

Book 3: CRUEL GHOSTS (coming 2026)

About the Author

Hazel St. Lewis is a Northern California-based Fantasy Romance author. Diagnosed with dyslexia at a young age, she struggled to read and write, but fantasy stories inspired her to start story-telling. Unfortunately, now, she is a little too obsessed with Dracula (this will become important soon... wink, wink). When she isn't writing, she can be found playing with her hoard of cats (too many to count...it's a problem), singing songs to said cats—like Cinderella—or painting.

Facebook Group: Shadow Daddy Books
    TikTok @hazelstlewis
    Instagram @hazelstlewis
    Email: Info@hazelstlewis.com
    Patreon: patreon.com/HazelStLewis

Stay in Touch!

Newsletter Sign-Up

Sign up using the link below for Hazel's newsletter to be the first to receive exciting news, updates, and bonus content.
Newsletter Sign-up

Follow me:

Facebook Group: Shadow Daddy Books, TikTok @hazelstlewis, Instagram @hazelstlewis

Join my Patreon:

Want to read books as I write them? Or see the covers early? Join my Patreon here: patreon.com/HazelStLewis

Please Consider Leaving a Review!

If you enjoyed this book, please consider leaving a review. One of the best ways to support authors (especially new ones like me) is to leave a review!